I0719696

Manna tree

Savannah J. Frierson

For my sister, Karma, who has waited almost a decade for this book
to be dedicated to her. That is poor of me, but my life has been
infinitely rich because of her.

ACKNOWLEDGMENTS

My sincere gratitude to my advanced readers for this novel: Sylvia Bullock, Karma Frierson, and Gracia Rich. Your comments were insightful and encouraging. I would also like to thank all of my Patreon Patrons for your support throughout the year. You have made my endeavor in authoring that much easier and I'm so grateful.

Many thanks to my agent, Saritza Hernandez, for being one of my biggest cheerleaders! It's great to have someone believe in you as much as she does. I would like to thank my family and friends for their encouragement as well.

And finally, thank you to my readers! I would be absolutely nothing without you and your support. I hope you enjoy Cole and Margot's journey from tragedy to joy.

Chapter One

He should've stopped him. He *could've*....

So, why hadn't he? They weren't little kids anymore. Cole Patterson was old enough and big enough to take a punch and throw a good one of his own. He should've wrestled his brother to the ground until he'd called uncle and relinquished the keys.

Cole should've, but he hadn't. Now two people were dead because of him and a third wasn't far behind.

A hand squeezed Cole's shoulder and he smelled coffee. Cole took it without looking at the bearer, muttering a thank you before blowing the black liquid and drinking a sip. Bitter. Gritty. Massachusetts General Hospital was no Dunkin' Donuts, that was for sure, but it was something.

"Ma'am, you can't—"

"Don't even *think* about telling me what I can and cannot do!"

It was the first time Cole had looked up since coming to the hospital, and he saw a tall, dark-brown woman wearing paint-smeared sweats and a deadly expression. The cop who'd been standing sentry amid the two emergency room curtains abruptly stepped back and let the woman pass, shooting Cole a look that said he had a healthy sense of self-preservation.

"Goddamn you, *wake up!*"

It was the same tone she'd used with the cop, but she wouldn't get the same response; in fact, she wouldn't get any response because the person she was talking to was dead. Because of Cole. Because he hadn't had the guts to stop his too-drunk brother from getting behind the wheel; because he'd trusted his brother's promise to get a taxi and had remained at the bar instead of driving his brother home himself.

The one good thing about this was that it was three in the morning, which meant there were at least two more hours before the local media swarmed outside the hospital for statements, details, and analyses it could glean about one son of an aspiring attorney general crashing headlong into another car carrying two people, while the other son could've prevented the whole mess but hadn't.

"WAKE UP!"

The scream tore at Cole. The raw anguish in her voice, the guttural grief, shook him to the core. Even the orderlies and the nurses murmured in fear and concern, staring at the curtain with cautious curiosity. Cole closed his eyes. That voice reverberated throughout his entire body.

It was his fault.

He heard the woman come from behind the curtain and he looked up again, his eyes locking with hers. He could tell she hadn't cried yet and she didn't look on the verge of tears, either. He understood that. He was still in too much shock to do anything but the most basic actions required for survival. Should he comfort her? It was his fault, after all; and as much as he would deserve any slap or punch she could give him, he didn't fancy being on the receiving end of one or several.

Nevertheless, he stood and approached her because he was a Patterson, damn it, and he would take responsibility for his actions and inactions.

"Ma'am?" Her eyelids fluttered but she didn't say anything. He cleared his throat. "My name is Cole Patterson and I'm *so* sorry—"

"Where's the bathroom?"

He blinked. That had been the last thing he expected her to say. He also hadn't expected her normal voice to be so pleasant in tone. He frowned briefly, especially when she started swaying. Forgetting he was in a hospital where there were people who helped the woozy for a living, he grasped her arm gently and gave her a crooked smile.

"I don't know, but I can help you there."

"You can?"

"It's the least I can do."

Her eyes dragged away from his and she sighed as if to grant permission. They began walking slowly, he ignoring the looks they received and glad the bathroom wasn't far from where they'd been. He knew he should've left when she entered the bathroom; but for some reason, he couldn't. This woman seemed dazed, confused, lost—much like he was. It was comforting to know he wasn't the only one, and he needed their grotesque camaraderie for a few more moments.

It was by the grace of God Margot made it into the bathroom before she threw up the ice cream and cookies she'd been eating before getting the call. She'd known something was wrong when she'd awakened abruptly from her superficial sleep with dread plopped into the pit of her stomach. She couldn't figure out *what* was wrong, however, and had checked her apartment to make sure nothing was burning, everything was locked, and the various detectors were working. When that still hadn't made her feel better, she'd pulled out a carton of Moose Tracks ice cream and a tin of chocolate chip cookies to eat while watching *Nightline* and waited for the dread to pass.

It hadn't, instead growing worse when her phone had rung almost thirty minutes later. She'd almost choked on the cookie she'd been chewing; and when the voice on the other end had begun, "Mrs. Reed, it is my sad duty to inform you…," she'd slammed the phone on its base and tried to swallow the remainder of her cookie down her highly constricted throat. Of course, phone calls like that never meant good news; and after having been on the receiving end of one almost four years earlier, she wasn't in the mood to hear another. God wasn't so cruel. God wouldn't take the two people in her life who meant the most to her so closely to each other. Shouldn't she get a ten-year grace period at least? She'd *just* come to terms with the first loss, and now here was some random voice telling her she was about to endure a second.

When person had called again, she'd forced herself to listen to the message: head-on collision; drunk driver; instant death for two, critical condition for a third. When the informant had realized she wasn't responding, he'd offered the vital information of which hospital and who was the survivor.

"George Butler."

Georgie. Her baby...well, not really since they were only two years apart, but Georgie? The successful resident at Tufts Medical Center studying to be a general surgeon? The little brother who had gotten her in so much trouble in high school when he'd told their parents she'd gone on a date with Conrad Rull? The man who had just married his partner of two years and was trying to start a family?

Margot was glad she lived near Harvard Square because there were always taxis around. She'd marched out of her apartment, uncaring she looked a hot mess, and demanded to get to Massachusetts General Hospital. The driver had known better than to make small talk given her expression and mood, and she'd rewarded him with an incredibly generous tip. She had other, more pressing things to worry about other than if she'd done her math correctly. She had to convince her brother to wake the hell up because he would be a father in seven months.

"Oh God," she muttered, her raspy voice bouncing off the tiles. She was still in the bathroom, sitting fully on the floor and leaning against the commode. God *couldn't* be so cruel—

"Ma'am?"

She frowned, wondering if the male voice she heard were real instead of a figment of her exhausted mind. She groaned, not having the energy to formulate a more coherent response.

Footsteps echoed and soon she could see shoes underneath the stall's walls and doors. They looked expensive, gleaming and without the tiny creases in the leather that let one know the shoes had been worn often. She stamped down the urge to caress it, balling her fist into her lap.

"Ma'am—"

"Margot," she mumbled. "Ma'am makes me sound old, and I ain't old."

"Margot?"

"Why you in the ladies' restroom?"

He didn't answer immediately. "I was concerned....I wanted to make sure you hadn't passed out."

There was no reason for her to be touched by this, and yet she was.

"What's your name again?"

"Cole."

"Cole? Like Nat King Cole?"

"Yeah."

"White boy like you know who that is?"

A breathless chuckle. "Yes. I'm down with the old school!"

She laughed heartily at that, so much so that her sides began to hurt and she took in deep gulps of air in between laughs. This was far too surreal. Here she was in a hospital women's bathroom, laughing talking to a random white boy while her brother lay in the emergency room clinging to life.

"Ma'am—Margot—"

"I'll be all right," she croaked.

She barely registered him sitting on the other side of the stall's door; but when his pale hand reached blindly back, she let out a watery chuckle and grasped his hand in return.

She didn't feel so alone anymore.

Margot's hand was strong around his. Though he'd offered his to provide her comfort, she was giving it instead. Cole squeezed his hand around hers and took a deep breath, uncaring he was sitting on the floor in the women's bathroom in clothes he'd been wearing to a swanky party mere hours beforehand. Everything was stripped bare, simpler; death had an excellent way of putting things in perspective. Other than his paternal grandmother five years ago and his maternal grandfather when he'd been three, no one close to him had ever died. Why would he think about death, anyway? He was twenty-five years old and just beginning life, living it up between Boston and New York and taking full advantage of the fact his father, a partner at a prestigious law firm, was now running to be the Commonwealth's attorney general. He had status, classic good looks, and all the women he could ever want. Yet none of that mattered with his brother now lying in the morgue.

"Why are you here?"

Her voice startled him. It was still raspy, still deep, and still calming. His mind briefly replayed the bawl she had let out earlier and he tightened his hand around hers again.

"I needed to apologize."

"Apologize?"

"It was my fault—"

"What? Your fault?"

"I should've stopped him—"

She'd bounced their hands against the floor and he stopped talking. Since he couldn't see her face, he couldn't tell what she was feeling; but considering she hadn't tried to rip his hand from his arm, Cole reasoned she hadn't heard him or she was biding time.

"I've been through this twice now," Margot said flatly. "No matter how many times the preacher says, 'It was just his time,' you curse God for not giving you a damn calendar so you could be prepared!"

Cole wanted to ask who the other person had been, but it wasn't any of his business really. "Yeah."

"I gotta tell my brother his husband died in the crash when he wakes up."

Cole's ear twitched at that. He hadn't known her brother was gay. "Oh."

"That's not something I ever wanted to say to him. I've been on the receiving end; it's not pretty."

There was his answer, he guessed. "I'm sorry."

"'Sorry' doesn't mean a damn thing. 'Sorry' doesn't bring my husband back or Georgie's. 'Sorry' doesn't bring back that third driver. 'Sorry' doesn't erase the fact he'd been drunk and took out two people instead of doing the world a favor and killing his damn self by himself!"

Cole smarted at that, but he couldn't blame her for saying it. Jacob had always been a selfish bastard, but Cole had still looked up to his older brother with a mixture of awe, envy, and emulation. He'd wanted to be Jacob Patterson when he grew up, with the complete, unadulterated adoration of his parents, the unfailing respect of his peers, and the abandoned swooning of the ladies.

"He was my brother."

"Who?"

"The third driver."

Her hand tightened painfully around his and he let out a soundless gasp. Her grip reminded Cole of the kind his father would give on his shoulder whenever he did something disapproving. Yet earlier, when his parents had met him at the hospital, Frank Patterson hadn't even spared Cole a glance, too busy staring at the burned and mangled body of his oldest son lying in the black, leather body bag.

"I'm sorry."

He frowned. "Sorry?"

"Yeah." Margot sighed, loosening her grip a little. "I know it's hollow, but that's the most I can give you right now."

Cole reclined fully against the cool stall door, his thumb running along the back of Margot's hand idly. "That's more than I deserve."

His thumb felt very good against her skin and Margot sighed. Why was he sitting there with her instead of mourning his brother with his own family?

"It's my fault."

Margot frowned. "What?"

Cole cleared his throat, and he moved his thumb to caress her palm instead of the back of her hand. "The blame. I see it in my parents' eyes. I know it's my fault this all happened. I don't need them to tell me that as well—"

"You weren't driving."

"I made him promise not to drive, and then I let him go off," Cole said, giving a dry chuckle. "I trusted him."

"Are you the oldest?"

"He is." Cole cleared his throat again. "He *was*."

"You should go be with your family."

"What about you?"

Margot gave a laugh that was anything but humorous. "Me? Don't you worry about me. I'll be fine. I've done this before."

"I haven't," Cole admitted. "I don't know how to go about this."

"One day at a time."

"You're awfully philosophical about this."

"I'm tired and nauseous. There's nothing for me to do *but* philosophize."

It also helped her brother was just in a coma; that meant there was hope…that he could come out on the other side of this alive…that she wouldn't have to cremate two bodies in a few days' time.

"God wouldn't be so cruel," she murmured, then sat up quickly, a shiver going through her body. The dread in her belly increased and she took long, slow breaths to quell the panic starting to rise.

"Margot?"

"Something's wrong."

"Open the door, Margot."

That would require her to stand, and she didn't think her legs would be able to support her. She reached up blindly, the tips of her fingers grazing the door's lock as she tried to turn it. After a few failed attempts, she finally succeeded and slid against the stall's wall closer to the toilet as Cole entered.

The stall was too tiny for his frame and hers; but when he looked down at her huddled form and his eyes grew soft, she suddenly felt no bigger than a baby doll. He grasped her upper arms and helped her to her feet, looking at her with blue eyes so clear and concerned for her.

"Oh God…"

Cole's thumb caught the solitary tear that trailed down Margot's cheek, surprising both of them, it seemed, for he immediately jerked his hand away from her face and she gasped. Wordlessly, he grasped her elbow and led her out of the stall, taking her to the sink so she could splash water on her face. Cole suddenly felt very foolish and out of his element. What was he *doing*? Why with her? What was it about Margot that had him needing to make sure she was okay? She was older than he was, he knew, given the faint wrinkles around her eyes and the maturity with which she carried herself. Her hair was cropped short and natural in tight curls, so different from the long, silky hair he was used to admiring. Her sweats couldn't hide her curves, and she was far too voluptuous and intimidating for a man like him...a boy.

He felt like a little boy around her.

"You're staring." His eyes snapped to hers in the mirror and he saw the red creep into his cheeks. Her mouth quirked slightly and she shook her head. "Never seen a black woman before?"

"Of course! I just—"

"Thanks."

"Thanks?"

"I feel like a whale. You staring at me like that made me feel good for a little bit."

He gave her another crooked smile and dragged his hand through his blond hair. "You're welcome, I guess."

She dropped her head and hunched over the sink. "I doubt I'll be feeling that way again for a long time to come."

Cole approached her, putting a hesitant hand on her back. "I know I've just met you, and not under the best of circumstances. But if anyone will be able to survive this, it's you."

"This is surreal."

"Very."

Margot blew out a deep breath and stood straight again, turning her head to meet his eyes. "You should be with your family, Cole."

Cole clenched his jaw and guided her toward the door. "Come on."

When they went back to the main room, there was a doctor by her brother's bed. Margot stutter-stepped and Cole hooked his hand into the bend of her elbow to keep her upright and moving.

"Mrs. Reed?"

"Yes."

"May I speak with you privately?"

She leaned slightly into Cole and he squeezed her arm. Her nod was imperceptible, but she went with the doctor toward her brother's bed. Why had he wanted to insist he go with her? Cole had meant what he told her—she would survive this. It was an instinctive knowledge in regards to her, but it was as if he wanted to make sure she did.

Cole groaned, retaking his seat where his now-tepid coffee still sat underneath it. He threw the cup in the trashcan next to him and then leaned his head against the wall, closing his eyes as the adrenaline seeped out of his body. He should go home. There was no reason to be here anymore. He'd stayed because his parents had needed time alone with Jacob. He'd stayed because he'd needed, for some reason, to apologize to the family of his brother's victims.

He'd stayed because he had nowhere else to go. Being here kept him from dealing with his own feelings of guilt and anger...relief. What kind of brother was he to be relieved Jacob was dead? It wasn't that, Cole knew intellectually, but there was a sense of *finally* that he wouldn't have to deal with Jacob's drinking problem anymore. He couldn't help welcoming that particular freedom.

Suddenly, Cole heard a sickening splat and a doctor call for help. He sat up, his eyes snapping open, and saw the physician half-carry, half-drag Margot's form onto a gurney. Nurses and orderlies swarmed them; and before Cole could even stand, she was wheeled away to somewhere unknown.

Impulsively he followed them, calling out to the doctor before he got on the elevator. The doctor stopped, looking at him curiously and a little impatiently.

"What happened? Where are you taking her?"

"She threw up, then fainted. She hit her head pretty hard on the bed railing, so we're making sure she doesn't have a concussion."

Cole looked worriedly at the elevator doors. "I just met her but I..."

The doctor nodded, picking up the thread of Cole's unfinished request. "I'll keep you abreast of the situation, Mr.—"

"Patterson. Cole."

The doctor nodded again and Cole stepped back against the far wall as he watched the doctor enter the elevator. Cole remained there for who knew how long; but with each moment that passed, he grew more nervous. Cole hoped Margot would be all right.

"Mr. Patterson?"

He jerked at the sound of his name, frowning at the nurse who had just stepped off the elevator. "Yes?"

"Dr. Pierce says you can come up now."

The ride up to Margot's floor didn't last long. When he reached the door to her room, Cole could see she was still out of it. Dr. Pierce approached him with a mildly concerned expression, closing the door behind him.

"She had a mild, grade I concussion," he began, adjusting his eyeglasses as he glanced over her chart. "She doesn't seem to be in any serious danger, but we're still going to keep her here for observation."

"Okay," Cole said, frowning slightly. Margot couldn't catch a break, could she? "Why did she faint?"

Dr. Pierce pursed his lips and slid a pen in the clipboard. "Do you know Mrs. Reed well?"

Cole bit his lip and shook his head. He didn't have any right to the information, after all, but...he needed to know.

"Is there anyone else I can contact for her? Husband? Parents?"

"Her husband is dead and...I don't know about her parents," Cole muttered.

Dr. Pierce regarded him closely. "You can come visit her later this morning after ten. In the meantime, I'll see if I can contact her parents."

Cole nodded absently. "Thank you." He realized the doctor didn't even have to give him that much. It was obvious to everyone he and

Margot were strangers, yet still, he had to make sure she was okay. It seemed he was the only one around to do so.

"My number," Cole said as the doctor passed him. "Just in case something happens?"

"Mr.—"

"Please take it?" Cole insisted. Dr. Pierce seemed to debate himself before finally handing Cole the clipboard. Cole wrote down his cell phone number. "I can be the last to know but I just…I need to know."

"Okay, Mr. Patterson," Dr. Pierce said. "See you after ten."

Cole went to Margot's side, taking her hand in his and squeezing. "After ten, Margot."

He dropped her hand and left the hospital room, praying he didn't get another ominous phone call like the one he'd received not three hours earlier.

Chapter Two

Margot had difficulty opening her eyes, knowing instinctively she was not where she should be; and from the foreign object sticking in the back of her hand and the hum of machines in her ears, she was afraid of what had happened last night.

Why was *she* in a hospital bed?

She sat up quickly, the world swimming in her vision and the heavy pulse of blood pounding in her head. She grunted and reclined back in the bed, eyes closing. A trembling hand rested on her middle.

Now was not the time to panic.

"Mrs. Reed?"

Her eyes opened reluctantly to see a tall, bearded man wearing a white coat and a stethoscope around his neck. He smiled at her softly.

"Where am I?"

"Mass General Hospital," he replied. "I'm Dr. Pierce. You knocked your noggin good last night!"

Why in the devil did he sound so cheerful? "I did? Am I all right?"

"Medically, you will be, yes," he said but his face turned serious. "You fainted."

"Fainted?"

"Yes. Do you remember what happened?"

"Remember?"

"Why you fainted?"

Margot frowned and closed her eyes again, sifting through the dark and muddy memories of the past twenty-four hours. She remembered being in the studio she and Oscar shared as they worked on the storyboard of his latest children's book. She remembered them getting a call from the OB/GYN, then she and Oscar celebrating the good news. She remembered Oscar rushing out to plan a big night to reveal the surprise to Georgie. She remembered battling a brief onset of grief when she realized she and Marcus would never have a child together. She remembered—

"Oh God!"

She sat up quickly once more, only for the pain to shoot into her head again and for Dr. Pierce to ease her back onto the bed. "Take it easy—"

"Georgie! Oscar! They're—!"

"Mrs. Reed—"

"I need to get to them! I need..." Her eyes stung and she gasped for breath. Last night was supposed to have been a nightmare, an awful, monstrous nightmare she'd joke about with Oscar the next morning. But there was no more Oscar. Oscar had died instantly in a head-on collision the night before. Oscar was now in the hospital morgue waiting for her to claim and prepare for his final rest.

"No."

"Mrs. Reed—"

"No!"

"You have to—"

"My brother..."

"It doesn't look good, Mrs. Reed. But he's also not gotten any worse, so that's a good sign."

Worse. Worse was death. Worse was she having to spread his ashes after she finished spreading Oscar's, his husband's ashes, in the White Mountains—but not before Georgie's organs were harvested.

"I can't..."

"I know this is a lot to take in—"

"Do you?"

Dr. Pierce didn't respond, seemingly knowing his words would be hollow and exacerbate her sorrow. Now wasn't the time for her to hear silver linings and whatever other empty words people said at moments like these.

"You have a mild concussion from when you hit your head after you fainted. Everything seems to check out, other than the pain you're having in your head. Do you have anyone who can look after you for the next few days?"

That was the absolute worst question for Dr. Pierce to ask. She had no one, not anymore. Her husband was gone. Her brother and brother-in-law were gone. She was alone.

No, not completely.

Margot gripped the cloth of her hospital gown draped along her abdomen and looked at the doctor in fear. He smiled softly at her again.

"The little one is all right."

At least someone was.

"Dr. Pierce?"

Two pairs of eyes swung to the hospital door where a tall, young-looking blond man hovered in its frame. There were pink daisies in his hands and red stained his cheeks.

Was he lost?

"Ah, Mr. Patterson, right on schedule," Dr. Pierce said and grinned at Margot. "Do you remember him?"

She stared as the blond man came into the room, her eyes barely blinking when he set the flowers on the table beside her.

"How are you feeling?" he asked softly.

Margot looked to Dr. Pierce for help.

"She's a little worse for wear, but I don't foresee any major problems," the doctor responded. "I asked if she had anyone to look after her, but she never answered."

Margot licked her dry lips. "I…"

"Mr. Patterson—"

"Cole," the blond man corrected the doctor.

"Cole watched out for you last night. Do you remember?"

His eyes were vaguely familiar, as was his voice; but when he slowly took her hand, as if giving her time to deny him, and squeezed, recognition overwhelmed her.

"Nat King Cole."

He smiled and squeezed her hand again. "Yeah."

Margot returned his smile and squeeze. "I didn't think I'd see you again."

Cole shrugged. "I wanted to make sure you were all right."

"And you? How are you doing? Your family?"

Cole shook his head. "Let's worry about you first before we talk about me."

Margot frowned at him but gave her attention back to the doctor. "Do I really need someone to stay with me?"

"I'm afraid so, especially considering the circumstances. You could stay here for more observation, but you'd be more comfortable at home."

"I need twenty-four–hour care?"

"No, you don't, but given your condition—"

"Condition? What's wrong with her?" Cole asked, a slight panic lacing his voice. Margot patted the back of his hand to calm him and his concerned eyes met hers. "Are you sick?"

"At random times in the day," Margot said dryly, snickering when Cole's eyes widened.

Cole looked to Dr. Pierce for more information, but the doctor chuckled and held his hands up in surrender. "Not my news to tell, unfortunately, but suffice to say I'd feel better if there were someone with you, Mrs. Reed."

"Ah—"

"I can," Cole said, surprising all three of them.

"Now, wait a minute—!"

"Do you have someone?" Cole challenged. Margot sucked her teeth and looked away from him. "I can stay with her."

"Your family—?"

"Is too concerned with press conferences and damage control. You need someone, Margot, and I'm offering myself. It's the least I can do."

She shook her head. "You're not responsible for—"

"Humor me, Margot. Please?"

Margot stared at her feet. The closest person she could call was Gail in New Jersey, and she wouldn't feel right having the woman make the seven-hour drive just to babysit. Her parents were even farther away in Virginia, but she doubted they would've come to see her even if they'd lived up the street from Mass General.

Margot shook her head, unwilling to think about that.

"You'll have to stay here if you can't find anyone," Dr. Pierce said after a few moments. "And Mr. Pat—Cole here seems trustworthy."

"I'm very trustworthy," Cole insisted.

Margot didn't doubt it. This could've been an incredibly difficult, overwhelming, and lonely time for her, but Cole had made all of that less so. She was thankful for this young stranger coming into her life; it reaffirmed God wasn't nearly as cruel as she suspected He could be.

"All right," Margot said, looking first at Dr. Pierce, then at Cole. "Cole it is."

Cole glanced at Margot as he maneuvered the car into the right lane, preparing to get off Storrow Drive onto the Anderson Memorial Bridge. He hated driving through Harvard Square—too many pedestrians who didn't pay attention to traffic. That was what he told himself, at least. Had he been admitted into the prestigious university, perhaps he wouldn't be so sore about its square.

"Bear right and go under the overpass," Margot said softly once they made it through the main intersection. Cole nodded and did as was told. "Keep right until you reach the light. You want to be on Broadway, not Cambridge Street."

"Yes, ma'am," he murmured.

"What I told you about that 'ma'am' mess?"

He grinned. "Margot."

"Much better."

Cole was glad she seemed in decent spirits. Before they'd left the hospital, Margot had spent some time with her brother. The only sounds in his room had been her low whispering, the droning hum of the machines, and the television the roommate was watching. The fact Margot's brother had made it through the night was a cause of relief and a little more hope. Yet considering what the doctors had told Margot, too much hope could be dangerous in this case.

It wasn't long until he pulled up in front of an unassuming brick building. Luckily, there was a parking space not far from the entrance and he parallel parked smoothly. The pair of them sat for a minute, no one moving, but Margot kept inhaling sharply as if trying to say something but changing her mind every time she attempted.

Finally, she committed. "You know, it's not too late to back out—"

"So you used me for a free pass!" Cole teased, unbuckling his seatbelt.

Margot rolled her eyes and unbuckled her belt as well. "No, but...this is very unusual, isn't it? And I'm sure you have *things* to do."

Cole clenched his jaw and opened his door. "I *am* doing the *things* I have to do," he replied. "Now get out so I can get on with it!"

Margot gasped with indignation and he grinned a little, going over to her side to help her out. She refused to look at him but he didn't take offense. If he'd really done something to make her mad, he was certain he would've heard about it long before now!

"And again, I thank the Lord for letting me find a building with an elevator," Margot murmured, pressing the UP button as they stood in the small lobby. The place wasn't too big or too small; he thought it fit Margot perfectly based on what he knew of her thus far.

"How long have you lived here?"

"Two years," she said. "Rent isn't through the roof and I have a skylight!"

The elevator doors opened and they stepped inside, Margot pressing the button to take them to the top floor. The ride wasn't long and soon they were entering her home. Her apartment was open, airy, and bright in the early spring sun. There was very impressive artwork hanging on a wall in her living area and he took a closer look.

"Who did this?" he asked, fascinated by the bold colors and textures of the abstract painting. His mother would love something like this; he'd try to buy a few paintings for Mother's Day.

"Ah..."

Margot mumbled something and started down the hallway. Cole followed. "What? I didn't hear you."

"Just a painting," Margot said with a shrug as she entered her bedroom. Cole hovered at its door, watching her throw her purse on the bed. The covers were piled in the center of it and the closet door was open with clothes hanging from its knobs. Some of the drawers of her chest were slightly opened with clothes peeking out, and her shoes were in a haphazard pile at the foot of it. There was another painting above her bed, not abstract, but just as stunning. It was a garden of some sort, and there was an explosion of reds, golds, greens, and pinks. The flowers he couldn't recognize—he didn't pretend to be a plant expert—but they were beautiful.

"That's amazing," he breathed, still staring at the artwork. "Whoever did it is amazingly talented."

"You say amazing, my parents say a tremendous waste of time."

Cole gaped at her, surprised. "Really? You?"

"I dabble—"

"If this is a dabble, I don't even want to know what a serious attempt would look like!"

She gave him a shy smile and rolled her eyes. "Now you're being silly."

"I'm serious, Margot," Cole said, turning his attention back to the painting. "It's really good."

"Thanks."

Now that the topic of the painting had been exhausted, Cole felt awkward again. Perhaps he should leave her room so she could get comfortable. If he'd known how to cook, he would've made her something.

"Do you like Chinese?" he asked.

"Yes. Call your parents."

He looked at her weirdly. "How did my parents get into this?"

"I feel guilty for taking you away from them. I can get a neighbor to—"

"I promised Dr. Pierce and I owe you—"

"Why?"

Cole swallowed and shook his head. "I'll go search for a Chinese place online."

He closed the door as he left her room and went into her living area, pulling up a search on his phone. He sat on the couch and began scrolling through it, then turned on the television so it wouldn't be so quiet.

"At three this afternoon, Frank Patterson will give a press conference at his campaign headquarters to talk about the death of his oldest son Jacob in a car crash last night. There is speculation he was drunk at the time of the accident, killing him and one other person while critically injuring a third—"

Cole shut the television off. He could deal with the silence for now.

He was debating between two different Chinese restaurants when his cell phone rang. He answered it blindly.

"Are you coming to the press conference, or are you going to be AWOL as you've been thus far during this time of crisis?"

As tempted as Cole was to end the call, he merely swiped a hand over his face and sighed. "I'm surprised you even noticed I wasn't there."

"Your brother is dead, Cole."

"I know that."

"Your mother wants you to come."

"And you couldn't give a damn if I were there or not—"

"Cole!"

Cole leaned against the back of the couch and stared at the ceiling. He'd never had a good relationship with his father, and Frank had never seemed interested in one with him since he had Jacob. Father and firstborn son had attended hockey games, discussed law cases, and listened to lectures because they were fun. Cole thought all three were incredibly dull. Now Jacob the Golden Boy was no more, and the future partner of Patterson, Irving, and Rouche wouldn't be the eldest Patterson son.

"Are you with one of your girlfriends?" Frank asked scathingly.

Cole laughed at that. If only he knew. "How long will this press conference take?"

"As long as necessary!"

"I'll stay long enough for you to make your statement, but the Q&A section I'll pass. I have things to take care of—"

"What could be more important than being with your family?"

"Being with someone who needs one but doesn't have one," Cole said flatly. "I'll see you at three."

Cole ended the call and threw his phone on the couch cushion, exhaling a deep breath. This would certainly put his father up in the polls—voters loved a good sob story. He'd have to call the Chinese place when he got back from the conference. Better yet, he'd pick up something. Maybe Margot would like Greek.

"Margot?" he called, knocking on her bedroom door. It was far too quiet on the other side of it for his liking, and he knocked harder.

"Margot?"

He tried the knob, relieved to find it unlocked, and entered her room. She was sitting on the floor against her bed, a towel barely covering her nude frame. She didn't even glance his way when he entered the room, steadily staring at a spot on her dresser and barely blinking.

"Margot?"

"You know they tried almost a year—a *year*?"

"Who tried?" he asked, approaching her slowly. There were still droplets of water on her shoulders and arms.

"Georgie and Oscar. They wanted to be parents. They would've made such good parents too. Oscar wrote children's books and Georgie was going to med school. They would've had very healthy, literate children between the two of them."

"Margot."

"Now there's a baby with no parents," she said, her eyes finally sliding to his. "An orphan before it's even born."

Cole crouched down in front of her. "I'm sorry."

"I was only supposed to be the aunt," Margo moaned, resting her head against the bed. "I can't be anybody's mother!"

His eyes dropped to her middle, which was hidden by the terry cloth. "You're pregnant?"

Margot nodded and exhaled harshly. "Found out yesterday—I'm two months along! When I agreed to be the surrogate, I didn't expect any of this! I didn't plan on being this child's mother!"

Cole didn't know what he could say to reassure her, so he patted her knee gently. He would panic, too, if in her situation and he felt sympathy for her. Her life had changed irrevocably, and now she would be responsible for a baby in seven months

"I have to go for a few hours," Cole said after some time. "Family."

"That's where you should be in the first place."

He quirked his lips at that. Even in her grief, she had time to chastise him. "I'll be back."

"If I'm asleep or something, there's a key hidden in the door frame of the apartment on the left side."

Cole nodded and he reached out and cupped her cheek before he had time to think about what he was doing. "I don't want to leave you alone."

"I'll be all right," Margot said softly. "Maybe you're taking this thing a bit too seriously."

Perhaps he was; but with Margot, he didn't feel so helpless and forgettable—a prop. He didn't feel like background scenery or the backup to the preferred son. He liked feeling needed.

"This is weird, isn't it?" Cole surmised.

"Very," Margot admitted. "And not in a bad way?"

"Why the question?"

She shrugged, tightening the towel around her as she tucked her legs underneath her. "I just met you yesterday and yet I don't feel threatened or wary of you."

"You'd tell me if you did, right?" Cole asked. The last thing he wanted to do was freak her out.

"I would, but...I shouldn't get used to you."

Cole looked into her dark-brown eyes wistfully. This *should* only be a temporary circumstance between them, at least until Dr. Pierce cleared her. He did have his own responsibilities, contrary to what his father thought. He was a private consultant for financial companies, which meant he could set his own hours and caseloads. Between that and his trust fund, there wasn't a need for him to work eighteen-hour days every day, and he lived the life of a young, wealthy bachelor with gusto.

And yet, "I wouldn't mind," he found himself saying, more shocked by the truth of his words than the fact he'd actually said them.

Margot sighed and gave him a wan smile, pulling his hand from her cheek and squeezing it. "You should go so you won't be late."

He nodded, sliding his hand away from hers and standing slowly. "You have my cell?" She shook her head. "I'll leave the number on the refrigerator for you just in case—"

Margot snickered. "Yes, Dad."

Cole blushed and smiled, rolling his eyes. "See you."

"Yeah."

He left the room and stopped in the kitchen. There was a pad with a pen stuck to the refrigerator door with a ladybug magnet and he wrote down his information. He left the apartment, grabbing the hidden keys before getting on the elevator and exiting the building.

This press conference couldn't end soon enough.

Chapter Three

Jill Patterson was a stunning woman of fifty-two, with a head full of auburn hair and bright blue eyes; yet for the past day and a half, they weren't as bright as usual, and her hair appeared flat and lifeless. She still looked impeccable in her cream linen pantsuit, but the zest with which she usually approached all she met was gone.

"Mother."

Watery blue eyes met Cole's. He handed her a steaming cup of Earl Grey tea. She thanked him silently but didn't take a sip, merely staring into the warm liquid held in the paper cup.

"It was a very nice press conference," she said, not looking at Cole. "The reporters were very nice."

Cole sat down next to her and clasped his hands in his lap. He'd decided to stay for the entire thing, knowing his mother needed him there. The reporters definitely weren't as gung-ho as they could've been about Jacob's too-high blood alcohol content levels, and rarely mentioned the fact that the couple he'd hit was gay and married. The politics of the situation were kept to a minimum—it seemed even the press was willing to give them a twenty-four–hour grace period.

"Have you spoken with the family of the victims yet?" one reporter had asked Cole's father. Frank had said no because he wanted to give the family its time to grieve without him interfering, but he certainly would within the next day. That had made Cole panic slightly. He didn't want his father turning Margot's grief into another advantage for him. As unfortunate as the accident was, Cole would rather his father not talk to Margot at all in order to keep something in her life sane and private. If Frank Patterson wanted to send condolences, he could mail a sympathy card.

"How does Saturday sound?" Jill asked again, her voice a ghost of what it usually was. "For the funeral? The forecast says it should be sunny and mild. I don't want it to rain while Jacob's being buried."

He didn't want to answer that, his throat growing tight. As angry as Cole was at his brother for doing the incredibly stupid thing of getting behind the wheel, the amount of anguish he hadn't allowed himself to feel suddenly hit him, the realization Jacob was no longer with them overwhelming him.

"Cole?"

"Yes?" he asked gruffly.

Jill looked ahead, a tear falling down her cheek. "This isn't really happening, is it? I don't have to bury my baby boy, do I?"

Cole sighed deeply, removing the long-ignored cup of tea from her hands and setting it on the floor underneath her seat. He then wrapped his arm around his mother's shoulders and she rested her head on his shoulder. He heard her sniffle, but she didn't break down into body-wracking sobs as she'd done when she'd first arrived at the hospital last night. Jill was a shell of her former self, but how could she not be? Suddenly she had one fewer person to be a mother to, and Cole was sure it would take a long time for her to get used to it—if at all.

"We'll get through this, Mother," he said quietly, squeezing her.

"We shouldn't have to," Jill said quietly. "A mother should never have to bury her child."

Cole couldn't disagree with that, and yet, she was. If he could make it two days ago, he would. If he could've been more aware of how many drinks Jacob had had, or felt his brother steal the keys from his slacks pocket instead of making out with an insanely attractive brunette, he would've stopped the entire tragedy from happening.

Cole clenched his jaw. Just *who* had been the older brother? Jacob was four years older, which should've meant he had more life experience and the common sense to go with it. Jacob should've listened to his own advice! How many lectures had he given Cole about responsibility and buckling down?

"You're not going to be young forever, baby bro," Jacob had said even as he knocked back a shot of whiskey at the bar last night. Cole had rolled his eyes, mildly concerned at the fact Jacob was drinking, but he'd been doing so well recently in terms of his alcohol intake; the stress of the major Brickson case now dissipated since the judge had ruled in Jacob's favor. It was one celebratory drink, Jacob had promised. There would be no more.

Frank came into the room, talking with his aides and directing people to do various tasks. His father didn't appear as tall as he usually did, especially without the lectern of microphones to add to his stature. He seemed to have aged years during the last few hours as well.

"Glad you decided to grace us with your presence."

Cole smiled, though there was little warmth. "This *is* a family crisis, as you said; and last I checked, I was still a part of the family—"

"Never said you weren't."

"There are a lot of things you've never said to me."

Frank glanced at Jill, whose eyes were closed as she continued leaning on her son. "She's not slept since the night before."

"And you?"

Frank sighed, pushing the sleeves of his dress shirt up his forearms. "I've been planning and doing press and taking calls and trying not to completely disintegrate because of all of this."

"Dad—"

"And where have *you* been?"

Cole bit his bottom lip, looking briefly away from his father's gaze, trying to figure out how to phrase his comment. "I've been...helping out a friend."

"Is the friend dying?"

The way Frank asked the question made Cole bristle and he cleared his throat. "No, but her brother-in-law did and her brother is!"

It took Frank a minute to understand what Cole meant. Once he did, he came closer to his son and lowered his voice. "Good job."

"Good job?"

"Yes. You befriending her will make her less likely to sue—"

"Dad!"

Jill jumped at Cole's outburst, and Cole murmured an apology. Sue! If Margot *did* sue, Cole wouldn't blame her. She was wholly unprepared for what lay ahead—a new baby, two funerals, and no one to help her with any of it.

"We can't handle a lawsuit on top of a funeral—"

"Jacob *caused* the accident! He broke the *law!*"

"And where were you? You two were at the bar together. You could've stopped him!"

Cole clamped his mouth shut, anger, guilt, and frustration overwhelming him to the point he couldn't think of anything to say. How many times had he thought, "what if?" It was exhausting and futile.

"You're not being fair, Frank," Jill said softly. She brushed hair out of Cole's eyes. "He lost Jacob too."

"Yet he's more concerned about some stranger—"

"Weren't you thanking me not two seconds ago?"

Frank clenched his jaw, looking between his wife and son before walking away from them. Jill sighed and pressed her forehead against Cole's temple.

"He's hurting."

"We all are, Mom."

Jill's fingers were comforting as they ran through his hair and he almost wanted to purr. "Is she okay?"

"Who?"

"Your friend. How is she?"

"Still in shock, I think," Cole said. "She's kind of going through the motions right now."

"Well," Jill began, putting her chin on Cole's shoulder. "Everyone grieves differently. You helping this woman is your way. I'm proud of you."

"Really? You're not mad I haven't been around?"

"You were the first on the scene," Jill said. "The last to see your brother alive. This friend of yours—where is her family? They should be helping her."

"She doesn't have anyone," Cole said quietly.

"The poor woman," Jill bemoaned, moving her hand from Cole's hair to his back. "You're doing the right thing, Cole. I'm glad you're with her. She shouldn't be alone at a time like this."

"Mother."

"If I didn't have you or your father right now..."

Cole kissed his mother's temple. "I love you."

"I love you, too, baby boy," Jill whispered, her eyes becoming teary and her voice trembling. "You're all I have left."

He kissed her again, rubbing her back as she worked through this latest bout of sorrow. Cole was glad and relieved his mother understood, but he'd stay with her should she ever ask it, even if his conscience would bother him about leaving Margot to fend for herself. His connection with her still didn't make any sense to him, but his instincts told him there was a reason for it.

He'd try to figure out that reason later.

Frank approached them again, his expression difficult to decipher. Jill sat up, wiping away stray tears as she waited for her husband to speak.

"Do you think your friend would be willing to meet with us?"

Cole glanced at his mother before answering. "In what context?"

"What kind of question is that?"

"I mean, are you going to bully her into signing a statement saying she won't sue or something equally tacky?"

Jill sighed. "Cole..."

"You should have a bit more faith in me than that," Frank said, narrowing his eyes. "Like you said, Jacob caused the accident. I just want to make sure your friend knows we offer condolences."

"And which campaign strategist told you this would be the best way?"

"Cole—"

"No, it's all right, Jill," Frank said, eyes still narrowed but his posture relaxing somewhat. "Like you said, the boy did lose Jacob too. His insolence is a show of his grief."

Cole rolled his eyes and removed his arm from his mother's shoulders. "She's going through a lot right now. The last thing I want her to be is intimidated."

"You don't intimidate her?" Frank asked skeptically.

Cole shrugged, then chuckled slightly. "If anything, she intimidates me."

It was true. Margot made him think of someone else's welfare besides himself, and Cole knew that had this accident not brought them together, he would've never fathomed a Margot Reed ever being in his life. He didn't know how long she'd remain there—perhaps after the doctor cleared her she wouldn't want to see him again, the brother of the man who had destroyed her family. Perhaps he'd go back to his routine of consulting financial firms during the day and hopping from one bedmate to another at night.

Cole doubted it. This was one of those life-changing events. Even if Margot Reed didn't remain in it physically, he'd never be able to forget her.

Frank put his hands in his trousers pockets and looked at the ceiling. No one spoke for a while, each lost in thought.

"I would like to meet her," Frank said finally, "but when and if you think she'd like to meet with us. I...we...should probably talk."

Cole felt his mother take his hand and squeeze it as if silently asking him to heed his father's request. "Okay," he replied, looking first to his mother, then to his father. "Okay."

Frank nodded briefly. "Excellent. Are you coming home tonight?"

"I can't," Cole said.

"Your friend?" Jill asked.

"Yeah."

Frank quirked an eyebrow yet blew out a breath and shrugged. "Fine. I'll call you to let you know if anything changes."

"I'll do the same."

"Good. Tell...your friend that the Patterson family has her in our prayers."

Cole nodded, watching his father go off silently. Jill tugged his arm and he turned his attention to her. "Yes?"

"I'd like to meet her too," Jill admitted. "I just...I don't know..."

Cole did; he'd waited for Margot at the hospital for the very same reason—to put a face on a common survivor of the tragedy.

"When I think she might be up to it, I'll let you know first thing," Cole promised.

"Thank you, darling."

They stood, arms still interlocked, and walked to the entrance of the headquarters. "I'll have my cell phone on me at all times," Cole said as his mother helped him in his jacket. "Anytime—day or night—call me if you need anything."

"I will, my love," Jill said, framing his face, her smile tremulous. "I really am proud of you."

Cole gave her a long kiss on the forehead before whispering goodbye and leaving. On the way back to Margot's apartment, he decided to forgo the Chinese and the Greek to get a pizza from Papa Gino's instead—cheese, since that seemed to be the safest option. Then again, if she didn't want the pizza, he had no problem getting something she'd like—she *was* eating for two, after all.

The sun was just beginning to set when he pulled onto her street, but his former parking space was gone so he had to go around the corner to find another one. He used the key to get into the building and made the trip up to Margot's floor, the bottom of the pizza box a little too hot to the touch for his liking. Once he reached her floor, he went to her door and unlocked it, sticking his foot between the door and the frame so he could re-hide her keys and still get inside.

It was quiet. He set the pizza down on the table in the kitchen before going to her bedroom and knocking on her door.

"Margot?"

He heard humming, low, husky, smoky, like warm bourbon. He cracked open the door to see Margot sitting in the middle of her bed wearing a tank and shorts with headphones on her head and a pencil and sketchpad in her lap.

"Margot," he tried again, knocking louder for emphasis.

She physically jumped, her hand going to her heart as her chest heaved from her startle, and then she glared at him when she realized who he was. "Boy!"

Cole grinned and leaned against the door frame. "Sorry."

Margot sucked her teeth as she took off her headphones. "I'll bet."

"Have you eaten?"

She pulled her bottom lip between her teeth and shook her head. "Not hungry."

"You have to eat."

"Do I?" His eyes dropped to her middle and she sighed, pressing a hand to her abdomen. "I do."

"I got a cheese pizza," Cole said. "Is that okay?"

"If you had gotten pineapple and anchovies it would've been even better, but I can do cheese," Margot said, stretching her arms over her head before getting out of bed. Her movements were deceitfully graceful for someone who'd had a concussion the night before, and he couldn't help but stare.

The sweats hadn't done her body justice; not even the towel had offered such clues. There were too many curves for a heterosexual male like him to take, and he was struck with the sudden urge to pull her into his arms so he could feel every single one.

He coughed and turned quickly, willing his body not to go into the direction his mind was leading him. Her brother was still in critical condition and her brother-in-law was dead. *His* brother was dead. Now was not the time to be thinking of anything else.

Seemed Margot could do more than intimidate him.

Margot looked at Cole out the corner of her eye as they sat on her couch and half-watched some entertainment news program talking about some young teenage celebrity and her continuous escapades across Hollywood.

This boy should be going out and doing the same thing, not babysitting me! Margot mused, watching him take a bite out of his third slice of pizza. Her stomach had begun to protest midway through her second slice, so she'd grabbed a bunch of grapes she'd put in her freezer and began snacking on that.

"How was the press conference?" she asked. Cole's eyes bugged out and he began coughing frantically. Margot snorted and rubbed his back, cooing nonsensically as he got himself together.

"That good, huh?"

"Ugh."

Margot chuckled and patted his back before removing her hand. "I would've watched it had I not completely passed out in my room three minutes after you left!"

"I'm glad you didn't," Cole said. "You need your rest."

"Do I?"

Cole gave her an incredulous look as he bit into his pizza and Margot snickered softly. Her young stranger/friend was taking the role as caregiver very seriously and she didn't know whether to be touched or annoyed. She was a grown woman, after all, and Dr. Pierce only needed him there to make sure she didn't get any worse. On the other hand, Cole distracted her from her mourning, so she couldn't be too upset with him.

"Were your parents well at least?" Margot popped another frozen grape into her mouth, the sweet fruit bursting inside her mouth.

"As well as could be expected," Cole admitted. "Mom broke down every now and again, but I think she got most her first tears out last night."

Margot nodded, saying nothing. She hadn't cried yet, too afraid that once she started she'd never stop. She knew she'd have to go to the morgue tomorrow to claim Oscar since both of his parents had died and he'd made these arrangements about his death (far too soon, Margot had thought at the time) when they were all trying to get pregnant.

Margot had always thought Oscar had a bit of clairvoyance, but she wished she could've been warned about this particular event.

"She said she was proud of me," Cole said after a few minutes.

Margot smiled at him. "That's good, isn't it?"

"Yeah."

"So they're not angry you're with me?"

"They want to meet you."

"Meet me? You told them about me?"

"Considering you're just as affected by all of this as they are, yeah."

Margot put down the bowl of grapes and snuggled into the couch. She stared at the television, not even jumping when Cole unexpectedly grasped her shoulder.

"I'm sorry."

"Why are you apologizing?" she asked, still not looking at him. "You're right, after all. We're all connected by this."

"Margot?" She turned her head toward him and he gazed deeply into her eyes. "I won't let you be alone through this."

She stared at him, for a moment unable to be anything but touched by his sincere statement.

"I haven't told my parents yet."

"You haven't?"

Margot shook her head and dropped her eyes to her lap. How funny it was that Cole was so willing to be there for her when her parents couldn't even be bothered. Neither Georgie nor Margot had spoken to Robert and Faye Butler for years, the parents abjectly disappointed at their children for being true to themselves and their wants instead of who they'd been groomed to be and want.

"Why not?"

Margot shrugged. "Same reason you haven't wanted to go see your folks, I guess. Then again, I *have* had a concussion....I shouldn't exert myself by dialing ten numbers that would get me a direct line to an argument!"

"Margot..." Cole began with a frown, but she steamrolled over whatever he could say.

"Besides, *technically* I won't be alone." She glanced down at her still-flat tummy. His eyes followed hers.

"That's true," he conceded, chuckling. "But still..." He shrugged, meeting her eyes.

Margot couldn't keep the contact for long and dropped her eyes to her lap again. She was becoming too entranced by the sky blue of his eyes and the warmth of his palm on her shoulder.

"Do you know what you're saying?" Margot asked after a few minutes. "Those are some lofty promises!"

"And I'd like to try to keep them, with your permission, of course."

Margot shook her head in disbelief. Cole was making it very hard not to get used to him, to make him the non-issue he should've been. She'd not had someone make promises to her like that since Oscar and Georgie...Marcus.

Cole was like Marcus: optimistic, a big heart, considerate, and far too attractive for her own good.

At that thought, Margot sucked in a breath and left the couch. *Where had* that *thought come from?* She couldn't let her mind go there; that would only compound the sadness she felt from this tragedy.

"Did I say something wrong?"

Margot shook her head, leaning against the wall of the hallway. She *could not* become attached to Cole Patterson, especially not right now. She was just vulnerable to any kind of affection she could get, and Margot didn't want to complicate matters by entertaining thoughts of something more than appreciating a Good Samaritan's care. Besides, she'd just started to move on with her life without Marcus in it; and though this accident was a gross step backward, Margot was determined to work through this and persevere.

Yet when Margot felt Cole behind her, his breath warm and moist against her neck, it was all she could do not to lean into him automatically. There was something about this man that drew her to him and it scared her. She'd not been prepared for Cole's introduction into her life, or for how quickly her comfort level with him grew with each moment they spent together.

"Margot—"

"I don't even know how old you are," Margot whispered, more to herself than him. None of this was making any sense to her, and the scarier part was she didn't particularly care. How she did feel overruled how she should've felt—uneasy, unsure, unsafe. She felt the complete opposite with Cole.

"Twenty-five," he said, and there was humor in his voice. "Is that a problem?"

She was thirty-two; and while they were both adults, Margot couldn't help but feel a little uneasy about the age difference. Then again, why should she? They were just friends helping each other out in a time of crisis, right?

"I know you're older than I am, Margot," Cole admitted. "You have a maturity few twenty-five-year-old women possess—"

"What do you know about maturity?" Margot asked lightly, glad Cole was distracting her from her thoughts. "I was twenty-five once; and though I probably wasn't as crazy as most, I did have some moments—"

"Really?" Cole asked, moving to her side and looking down at her with amused eyes. "Like what?"

Margot sucked her teeth and turned to face him fully, her back and hands against the wall and her feet crossed at her ankles. "I got married."

"How is that crazy?"

"Are *you* thinking about marriage now?" He blushed and ran a hand through his hair. "That's what I thought—"

"It's only crazy if you didn't love him," Cole challenged.

"I did, very much," she said, her voice softening as she thought of Marcus Reed. "The crazy part was my parents didn't."

"Why?"

"They didn't think he was appropriate for me."

Cole frowned and slipped his hands into his pockets. "What was wrong with him?"

"He was a mechanic from DC—not in the right tax bracket, didn't have an appropriate last name, very little prospects. 'We didn't work so hard for you to have all these opportunities so you could marry a bum!' they'd said, but he wasn't a bum. He was the furthest thing from it."

Her car, a late-model Toyota her parents had frowned upon, had been giving her problems again, and she'd gone to an auto shop one of her coworkers had recommended. Marcus Reed had been dirty, grimy, and a bit short with her, rubbing Margot's already tightly coiled nerves even more raw with his treatment of her. She'd been about to leave and take her business elsewhere, or as far as her car would have let her, when Marcus had apologized and told her he'd just received troubling news about his grandfather and she didn't deserve his rudeness.

Had Margot not seen how his whole body had sagged as he'd explained his behavior with no inflection in his tone, or how his eyes had suddenly gone flat, she would've thought he'd concocted the sob story so he wouldn't lose her business.

"Did he own the shop?" Cole asked.

"His uncle. He was raised by him. His mother was dead and his father was in jail—not the best home life, but somehow Marcus managed to be successful," Margot said, smiling slightly at him. "His bank account might not have said it, but his spirit did. That's why I fell in love with him."

It hadn't taken long for her to fall, especially when he'd been so dogged in his pursuit of her. Instead of making her wary, it had excited her—very few men had given her the kind of attention he had. He'd courted her, called her at night just to talk, sent her little cards in the mail to let her know he was thinking of her. In fact, he'd been the person to introduce her to Oscar Delgado.

"You're very talented, Mar," he'd tell her, so different from the disregard her parents gave her craft. His unfailing support had meant so much to her growth as an artist.

"I agree with him, about your talent, I mean," Cole said, shuffling his feet slightly. "But I've already told you that, haven't I?"

Margot grinned a little. "That doesn't mean I don't like hearing it again."

Cole laughed. "Well, you're an amazing artist, Margot."

Even if the reassurance was good to hear, it still made her uncomfortable. "You can make a judgment like that based on two paintings?"

"Gut instinct," Cole said with mock seriousness.

"I'm sure!"

"I mean it! I make a living going off my gut instincts!"

"Doing?"

"Consulting."

Margot groaned and hid her face in her hands. "You've been caught by the monster!"

"Monster!"

"Consulting is evil and the hours are evil and getting no sleep is evil!"

That was what she'd been doing in DC when she'd met Marcus and Oscar, consulting for a public opinion research firm. While the pay had been good and her job in high demand, it hadn't fulfilled her at all. When Oscar, upon seeing some of her sketches, had offered her the opportunity to illustrate the children's books he'd written, she'd done so on a lark, not thinking anything would have come out of it. Something had—a deal with one of the leading children's book imprints in the country—and Marcus had been the one to encourage her to quit her job and take the partnership Oscar had offered as a permanent illustrator for the children's books he'd write.

"And your parents weren't pleased," Cole deduced.

Margot sighed heavily and leaned more against the wall. "That is a severe understatement."

"Are you tired? We should sit," he said, already taking her elbow and leading her back to the couch. She let him, not even minding when he sat much closer to her than he had before. His arm was strong around her shoulders and his fingers drifted along her bare skin aimlessly. She remembered when she and Marcus used to sit like this just listening to jazz or watching a movie or talking in their small apartment. Simply being together had meant more than any gift he could've ever bought. Cole doing the same was better than any reassurance he could verbally give.

"All he ever wanted me to do was fulfill my dreams," Margot said quietly. The television was still on, but neither of them watched it. "I *loved* drawing and painting and sketching, and I finally had an outlet to do it, instead of doodling in the margins of my legal pad whenever I had to sit through incredibly dull meetings. And Oscar's children's books were so brilliant—he wrote about diversity and different types of families and different cultures—especially his Dominican one. He was such a joy, and they had so much faith in me."

"What did your parents want you to do?"

Margot bit the inside of her lip to keep the tears from forming. They'd told her to forget Marcus and her silly dream of becoming an artist. When she'd told them she couldn't do that, they'd said they no longer had a daughter. She'd lost a lot of weight during the following months, and yet Marcus and Oscar had been so patient with her. As much as her parents' dismissal had broken her heart, Margot never regretted her decision. With Marcus and Oscar by her side, she'd never had a reason to do so.

"Georgie said my standing up to our parents had given him the courage to come out," Margot said, sniffling as a tear escaped her cheek. "They blamed me for it and they cut off his funding for medical school. They had a daughter who was a bum and a son who was gay—our standing in Bougie Black Richmond went down considerably after that."

Georgie had gotten another job as a bartender, and Margot, Marcus, and Oscar had all pitched in some money to help with expenses. She and Marcus had even moved from DC to Boston where Georgie was attending medical school so he could have affordable housing. Marcus had gotten a job as a mechanic at an auto shop specializing in foreign cars in Somerville and she and Oscar had devoted much of their energy to their books while she did extra freelance graphic art projects on the side.

"We were making it," Margot said, her voice becoming strained. "We were *happy*—everything was falling into place. And then Marcus died…and now this. I don't want to call my parents and hear, 'I told you so!' I don't think I could handle that right now."

There was a light, moist pressure against her temple, and it was then she realized Cole had kissed her. That simple act of empathy let loose the torrent of tears she'd been damming since the nightmare began. Cole whispered softly, gathering her frame close to his as she cried.

She was exhausted by the time her tears were spent, and, judging by the way her stomach growled, hungry as well.

"The little one needs nourishment," Cole deduced, squeezing her shoulders gently. Margot made to get up but he kept her on the couch. "What would you like? I'll get it."

"Actually, I was going for the pizza," Margot said, blushing slightly.

Cole chuckled and he opened the pizza box. "I'll go warm it for you."

"And some water, please?" she asked as he passed by her with her slice of pizza.

"Okay."

She stared at her stomach, still disbelieving there was a baby growing inside her, and Oscar and George's at that. They'd wanted DNA from both parents, so Oscar was the biological father and she was the biological mother. The in vitro processes had been exhausting and the drugs had made her weak and sick. After of year of unsuccessful attempts and ridiculous expenses, Oscar, especially, had been ready to give up on having their own biological child.

"Just one more time," Georgie had pleaded, looking to his husband and sister. "I think we should take one more shot at it."

Margot thought Georgie's optimism was the single reason she'd conceived this last time. She touched her abdomen, hoping he'd make it through in order to hold his child in seven months since Oscar wouldn't.

"Are you all right?"

Cole put the plate of pizza and the glass of water on the coffee table and sat down next to her, concern in his eyes. Margot gave him a tiny smile and nodded. "Working on it."

"The baby?"

"Two days ago I didn't even know there *was* a baby inside of me. Luckily, I've been so used to being without alcohol during this entire process or else we could be in serious trouble!"

"How many do you think are in there?" Cole asked. "Don't these things usually make you have eight children—?"

"Eight? Oh, *no*, not eight!" Margot laughed, though apprehension did make her heart beat faster. There was no way she could support eight children alone!

"That is a lot," Cole conceded.

"Too much!"

Her stomach growled again and Cole handed her the pizza. "Well, eight or one, you still need to eat."

Margot moaned as she took a hearty bite. She didn't care how fattening the pizza was, or how much grease there was in it, or even the fact she could easily spend much of her night hovering over the commode because of it. Right then, at that moment, it was the best thing she'd ever eaten, and she adored the Chinese and Italians for thinking up such a culinary feat.

When she finished, Cole threw away her trash and she stood up, watching him take care of her. She slipped her hands in the elastic of her pants as if to support the weight of her upper body.

"Are you going to go home?"

The question had apparently surprised him for he slowed his movements and frowned at the trashcan he was putting back in the cabinet underneath the sink. "Um…"

What did it mean for her, for *them*, that she hoped he'd stay? Last night had been a fluke—a concussion had made her remain in the hospital and therefore under someone's supervision the entire night. Though she hadn't known any of those people, and the reason for her forced stay wasn't the best, at least she hadn't been alone. If he left, she would be, and Margot didn't think she could handle that.

Yet he was a young man; and though he'd suffered a loss as well, Margot was sure he probably could find a better way, with better company, to work through his grief than being with her. Suddenly she felt silly and exposed. She laughed in embarrassment and started for her bedroom, waving her hand as if to erase her vulnerability.

"Ignore me—"

"Do you want me to stay?"

"You don't need to. I did fine by myself when you left earlier, and if something happens I'll call you—"

"Margot."

He was directly behind her now and she could feel his presence and his heat against her back. Unable to think about what she was doing, and thus stop herself, she leaned against him, sighing softly when his arms came around her waist and his lips brushed against her temple.

"I'll stay."

Her voice was shaky and breathy when she replied, "Thanks."

Chapter Four

Margot stared at her cell phone's display, the seldom-dialed, yet well-known number almost intimidating her to the point of throwing the device far away from her. She wouldn't, though. It'd been two days since the accident. This call was long overdue.

She pressed Send and listened to her phone make its ringing sounds. It was a Saturday morning, not too early, but just before breakfast. She wasn't hungry herself; but when she finished the call, she'd have a bowl of cereal so she could say she ate. The last thing she wanted to do was endanger the baby she carried.

"Butler residence."

Margot didn't recognize the voice, and that made her even more nervous. Perhaps they'd gotten a new housekeeper. "May I speak to Robert and/or Faye Butler, please?"

"May I ask who is calling?"

She'd dreaded that question, and something told Margot this woman wouldn't get her parents if she didn't say who she was. "It's Margot...their daughter. It's important I speak to them."

"Daughter?"

The absolute surprise in the housekeeper's voice hurt, but Margot swallowed and took a deep breath. "Please get them."

"Just a moment."

Margot sat cross-legged in her bed, her covers tangled with her limbs. She rubbed her hand over her hair and chuckled slightly. That had been her first act of rebellion, at least according to them. She'd returned home during her senior year in college with her hair short and natural, and her mother had thrown a fit of epic proportions. "You'll never get a job with your hair like that!" she'd cried. "All that pretty hair you had...gone. What's *wrong* with you?" The money and time Margot had saved by not going to the hairdresser every six weeks for a touch-up, and every other week for a wash and set, had overruled whatever objections her mother had made. And though her father hadn't said anything, his disappointed look had been just as vocal.

"I'm sorry, ma'am, but your parents aren't available—"

Another pain shot through her, but Margot couldn't hang up the phone yet despite everything in her body telling her to put an end to her misery. "Did you tell them it was important?"

"They said they don't have a daughter."

"They *do* have a daughter," Margot said. "They have a daughter and a son; well, they actually may *not* have a son in the next twenty-four hours because he's currently in a coma fighting for his life!"

The housekeeper gasped. "Ma'am—!"

"I am Margot Elise Butler Reed, their firstborn and only daughter, and George Paul Butler, their second-born and only son, was hit by a drunk driver almost two days ago and has been in a coma ever since. I know we aren't on speaking terms, but I thought they should know their children need them, and one of them is dying. I just hope that should one of them be terribly sick or dying, they could extend us the same courtesy. *We* still love them, irrespective of how they feel about us. *We* still need them!"

Margot had whispered the last part and dropped her face in her hands. It didn't matter if they were grown or estranged, Margot needed her parents right now.

"I will...try to relay that message to them," the housekeeper said, clearly shell-shocked by Margot's monologue.

Margot exhaled harshly and nodded, understanding that was the best the woman would be able to do. "Thank you. Let me give you my number so they can contact me."

The call ended after the housekeeper repeated the numbers for assurance, and Margot fell back on her bed and stared at the ceiling. Her hands went to her abdomen, her mind wandering and wondering. At this moment, the little one inside of her was the closest thing she had to a family. Her parents weren't talking to her, her brother *couldn't*, and Oscar and Marcus were dead. Maybe God was punishing her for going against her parents' wishes; but as soon as the thought had come, she dismissed it. Death was a part of life, right? That was what Georgie had said when Marcus had died, and that death had been just as senseless as these were. Carbon monoxide poisoning, of all things, because someone had left the car running in the garage while Marcus had been taking a nap in the auto shop's office. The owner, Mr. Reagon, had felt so guilty about it that he'd closed the shop for a month and had offered her a small ownership in the business as a settlement. Marcus had been one of his best employees despite being among the newest and they'd forged a very close relationship during Marcus's three-year tenure there. Margot had felt guilty about taking it, but both Oscar and Georgie had told her to accept it because she'd need the finances later.

She'd been pregnant at the time.

Everyone had been so excited about the new baby; but shortly after Marcus's death, she'd had a spontaneous abortion. It had been a double blow, both events unexpected and unwanted. Her depression had gotten so bad Gail had come up to make sure she wasn't starving herself to death, and the book she and Oscar had been working on had been pushed back to a later publication date. It was hard to illustrate a cheery children's book when she felt anything but, and it wasn't until Georgie, Oscar, and Gail had taken her on vacation in New Hampshire's White Mountains for a change of pace did she finally work her way out of her gloom. Not only had it done well for her, but everyone else who'd gone on the trip had been recharged. The nature, peace, and crisp air of the mountains had left them grounded and closer to that Higher Power, and all had returned to their daily grinds better than before.

Incidentally, that was also the place Georgie and Oscar had chosen to have their ashes spread when they died.

"What if you two don't die at the same time?" Margot had asked. They'd been discussing their funeral plans during her intervention in New Hampshire. Gail had gone to bed for the night and the three of them had been reminiscing about Marcus and the funeral—a small affair in DC so his uncle could attend. Marcus's death had highlighted their mortalities; and since Oscar and Georgie had been newlyweds, they'd begun thinking aloud about how they wanted their final arrangements.

Oscar had been very specific—a purple urn for his ashes, the ashes spread at sunset, his ashes spread first. Both she and Georgie had teased him about that, especially since there was no deeper reason for his preferences except for the fact sunset was Oscar's favorite time of day. Georgie had been more flexible, only saying he wanted his ashes spread with Oscar's. He didn't care what color the urn was or what time of day because he wouldn't be around to see it.

"We can wait on each other too," Oscar had said, linking his fingers with Georgie's. "I don't care which sunset, just as long as it's with George."

"But we don't plan on this happening for a long time, so don't worry, Mar," Georgie had said, giving his sister a warm smile. "We won't make you go through this again anytime soon."

And yet, that decision wasn't up to them. It had never been and it never would be, and today she'd search for funeral homes before she visited Georgie and claimed Oscar's body. She'd been granted a three-year reprieve from one funeral to the next, and she prayed it wouldn't be the double whammy it had been the last time around, either.

Or triple.

Margot shook her head, untangling the covers from her legs and leaving the bed. She needed to eat. They would *not* lose this baby. She would *not* lose another child.

"Jesus!"

Margot swallowed a yelp and stumbled back, barely dodging the fist that had been trying to knock on her door when she'd opened it. Her heart wanted to burst out of her chest and she took deep breaths to calm herself.

"I'm sorry," Margot apologized, staring at her sock-covered feet, then laughter replaced her fright. She'd completely forgotten Cole had slept on her couch last night.

Laughter turned into a caught gasp, however, as she moved her eyes up his body to his face. He was shirtless, his jeans hanging low around his narrow hips, and water still beaded on his slightly tanned skin.

She dropped her eyes again quickly, embarrassed. "So sorry!"

It wasn't as though she'd never seen a man's naked chest before, though it had been three years since the last time, and the ones she'd seen had never been white.

"I didn't think this out very well myself," came a rumble, and she looked up again. Cole was blushing, though there was something in his eyes that made her step back more and divert her attention.

"Was there something you needed?"

"I was just coming to check on you," he said sheepishly, zipping up his jeans and slipping on his shirt. "I thought I'd have some time between the knock and you answering the door."

"It's all right," Margot promised, slightly distracted by him buttoning his top. "Are you hungry? I am. I was about to get a bowl of cereal, but if you want something more I can make it."

"Cereal's fine. I don't generally eat breakfast."

Margot frowned. "That's bad. It's the most important meal of the day!"

"It's usually a Dunkin' Donuts coffee and a doughnut, if that. I get busy," he said with a shrug.

"Be lucky you're not my child," Margot muttered, brushing by him and going down the hall to her kitchen. "I'd force you to eat every morning!"

Cole chuckled. "Believe me, I'm *very* lucky we're not related!"

"You think I'll be a bad mama?"

"Not at all," he said quickly, stopping just at the entrance of the kitchen while she went inside and pulled down two bowls. "But...it'd be awkward."

"Awkward?"

He blew air out of his nostrils in silent laughter. "It wouldn't be good to check out your mother, would it?"

She'd been reaching for the cereal box when he'd said it, and she knocked it down accidentally. Tiny circles of oats overwhelmed the tile floor. "Lord..."

"Whoops," Cole said, coming to her to help. "Broom?"

"That tall cabinet by the fridge," Margot muttered, stepping around the mess to get the broom.

Cole refused to give it to her. "You handle breakfast. I'll clean up."

Luckily, there was another unopened box of cereal she'd purchased on her last grocery run and she prepared the bowls while he swept. When finished, the pair sat at the breakfast bar, Cole reading the cereal box while Margot focused on the far wall.

"You've checked me out?" That shocked her. At no point during their acquaintance had she ever been dressed to merit such a thing. Cole coughed and Margot winced, rubbing his back as he got himself together. "Sorry."

"That's all right," he said with a laugh, taking the napkin to wipe his mouth. "I didn't expect the question."

"I didn't, either," Margot admitted. "But...really?"

Cole glanced at her, running his fingers along his glass of orange juice. "You're a striking woman, Margot."

"I've looked a hot mess the entire time you've known me!"

"I disagree, and...you haven't been dressing to attract attention, either," Cole conceded. "But I'm not blind. I think you're very attractive."

If she'd been as light as her mother wished she were, Cole would've been able to see her blush. "In about three months, I'm sure you'll change your mind!" Margot said in an effort to defuse the tension that had suddenly enveloped them.

He didn't answer her for a moment. "In three months, huh?"

It was then Margot realized what she'd unwittingly insinuated, and she was so embarrassed she was sure she could fry an egg on her cheeks.

"Are you done?" she asked instead, looking at his empty bowl. She didn't wait for his answer and took it and hers to the sink, rinsing them out with nervous hands and nearly scalding water. Cole reached around her to turn on the cold water, clearly seeing the steam rising from the tap as she tended to her task.

"Margot—"

"Dr. Pierce only gave you a few days; I'm sorry to assume," she said, interrupting whatever he had to say. She wasn't in the mood for "thanks, but no thanks"; she'd rather just cut right to the end.

"You need me for longer than that, Margot," he challenged.

"You don't have to—"

"I do—"

"I don't want you around because of guilt or pity," Margot said, turning off the water and putting the bowls in the dishwasher. "I can do all of that by myself."

"Of all the things I feel right now, Margot, pity is not one of them."

He was closer now. Her heart raced in anticipation and fear. The timing was off; the situation was off; the *everything* was off, and yet…

She turned her head to face him and he touched her chin gently. She closed her eyes, unused to such tender contact from a man who wasn't family.

"Are you going to the hospital today?" he asked softly. She nodded absently, sighing when his thumb drifted along the swell of her cheek. "I need to make some calls and check in with my parents; but whenever you're ready, I can take you."

Margot opened her eyes and a tear fell down her cheek to his thumb. "Thanks."

He smiled and kissed the spot where his thumb had caught her tear. "You're welcome."

-SJF-

Cole trudged up the stairs of his condo to go to his bedroom and looked around it as if it had been the first time he'd ever seen it instead of returning from an unplanned, two-night vacation. Margot was currently at the hospital visiting her brother and claiming her brother-in-law. He'd asked her repeatedly if she wanted him to stay with her, but she told him it would take a while and he should handle his own business. Both had stopped by to see Dr. Pierce before going their separate ways. Margot was doing well, but she'd need one more day of observation before he cleared her. Cole couldn't help but feel a little relieved by that diagnosis; it meant he had at least one more day with a viable excuse to be with Margot.

"What is *wrong* with me?" he chastised himself as he plopped on the bed and stared at the ceiling, his body rocking with the bed's disturbance. They'd both suffered a traumatic, emotional blow, and yet he was *flirting* with her? He must be a sick bastard—was he really so one-tracked about his attraction he couldn't even let Margot grieve properly...let *himself* grieve properly? There was no shame in breaking down and crying, though he hadn't yet.

Did he think if he did, Margot wouldn't think him enough of a man? She'd been *married* for crying out loud, to a *mechanic*—one of the most macho jobs ever. He couldn't change a tire to save his life and he was more of a butterfingers than a handyman. He was younger than she was, too...irresponsible despite his lucrative job and nice condo. She was way out of his league.

"Way, way out," he muttered to his ceiling. Yet no matter how inappropriate he thought it was, he couldn't dampen his overwhelming attraction to Margot, so he'd decided not to try. She'd responded to him earlier that morning, but that was probably more from surprise than anything else. Besides, Cole had no idea if she'd been in any kind of relationship since her husband's death; and though his instinct told him she hadn't been, it wasn't any of his business.

He wanted it to be, though; in fact, he'd already started making it so. Earlier that morning, the apartment had received a phone call from one of the newspapers. Obviously surprised by the male voice on the other end, the reporter had stuttered a request to speak to Margot. Cole had refused, not wanting to subject Margot to a round of impersonal interview questions; and when the reporter had asked if he were her husband or boyfriend, he'd told the reporter goodbye and hung up the phone. Cole knew the reporter would try again; but, hopefully, it wouldn't be today. He didn't understand why the media didn't give people time to just *be* when tragedies happened. Perhaps they thought everyone clamored for his or her fifteen minutes.

Cole knew Margot wasn't that type of person; in fact, she'd probably be perfectly content to stay holed up in her apartment...by herself...if he hadn't crashed into her life. He wanted to show her a good time. After all she'd gone through the past few days, she needed it. Maybe he could take her to a nice restaurant; or if she didn't want to go out, bring the nice restaurant to her apartment or even here—

"Definitely her apartment," Cole said quickly. He didn't think he'd be able to function if she were in his home.

He called his mother to check in and ask for advice. Jill seemed to perk up at his call, especially when he said he wanted to do something nice for Margot.

"We can send Henri over to prepare something—"

Cole chuckled. "That may intimidate her. I just want her to feel special and like she matters."

"Believe me, that helps get you through grief," Jill said. "Your father hasn't been this attentive to me in months because of this campaign, but since...'the incident'...he's made sure I'm okay. We're there for each other, just as a married couple should be."

"I think you're lying," Cole deadpanned. Frank still seemed the workaholic, polls-obsessed man he'd been when he'd first started his campaign.

Jill laughed; and though it wasn't as strong as it used to be, Cole was so happy to hear it. "I'm not! We hold each other so tightly throughout the night, it's almost as if I've gotten my husband back."

"I'm glad you did," Cole said seriously. He didn't plan on "getting" his father back tonight, or ever.

"I just wish it hadn't taken Jacob's death for it to happen," Jill said, her voice growing soft and wistful. "We decided Tuesday for the funeral instead of Saturday."

"Okay."

"I would invite your friend to come, but...that would be a little awkward, wouldn't it?" Jill said. "To attend the funeral of the person who destroyed her family?"

Cole was surprised by his mother's bluntness, but what she was saying was exactly what had happened. "She's...we're...*friends* of a sort, and I'm the one who didn't stop him—"

"He made you a promise and he didn't keep it, Cole," Jill said firmly. "I know your father thinks one way, but I don't. If anything, we all caused that accident because we all turned away from the obvious signs of his drinking problem, all except for you. You know how addictions are; it's not until you hit bottom that you want to get better. Too bad bottom for Jacob left him in a body bag."

There was anger in her voice and Cole wished he were there to hug her. "Mother..."

"He'd get so angry whenever I tried to talk to him about it." Jill sniffed. "So I stopped. I didn't like him angry; he was so different from the sweet little boy I remembered. Jack Daniel's was not his friend, and yet they were thicker than thieves. How did that happen? When...?"

Cole had begun noticing when he'd visited Jacob in college for Pre-Frosh Weekend at Yale. Jacob and his friends had drunk heavily all night long; and while Cole had had some drinks himself, seeing his brother pass out had been a very scary experience for him. Cole had chalked it up to college living, but Jacob had never grown out of it.

"I'm sorry, Mother," Cole said finally, not knowing how else to offer comfort.

"Oh, Cole." She sighed. "Do not apologize. It comes in waves, you know. Yesterday I nearly died laughing watching old home videos of him and you. You two were adorable little cretins!"

Cole laughed as well. "I'd always get him into trouble."

"You were a troublemaker, all right," Jill agreed. "Always going against the grain. I'm proud of you, though. You've carved out a place for yourself and you've succeeded. I think you should start your own consulting firm too."

"Mother."

"I know. That's not what you want to do, but you could." Jill sighed and chuckled. "I just want you to be happy, darling. That's all I've ever wanted for the both of you. Besides, it isn't as if you're doing something illegal or not prosperous! Your father is just sore; he'll get over it."

"Will he?"

"Don't sound so unconvinced," Jill said.

"Is he there?"

"He's at the funeral home," she said, her voice growing sad. "We've decided not to make a big production out of it, either. He doesn't want anyone to think he's using Jacob's death for political gain."

"Did his handlers tell him that?" Cole asked dryly.

"No, actually," Jill said, some censure in her voice. "You know how much Jacob meant to your father."

He did know, and that was part of the problem between them. Cole could never measure up.

"Cole..." Jill began, seemingly just realizing what she'd insinuated.

"It's all right, Mother," Cole said, ignoring the brief hurt that had passed through him. "I know you didn't mean it."

"I shouldn't be so insensitive," she said. "I'm sorry."

"Don't ever apologize, Mother," he replied softly. "It's been a tough couple of days for all of us."

Jill sighed. "Okay, then. I'll let you go because I'm sure you're busy and I need to...yeah. When do you want me to let Henri know about the meal for your friend?"

"It'll be after Tuesday, probably not until the end of the week. Her brother is still touch and go, so I don't want to overwhelm her."

"I'm proud of you," Jill said again. "Very proud."

"I love you, Mom."

They ended the call. Cole checked his e-mail and snail mail. There were already condolences in his inbox and his terrestrial mail was predominately junk with a smattering of bills. Some of his clients had rescheduled their meetings to accommodate his bereavement. Had it not been for Margot, he probably would've worked right through as his father was doing. He didn't mind postponing his appointments. As long as he was busy being useful to someone, he'd be fine.

He wrote replies to the e-mails and changed his clothes before packing an overnight bag just in case Margot wanted him to stay again.

Cole arrived at the hospital thirty minutes later and went straight to George's room. He knocked quietly on the door before letting himself inside and noticed Margot holding her brother's limp hand in both of hers as she murmured to him.

"I have my first check up on Thursday," Margot was saying, a few tears slipping down her cheeks. "And afterward I'll come by and tell you everything the doctor told me. I won't lose your baby, Georgie. I'll do everything in my power to make sure you have a piece of Oscar with you."

The machines continued to hum and beep. Cole felt sadness at Margot's shoulders slumping from the lack of a response.

"Margot," Cole called quietly so not to startle.

She turned to him and gave him a tiny smile. "Dr. Pierce said talking would be good...talking and giving him something to live for."

"Yeah," Cole replied, unsure of what he could say. "How does the doctor think he's doing?"

"The lack of change concerns him, but I keep holding onto the fact Georgie's not gotten any worse," Margot said flatly. "Dr. Pierce keeps talking to me about organ donations and I wish he'd shut up because my brother isn't dead *yet*, and I won't think about it until he is—hopefully when he's old and senile and his kid has grandkids of his own!"

She'd grown more passionate as she spoke, but then she dropped her forehead on her clasped hands when she finished. Cole went to her and placed a comforting hand on her back. Waves. That was what his mother had said. This morning Margot had held it together very well; but now, staring at the bandaged and burned body of her brother with too many tubes sprouting from various places on his body, even the strongest person would have to be affected by it.

They stayed there for another half hour, mostly watching the monitors or remaining in their thoughts. Cole had brought up a chair to sit next to Margot. The pair spoke little during the visit, but he suspected Margot appreciated his presence.

The drive to her apartment was just as quiet. Yet when Cole pulled out his overnight bag, Margot arched an eyebrow at him before leading the way inside the building. Cole didn't know how to interpret the look, but he tightened his hold on the bag's handles and followed her.

"It always starts with a duffel bag," she said as the elevator went up to her floor.

"What starts?"

She didn't answer him. Instead, she stepped off the elevator and went to her apartment. He followed her inside and set his bag beside the couch, then sat at the breakfast bar, watching her rifle through her cabinets.

"What starts?" he asked again.

She glanced at him, then shrugged. "Dunno. I'm tired. I'm talking out my butt right now."

"Is that it?"

She abandoned her search for whatever and leaned her back against the refrigerator. "A friendship, maybe? Though I guess those don't always start with a duffel bag, unless you count sleepovers your parents let you go to when you were younger, or those inane 'get-to-know-each-other' camping trips during summer camps and college."

"Did you and Marcus start with a duffel bag?" Cole asked, raising an eyebrow in amusement.

Margot cut her eyes to him, but her mouth quirked slightly. "No. It was my portfolio. I'd left it in the car when I had dropped it off, and he called to tell me he had it. That's when he apologized. That's when..."

She let the thought hang, and Cole stared at her becoming lost in her memories. *Did* he want something to start between them that went beyond friendship? It was scary how quickly they'd come to depend on one another, how effortless it'd been. She was so different from any other woman he'd ever met—including his mother. Her strength and independence appealed to him, and yet vulnerability simmered under the surface as well. He doubted there had been any other duffel bags or portfolios in her life since her husband's death, and for him even to contemplate it probably made him the worst kind of jerk.

"There's no pressure, Margot," he said, dropping his eyes to stare at his fingers.

"No pressure?"

He nodded. "Me and my duffel bag. No pressure at all. I just...it was just in case you wanted me to stay again. I know Dr. Pierce said to, but...you're well enough and I didn't expect..." He stopped talking, his face heating badly. He wondered if he sounded like a blithering idiot to her too.

"You and your duffel bag are fine, Cole," she said. He looked at her then, noticing the faint smile on her face. "Very welcome here. You help keep me sane and not so alone. And the 'no pressure' thing goes both ways. The minute you become bored or fed up with all of this, you can leave and there will be no hard feelings. You had a life before all of this happened; it shouldn't be put on hold because of me."

"So did you," Cole said.

"I don't have much of one anymore," Margot said with a shrug. "Now that Oscar's gone I have no idea if the publishing house will need my services anymore after this book is published. I still have freelance contacts, though, and I get a small percentage from Marcus's uncle and Mr. Reagon. I'll be able to eat."

The guilt returned. "I'm sorry—"

"Shut up, Cole," Margot said bluntly. "You weren't the one driving, so just shut up."

He was taken aback. "Margot—!"

"Stop taking responsibility for things that aren't your responsibility!" Margot continued, her eyes snapping as they met his. "Besides, even if it *were* your fault, it doesn't change a damn thing!"

She was right. Jacob was still dead. Oscar was still dead. George was still in a coma. Margot was still alone.

She let out a deep sigh and averted her eyes from his again. "Like I said, no pressure. I won't be mad if you left right now."

That surprised him. "Why would I leave?"

Her laugh was little more than a harsh breath. "After the way I just wailed on you? Not many semi-strangers would take that and stick around, despite doctor's orders."

"I'd say after all we've gone through thus far, we're only quarter-strangers."

This time, she let out a genuine laugh. "You're such a smart-ass."

"Thank you," he replied, laughing as well. He liked her laugh and hoped he'd be able to make her do it more often.

Their laughter petered out and Margot rested more heavily against the refrigerator door, her eyes closing and her breathing deep. She looked exhausted.

"Why don't you lie down?"

She exhaled. "That would require me moving."

He grinned and sat straighter. "I could carry you."

She snorted. "You cannot."

"I'm stronger than I look," Cole assured her. He went to the gym regularly, though not at any fixed time every day. Sometimes it was early in the morning and sometimes it was late at night. "I think I bench press your weight, actually."

"I'm bigger than I look," Margot said, a corner of her mouth lifting. "I'm not like the girls you date."

"And what kinds of girls do you think I date?"

"The kinds that end up in mainstream fashion magazines!" Margot chuckled, opening her eyes to him. "Just a feeling I have."

So what that she was right? "Just because I date those girls doesn't mean I can't be attracted to other types. I thought we established that this morning."

"Right."

"And who said anything about dating?" Cole teased. "I just offered to carry you."

Margot rolled her eyes and managed to turn so her front rested against the refrigerator. "I'm comfortable."

"Liar," he said, standing and going to her. "Come on, Mar. Let me take you to bed."

She looked over her shoulder at him. "And now you're propositioning me?"

He blushed. "Margot!"

She giggled again, adjusting again so she faced him and tapped her finger against his nose. "You're so easy."

"And you're so difficult," he murmured, taking her finger and tugging so she stepped closer to him. "Hang on."

"Hang—Cole!" she gasped, clearly surprised that he'd lifted her. Her legs wrapped around him for leverage and her arms tightened around his neck. He couldn't move, though, not with her being so close and her curves molding into him the way they were. He was awed by her.

"See," Margot said breathlessly after a few moments. "I am heavy."

"You're not," he whispered, and to prove his point, he began walking them down the hall. She tightened her hold around him, the movement startling him a little, and he had to bite back a groan. Never had he wished her room to be so far away and yet so close at the same time. When he finally reached it, he set her down slowly, keeping her body close to his.

"Cole," Margot began, her eyes skipping to his. They were slightly glazed. "I don't think you should've done that."

"Yeah," he agreed, yet tightened his hold on her. Her eyes widened slightly and she gripped his shoulders. "Probably not."

"Are you going to let go of me?" she asked, her tongue licking at her bottom lip quickly.

Cole, transfixed by the movement, lowered his head to hers, their mouths barely a breath apart. "Do you want me to?"

"You should."

"I should." She spoke sense, and yet he wanted nothing more than to kiss her senseless. "Margot."

He settled for her temple instead, and Margot leaned against him, moving her hands from his shoulders to wrap her arms around his neck. They stood there and held each other, both clearly needing the affection, the contact. She felt so good.

"I haven't felt this safe since Marcus," Margot admitted after a few quiet moments. "I don't know how to feel about that."

"How about safe?" Cole teased, touched by her confession.

"I don't want to. I may become addicted to the feeling."

"Of all the things to be addicted to, that's not so bad."

"And when the supplier leaves?" Margot asked, moving her head to rest it on his shoulder. Her breath fanned against the side of his neck and he stifled a moan. "My parents left. Marcus left. Oscar left. Georgie…"

As much as Cole wanted to promise he wouldn't leave, he knew better than to do so. Life, as they'd been reminded, was unpredictable, and he didn't want to make a vow he couldn't keep.

"I need to eat," Margot said, changing the subject. She pulled away from him, not making eye contact. "I'm tired but I need to eat. I can't starve like I did last time."

"Starving is bad." Cole filed that bit of cryptic information away for later. She especially needed to eat now. "I'll order something—"

"There's no more pizza?"

He flushed. He'd polished off the rest last night. "I'll actually get Chinese this time."

"No seafood. Get either chicken or pork fried rice," Margot ordered.

"Yes, ma'am," Cole said, giving her a salute.

She sucked her teeth and crossed her arms over her chest. "What I tell you about that 'ma'am' mess?"

Cole winked and left her room, going into the living area to pull up the Chinese restaurant he'd found earlier on his phone. He made the order and scrolled through Margot's DVR list to find a program he wouldn't mind watching. Thirty minutes later, the apartment buzzed and he let in the deliveryman with the order. He took out the cartons from the bag and set them on the breakfast bar before going to Margot's room. He knocked lightly as he opened the door, smiling a little when he heard her snore. Apparently, exhaustion outweighed hunger.

He left the room, deciding to give her another hour before waking her up so she could eat.

Chapter Five

It was very odd for Cole to be standing there watching clump after clump of dirt hit the pristine white casket that held his brother's remains. A week ago, they'd been playing basketball in the gym; now Jacob was being buried. The service had been short and poignant. Cole had felt himself tearing up during it; but if he'd openly cried, his mother would've been inconsolable. She'd been close to it throughout the entire service, clinging to his arm as she sobbed. Frank had been stoic, though he'd rubbed his wife's back as she'd leaned on his shoulder.

No one had spoken unless directed by the pastor; and when Cole had given the eulogy, he'd had to stop a few times to compose himself. The past few days after Jacob's death, Cole had welcomed distractions—whether his mother, work, or Margot. He'd even written the eulogy at Margot's apartment at three in the morning two nights ago when inspiration had suddenly, and quite inconveniently, struck him. Even now he couldn't tell anyone what he'd written or said, but it had been the right thing for the occasion considering the large hug his mother had given him when he'd returned to his seat.

He didn't want to go to another funeral for a *long* time.

"We're about to leave."

Cole didn't look at his father as he came up beside him. "Okay."

Frank exhaled audibly. "That was a pretty moving eulogy you gave, Cole."

"Thanks."

"Didn't think you had it in you."

"Why?"

Cole saw Frank shrug out the corner of his eye. "Just didn't. I'm glad you did, though."

Frank clapped Cole's shoulder and walked off. Cole clenched his jaw, suddenly very irritated by his father. Why wouldn't he be able to give a good eulogy? Jacob was his brother, his best friend, his worst enemy...the closest person to him on the planet. Who else would give it!

The funeral procession drove back to their house in Weston where the other guests were having refreshments. Cole grew weary of meeting and greeting people, hearing, "I'm sorry for your loss" and "that was a wonderful speech you gave" ad nauseam. It got to the point where he went upstairs to a guest room and hid, needing a moment of peace...sanity.

He probably should check on Margot.

Last night had been the first night he hadn't stayed over at her apartment, Dr. Pierce giving Margot a clean bill of health. He'd dropped her at her place and they'd eaten leftover chicken fried rice together. When he'd been ready to leave, she'd walked him to the door and given him a kiss on the cheek as she whispered condolences.

He could still feel her lips on his skin.

Cole pulled out his cell phone and dialed her number. Her answering machine picked up, and he ended the call before the beep could sound. She was probably at the hospital. He would try again in an hour.

"Cole?"

"In here."

His mother appeared seconds later and she offered him a wan smile. "I don't blame you."

Cole chuckled slightly, watching his mother come sit next to him. She brushed the hair from his forehead and kissed his cheek.

"How are you doing?" she asked.

"I'm all right."

Jill nodded slowly, her thumb now caressing the swell of his cheek. "We all will be eventually."

"Yeah."

Jill stared at him a moment. "Are you staying the night?"

"I'm not," Cole said, a grimace forming before he could stop it. "I don't think...Dad..."

She sighed and dropped her hand from his cheek. "I'll talk to him—"

"Don't worry about it," Cole said flatly. The man had never been able to give him anything other than a backhanded compliment.

"You are still his son and he is still your father! Jacob's death should remind you both of that!"

He shook his head. "I just remind him of the son he lost." He stood and dragged his fingers through his hair. He didn't want to talk about it, still smarting from the earlier conversation with Frank. Even with Cole doing everything right, his father could still find something wrong.

"I give up."

"Don't do that," Jill chastised.

"Then what can I do, Mom?" Cole shrugged and kissed her cheek. "I'm heading out. I'll talk to you later."

They walked down the stairs together, encountering more people who offered their sympathies. He'd been half-tempted to leave without saying goodbye to his father, but the pointed look his mother had given him said he wouldn't get away with it.

Frank was in the living room talking to Eric Rouche, the most junior of the eponymous law firm, and didn't cease his conversation even when Cole had approached them.

Eric, however, offered him a conciliatory smile. "That was a very moving eulogy, Cole. Jacob would've loved it."

"I would've loved not to give it even more," Cole said, his jaw clenching when he heard his father scoff.

"I knew your mother forced you—"

"I meant I wish he wouldn't have died so I didn't have to give one in the first place," Cole ground out.

Eric eased into a standing position, clearly smart enough to remove himself from an impending family argument. "I'll call you later tonight with more details about the case, Frank. Give Jill my best."

Frank nodded but kept his eyes on Cole the entire time. "Will do, Eric."

Father and son glared at each other, neither willing to yield. Cole eventually did, however, because he was the son; and no matter how strained their relationship was, he still respected his father.

"I asked to give the eulogy," Cole said, his expression softer. "It was important to me, and I don't appreciate you belittling the fact I gave it."

"I haven't belittled you."

"Then why would you think the only reason I'd give it is because Mom made me? That's insulting!"

Frank shrugged. "Seems the only person you listen to is your mother. I know if I had asked you, you would've refused out of spite."

Part of Cole couldn't deny his father's charge, but he still couldn't believe the man's audacity. "So better not to ask at all?"

"You don't listen to me—"

"That's mutual!"

"You never have!" Frank said, his voice rising slightly, then he tempered himself with a deep breath. "Like whatever I think or want for you means so little as to merit complete dismissal—"

"You had your golden boy! You never needed to talk to me, anyway!"

Frank's blue eyes went hard and his jaw ticked. "I don't have him anymore. You did your part to make sure of that."

It was too much, and Cole all but staggered at the accusation. Without so much as a word, Cole left his father, and, upon finding his mother, dropped a final kiss to her cheek before hopping into his car and heading for the Mass Pike back to Boston. In a split-second decision, however, he got off at the Allston-Brighton tolls and made the now-familiar drive to Margot's apartment. He didn't even know if she were home, but he hoped she was.

He found a park around the corner and walked briskly to the building's entrance. He entered the first set of doors and pressed the buzzer to her apartment. When there was no answer after a few moments, he pressed it again. There was still no reply. He blew out a frustrated breath and briefly entertained waiting for her in his car, but that was too pathetic even for him. Yet, the only other person he would've talked to when upset was currently six feet under with fresh dirt adorning his coffin.

"Damn it!"

"Cole?"

He started and spun around. There was Margot, wearing black slacks and a red blazer, holding a purple psychedelic urn in one arm, a plastic bag from a corner store in the other, and her purse hanging precariously at the bend of her elbow. His heart constricted at the sight of the urn and his eyes began to sting.

"Let me help you," he said, his voice gruff, taking the plastic bag from her. Margot silently let him do all of this, merely accepting his presence, though she had every right to ask him what he was doing there. Cole watched her open her mailbox, heard her sigh when a deluge of cards and other pieces of mail fell out, and helped her situate herself and the numerous envelopes.

"Thanks," she said quietly, glancing at him before unlocking the door and letting them into the building. Neither spoke on the trip up to her apartment nor upon entering it. Cole set the plastic bag on the coffee table and watched her shrug out of the blazer to reveal a simple pink tank underneath.

She put the urn on the bookcase.

To think it held the remains of her brother-in-law, someone who had been a living, breathing person but a week before, was more than he could bear. Now Oscar Butler was nothing more than ash in a vase.

"Oh God!" Cole moaned, burying his face in his hands and letting out a gut-wrenching sob. Warm, strong arms came around him and he took the comfort Margot offered. He buried his face into the crook of her neck and released all the emotions he'd been squirreling away since this nightmare had begun. Margot allowed it, cooing and rubbing his back or combing her fingers through his hair, doing anything and everything to remind him she was there.

How long he cried he didn't know; but by the time he was done, his face was sore and his eyes were raw. His head pounded Margot whispered she'd be back, and eased his body away so she could stand. He sat there dazed, not really seeing the dark television screen before him, and jumped a little when he felt a soft, damp cloth on his cheek.

"I've been wondering when you'd finally fall apart," she said, her voice still soft. She handed him a glass of water. Cole remained passive and blinking as she moved the cloth to his other cheek. "I was starting to get worried."

"Worried?"

"Yeah. The longer you keep it in, the more intense the catharsis. I had to learn that the hard way," Margot said, the cloth now at his forehead. He closed his eyes and took a sip of water, soothed and relaxed by the ministrations. When he sensed she was done, he took her wrists in his hands and dropped them into his lap, his thumbs pressing against the pulse point as he stared at her hands.

"Seeing him in the ground..." Cole began on a shaky breath, squeezing her wrists slightly. "I think that made it real. Not even at the wake the other day. He'd looked like he was sleeping, and I'd allowed myself the delusion then. But today, in the ground with dirt covering his casket, I realized there would be no more pickup basketball games or lunches in Copley Square or impromptu visits to the ski lodges. My brother had moved on to a place where I couldn't follow, didn't *want* to follow until I was old, gray, and senile."

Margot adjusted their hands so their fingers could link. "Reality slaps you in the face in the most inopportune times, doesn't it?"

"Especially if it's your father's hand doing the slapping," Cole muttered, his eyes growing dark. He told her of what his father had said and Margot sighed.

"Our parents sound awfully similar," she admitted. "Because we don't fit their mold, they're perpetually angry at us. I never understood it. I'm not in jail. I'm not on drugs. I don't have children I can't support..." She let that trail off and chuckled. "At least not *yet*."

"Have you told them about the baby?" Cole asked, relieved for the momentary change in topic.

"I had to give them the news about Georgie through a proxy, so no, the fact I'm carrying his and his husband's child never came up," Margot said dryly.

Cole looked at the urn again, air trembling out of him as he exhaled. "Any help you need, Margot, I'll be more than happy to give it."

She smiled softly at him, cupping his cheek and pressing a long kiss to his forehead. Cole, moved by her affection, returned it by pressing his lips against the underside of her jaw.

Her body shouldn't get so warm at his kiss, especially when Cole was so distressed and needed her comfort. Margot shouldn't be wondering what it would be like to have those soft lips touch hers, or his hands caress her arms and back as if getting used to the feel of her.

She stood, needing to distance herself from him; but when he didn't let go of her hands, she stifled a groan.

"Cole—"

"I…" He frowned, tugging on her so she came close to him again. He scooted to the edge of the couch and locked her between his legs. His hands moved from her wrists to her waist, and he stared at her abdomen.

"I wanna be there for you and the baby," he said, staring at her middle. He dragged his hand to her stomach and slipped it underneath her tank as if he could feel the baby already.

"That's a lot of responsibility," she said, shaking her head. "And not even yours to take—"

"You don't have anyone," he said. "You're gonna need someone. And even if and when your brother awakes, he won't be able to help very much because of his recovery."

He was making sense, she knew, but, "We are friends. I don't need you to act as the surrogate father—"

"Godfather," Cole said, smirking a little. "I've appointed myself."

"Have you now?"

"You don't honestly expect me to just abandon you after all we've been through together," he said seriously.

"It's barely been a week—"

"A week that's felt like a year," Cole said. "And there are no rules for what we've been through."

Her body sagged wearily. She was unable to resist sinking her fingers into his hair. He closed his eyes and leaned his head back as if relishing in the contact, the hand at her waist tightening further.

"No pressure," Margot murmured, though she didn't know if that was for his benefit or hers.

"I don't mind."

She dropped her hands and wondered if she imagined him moan. "I...you've done more than enough."

"Do you not want me around?"

"I don't want to get used to you," Margot answered honestly. "I don't..." She didn't want to welcome someone in her life who could potentially leave it—and voluntarily at that. She was gun-shy about things like that now, regardless of context.

"Well, that sucks, because I've grown fairly used to you," he said, his mouth quirking.

Margot laughed and shook her head, pressing her palms against her face. "What a pair we make!"

"We are pretty unusual," Cole agreed, standing. He wasn't that much taller than she was, but she still had to tilt her head back a little to meet his eyes. "We first got to know each other in the ladies' room at the hospital, after all."

"Bonding at its finest." Margot snickered, shaking her head. Without him there, however, she would've snapped and probably started on her self-destructive path again. Why was this time so much different from last? Both times the deaths had been senseless and unexpected, and both times she'd lost someone very dear to her. Perhaps she was more prepared for grieving now than she'd been before; perhaps the fact she wasn't as deliriously happy as she'd been then made the impact of this tragedy more manageable.

Or maybe it was because God had provided her support that not even Oscar, Georgie, or Gail could have offered her at the time of Marcus's death. Cole was going through the same thing she was; their situations parity and parallel. They allowed each other space without being too unavailable, and yet gave support without being suffocating.

She hadn't been so attuned to someone since Marcus. She'd deal with the implications of that fact later.

"I know we still have a lot more to learn about each other," Cole said, breaking the silence. He cupped her shoulders and squeezed, "but from what I know right now, I doubt there's anything I could discover that would make me change my mind."

"Can I say the same about you?" Margot asked teasingly.

Cole shrugged, then laughed. "Probably not, but I still hope you don't change your mind."

"At least you're honest!"

"I try to be, especially with you."

"Why?"

"You demand it of me, I guess," he said, frowning slightly at the thought. "And because you'd not let me get away with being anything else!"

His assessment surprised her. "Really?"

"You're commanding, Margot. You don't seem the type to suffer fools gladly, and that's good because who wants to go through life being a fool?"

"I think you're mystifying me," Margot said, though she couldn't help but feel flattered by his comments.

"Perhaps, but this is the honeymoon stage of our friendship—everything is mystical right now," he joked.

She smiled and gave him a hug. "You're too charming for my own good."

"I try."

She laughed and pulled away from him. "Did you bring a duffel bag or are you just visiting."

"Visit," Cole said. "Actually, I hadn't planned on coming until I hit the tolls. I needed someone to talk to who wasn't my mother."

Margot chortled. "So you picked another older woman instead."

"If you're trying, even remotely, to put yourself on the same level as my mother, you'll fail because I could never think of you that way," he said.

"As a mother?"

"As *my* mother," he clarified. "I think you'll make an excellent mother; I just have no interest in you being mine."

"And what makes you think I'd want you as a son!"

He gasped indignantly. "I'm a good son!"

"Never said you weren't!"

He rolled his eyes and sighed. "I wish my dad realized I'm a good son."

"Grief."

"Jacob hasn't been dead all my life."

Margot shrugged, unable to think of something helpful to say. "Do you want to stay for dinner?"

He smiled at her. "I'd like that."

She smiled in return. She'd like that too.

Chapter Six

"Brace yourself, Margot. This is going to be cold."

Even with the warning, Margot couldn't help flinching as the doctor rubbed the chilly goo onto her stomach, and the pressure around her hand had her drawing her eyes to a pair of astonished blue ones.

"I can't believe there's a baby inside of you!"

Margot and Dr. Dennison chuckled at Cole's naiveté, and Dr. Dennison winked at him. "There may be more than one—"

"*Not* funny!" Margot insisted, forcing herself to relax against the bedding. Dr. Dennison was now moving the transducer over her stomach, but neither she nor Cole could see the monitor. There was a tiny crease furrowing between Dr. Dennison's eyebrows, and her hand tightened around Cole's. She hoped everything was all right.

"Just one as far as I can tell," the doctor said, and Margot breathed a sigh of relief. "You're lucky too. Though we only implanted one fertilized egg into your uterus, there's always the possibility of it splitting."

The sensation of the transducer had Margot jumping a little in reaction, earning a smirk from Cole.

"What you grinnin' at?" she muttered, all the while trying to fight off her own grin.

"I didn't know you were ticklish," Cole said, shifting closer to her so he could get a better view of the transducer gliding along her abdomen.

"There's nothin' to *know*," Margot insisted; but by the naughty look in his eye, she knew she'd have to be on her guard for the next few hours.

"All right, Margot, everything looks great—I don't see any major complications so far," Dr. Dennison said. Margot smiled and Cole squeezed her hand.

"For once, some good news in my life!" Margot said, and Dr. Dennison gave her an understanding smile.

"Would you like to see the first picture of the baby?"

Margot glanced at Cole briefly before nodding. Dr. Dennison turned the monitor around; and upon the first sight of the black-and-white pulsing mass on the screen, Margot felt tears sting her eyes. The baby was so tiny! Like Cole, there were times she would stare at her stomach, baffled by the fact that underneath it a baby grew—a baby that wasn't even supposed to be hers, a baby who could very well become an orphan before it was even born.

"Amazing," Cole breathed, looking at her with wonder before going back to the monitor. "Absolutely amazing."

Margot could only agree.

Not long after they viewed the fetus, Cole stepped out as Margot changed back into street clothes from the paper gown she wore, and Dr. Dennison looked at her sympathetically. She'd been the gynecologist throughout the entire ordeal and one of the first people Margot had called to inform about Oscar and Georgie's accident. Dr. Dennison hadn't had an opportunity to see Georgie in the hospital yet because of her own personal commitments but vowed to make her visit very soon.

"I can't possibly imagine how hard this is for you right now," she said. Margot shrugged. "I'm glad you have someone who could be there for you, although I will say I'm very surprised it's *Cole Patterson*—"

"Throughout all of this, it's been him," Margot admitted. "In fact, I doubt I would've been able to be here had I not had someone to keep me grounded. He lost his brother too."

The doctor acknowledged her comment with a short nod. "I caught his father's press conference about that a few days back. I'll admit I thought he was hanging around because his dad told him to—with the campaign and all. Not even August and he's campaigning like the election's tomorrow."

Margot paused at that. *Was* Cole only around because of his father? Were there political stratagems going on at her expense? November would be well after her due date by at least a month, but what could look better than the brother of the slain Jacob Patterson helping the sister of the couple he'd killed?

"You still think that, Nan?" Margot asked, holding her breath for the answer.

Nan smiled slightly and shook her head. "No. I'm usually pretty good at picking out the potential fathers who are incredibly excited and incredibly *not*, and he's definitely excited for you."

Margot relaxed and smiled at Nan's judgment. She was glad her gut feeling had been confirmed. Nothing had screamed political gain about Cole's actions, especially since he and his father didn't have the best relationship. Though it was entirely possibly he could be buttering her up to get on his father's good side, Margot didn't think it was probable. Besides, she remembered the night when they first met; nothing at all seemed fabricated about that.

There was a knock on the door and Cole poked his head into the room. "Is everything okay?"

"Fine," Margot assured him, giving him a small smile. He smiled in return and fully entered the room, coming next to her and nodding toward Dr. Dennison.

"So when's the next appointment?"

The two women gave each other an amused look, and Dr. Dennison chuckled slightly. "I think we can wait two months unless, of course, there are major complications, which I don't foresee. Margot's healthy and strong, and I think this baby will be too. Comes from good genes."

"The best," Margot said softly, her mind briefly going to Oscar. "The very best."

Cole squeezed her hand in support.

Dr. Dennison did prescribe prenatal vitamins, a recommended food and drink list for her to follow, and a "no-no" list for things she should avoid. As they left the office, Margot made an appointment for two months from now and paid for the visit. Cole eased the prescription and the list out of Margot's hands as she did both these things, and she gave him a weird look when he didn't return them as they went to the car.

He gave her a lopsided grin. "I can get these things on the list while you visit your brother."

That made good sense and Margot nodded. Cole always allowed her initial privacy when visiting her brother. Sometimes he'd come and sit with her later, sometimes he wouldn't. Margot realized it must be just as hard for Cole to see him as it was for her, knowing his brother was responsible for everything.

Cole walked with her inside the hospital though he wouldn't stay, and pressed a soft kiss on her forehead before he left.

"I'll be back soon," he promised, squeezing her shoulder one last time before going back to the car. Part of her wanted to call him back, suddenly unsure if she could give her brother the update about the appointment alone, unsure if the news would make him better or worse.

There seemed to have been no change from the last time she saw him yesterday, and Margot grew heartened and discouraged by that. No change meant Georgie wasn't getting worse. However, the longer there was no change, the more Dr. Pierce thought there wouldn't be, and the more he pressed her about organ donations. It was getting tough financially to keep him in the hospital too. All these pressures were weighing Margot down, especially since her parents had yet to return her phone call about Georgie. The burden was overwhelming and exhausting; and if Georgie didn't make any kind of change by the end of the week, she knew she would have to make a final decision one way or the other.

"Don't make me do that, Georgie," Margot murmured to him, picking up his hand and kissing the back of it. "You've still got something to live for. You've got your little son or daughter to live for, honey. You can do this."

He had to.

She told him about the appointment, quoting Dr. Dennison verbatim as much as she could, then of how their publisher, Family Books Publishing, would extend the deadline to release the final book Oscar had written and would establish a scholarship for Latino youth in his name. Margot had been touched when their editor, Tawny, had told her the news during their conference call yesterday afternoon. Margot had said Oscar would be very honored and humbled by such a gesture.

"I still need to finish the illustrations, of course," Margot continued, her thumb idly caressing the back of Georgie's hand, "but I've really not been in the right frame of mind to put a brush to canvas."

This usually would be the part where Georgie would tell her to get off her ass and beat her muse into submission if she wouldn't listen. That would always make her laugh, and, ironically enough, get her through whatever artist's block she'd been experiencing. Now there was no humorous pep talk, just his silence and the unbroken rhythm of the respirator breathing for him.

"Wake up, Georgie," Margot said, going back to the first words she'd said to him when this entire ordeal had started. "Wake. *Up.*"

Margot almost screamed when, *finally*, Georgie's eyelids opened to reveal red, unfocused eyes. Her entire body trembling violently, Margot stood and touched gentle fingers to his cheeks while the other hand that held his tightened.

"Hey, baby," she murmured, unable to stop the tears from falling. "Welcome back."

Georgie blinked, not saying anything, but she didn't care. His eyes were open! This was the sign they'd been waiting for!

She kissed his forehead. "I love you, Georgie."

He squeezed her hand in response, right before his hand went limp again and the abrasive drone of the heart monitor blared in her ears.

Before Margot realized it, she was being shoved out the room. Her face pressed against the high, thin window in the door as she watched nurses and doctors try to get his heart beating again. One nurse looked up and saw her, then came into the hallway and eased her away from the door, telling her they would let her know as soon as he was stabilized.

Cole found her staring at a tile in the floor fifteen minutes later, her face frozen in a frown of confusion and disbelief. When he sat beside her and took her hand in his, she didn't even blink.

"What happened?" Cole asked.

"He died."

Her eyes never moved from that spot when Cole pulled her into a side-hug, nor when Dr. Pierce came and offered his condolences. She didn't notice Cole pull her to her feet and walk her to the car, the drive from the hospital to her apartment, the fact Cole had taken her keys from her purse to let them into her building, the fact he'd led her into her bedroom and sat her on the bed. She noticed none of those things because her mind was fixed on that moment when Georgie had opened his eyes, something she'd wanted him to do since the moment he'd been admitted to the hospital, only to die seconds later.

"I gotta call our parents."

"Margot—"

"They should know...about Georgie...they should know he died today—"

"You're in no position to do anything but sleep."

"I can't sleep. I gotta call them..."

He framed her face in his hands, forcing her to meet his eyes.

"Margot."

His face became blurry, and two fat, warm tears rolled down her cheeks. "He squeezed my hand."

Cole nodded, brushing her tears away with his thumbs. "Honey..."

"He woke *up*."

"I know."

"Then why is he dead, Cole? *He's not supposed to be dead!*"

Cole pulled her tightly to him, but she couldn't commit to crying yet, too in shock and heartbroken for her tear ducts to work properly. She buried her face in the crook of Cole's neck, letting his warmth give her some sort of stability and comfort amid this horrendous turn of events. Today was supposed to be a good day—the first appointment with the obstetrician, telling Georgie about it, and going home to prepare for the next day's visit. She'd be going to the hospital again soon; but this time, it would be to claim the last member of her family who gave a damn about her.

She was now, officially, alone.

Cole held Margot long after she fell asleep, though he'd managed to convince her to change into something more comfortable. He'd left the room and warmed soup he'd found in one of the cabinets. Then he brought the bowl into her room to find her underneath the covers with her eyes closed and her head against the headboard. He'd thought she was sleeping and turned to leave, but then she'd called his name softly and he'd reentered the room.

"I don't want to be alone," she'd said, her voice a mere echo of how it usually was.

He'd set the bowl on the nightstand on her side of the bed, then sat at her feet, his hands rubbing along her shins. She'd closed her eyes again, her hands drifting along her belly to soothe. He hadn't forced her to eat, knowing she needed to deal with this latest loss in her own way and time.

But not alone. He wouldn't let her go through this alone.

Eventually, though he was sure neither of them had realized it, she was sidled next to him, her head on his chest and his arms tight around her waist and shoulders. He'd told her stories from his childhood—about the trip to Bermuda when he was six and Jacob had buried him almost completely in the sand, leaving him to breathe through a straw, and how he'd stayed buried for almost thirty minutes until his mother had been frantic that he was lost. He'd told her about the ski trip to Aspen when he was thirteen and how he'd found himself on a black diamond mountain by mistake, and how by sheer luck and the grace of God he'd made it down with little more than a sprained ankle and wrist. Now black diamonds were all he skied. He'd told her about when he'd been fifteen and he'd eagerly anticipated his first kiss playing Seven Minutes in Heaven; but in a twist of fate, the giver/recipient had been Larry Humes, so he didn't count it.

"But, maybe I should. A kiss is a kiss, after all."

That had earned a breathless chuckle from her.

"He wasn't half bad, either," Cole had mused, now that time had distanced himself away from the incident to where he could be objective about it. "I do remember hoping all girls' breaths didn't smell like root beer and jawbreakers, though."

"Incidentally, Georgie got his first kiss playing Spin the Bottle and his first kiss was a guy too. Needless to say, he had no trouble counting that."

"What was your first kiss?"

She'd chuckled again and shook her head. "Awful. I didn't even like him, but I didn't want to go to college without ever having a kiss; so when he leaned in, I let him. I promised myself never to be so desperate for affection again."

She'd snuggled deeper into him after she'd said that, and Cole didn't know if her words were ironic or as steadfast as she'd vowed they would be when she'd been younger.

"You like me, though," Cole had said.

"I do," Margot agreed. "You're pretty fly for a white guy."

Cole had laughed and pinched her side, causing her to jump and burrow even closer to him. "Quoting The Offspring? I didn't know black people listened to rock!"

"We invented it! Why wouldn't we listen to it?"

Cole just had shaken his head and kissed the top of hers. They hadn't said anything much after that, Margot falling asleep not long afterward. That had been almost four hours ago.

Now, Cole couldn't get to sleep, partly because it was still early, but mostly because he was far too comfortable to let go of Margot and leave her bed, and he knew he shouldn't be. She'd just lost her brother, for goodness sake, and all he could think of doing was holding her throughout the night as they slept. He knew how intimate that could be, especially when he'd done it with so few women—let alone with someone he considered his only true friend other than Jacob. He didn't want her to wake up freaked out and disgusted at him.

And this latest test wouldn't be so hard if Margot would stop pressing her body against his. Though she'd blessedly turned away from him, she still managed to follow his warmth, scooting back to find his body whenever he attempted to shift away from her.

It's not like she's doing it on purpose! Cole had reminded himself, but he had to dampen his desire to bring her snug against his front and wrap his arms around her, his body growing addicted to her lush curves. He kissed the back of her head, then nuzzled it, unused to her texture of hair but finding it soft and sweet-smelling, like a cloud. He liked her hair natural.

"Not now, Marcus."

Cole froze. She must be dreaming deeply if she thought he was her dead husband. He immediately felt guilty. His one little indulgence had taken her three years into the past, these latest events perhaps too much for her to handle. He tried to move back but she wouldn't let him, snuggling deeper into his body.

"You're killin' me, Margot," he muttered.

"Killin' *you*?" she asked incredulously, though her speech was slurred by sleep. "You're the one trying to 'spear' me with your weapon!"

She chuckled lightly and Cole blushed. He honest to God hadn't meant to react in such a way; but he was only a man, and Margot was an attractive woman. They'd talked about this; and though his brain knew, his body didn't care.

"Sorry," he apologized, smacking his forehead with the heel of his hand.

"It's all right...flattering, even, considering I feel like a whale."

"You're not a whale."

"Yet," she muttered. "I wonder if you'll have the inclination to 'spear' me when there's an entire house inside of me!"

There was no good way to respond to that, so Cole didn't, hoping she'd fall back asleep and they could reminisce on the ridiculousness of this night a long time from now, and after many pints of alcohol.

"Or maybe you're already starting to think that way," she murmured, moving away from him and curling her body tight.

He knew he had to reassure her, so he squeezed her shoulder and put his lips to her ear. "You'll always be beautiful to me, Margot."

She turned onto her back, eyes still closed with a faint smile on her face, whispering, "I love you." Then, to his surprise, she drew him down and gave him a light kiss.

Margot immediately opened her eyes at the contact, and they stared at each other in shock. Cole came back to his senses first and saw Margot's eyes dissipate from shock to abject horror. She let out loud, heart-wrenching sobs and he wordlessly gathered her to him, rocking her and telling her to let it all out.

This breakdown was more intense and longer than her last one, but that was to be expected. Her one hope had failed her, and to deal with its aftermath must be the worst thing in the world.

When this round of tears began dying down, Cole didn't shy away from her, tightening his arms around her and lying on his back so that she almost rested exclusively atop his body. She needed to know he was there for her completely, and no amount of tension he felt would prevent her from realizing that wholeheartedly.

Margot's lips tickled the skin covering his clavicle, and her fingers dragged idly against his right oblique. She didn't make a sound though he knew she was awake, and he didn't pressure her. He hoped she'd fall asleep soon so her emotionally exhausted body could refresh itself for the morning.

"Cole?"

He expelled all the air out of his lungs before slowly filling them up again. "Yes?"

"Don't leave me."

He kissed her forehead to avoid making a promise he couldn't guarantee.

Chapter Seven

Margot and Cole struggled to make that difficult transition back into the daily groove. However, it wasn't as bad for Cole as it was for Margot, especially considering he'd been allowed his "closure" earlier. Besides, he'd only lost one loved one, but Margot had to deal with two losses and handle all those affairs alone.

Though Cole hadn't been there when Margot had claimed her brother's body and had it cremated, he'd gone to her apartment after work so he could offer his support. Margot had accepted it gladly. The pair had sat on her couch with her curled into his body and watched the prime-time lineup on whatever channel happened to be on when Cole had turned on the television. They'd spoken little then, but their silence was the furthest thing from uncomfortable. To know there was someone there for you had said more than any audible words could.

The next day, Cole had met Gail Stewart, Margot's best friend since they'd been in second grade. He'd stopped over with a takeout bag of Indian food and had almost yelped when a nutmeg-hued, willowy woman answered the door instead of Margot's darker, curvier frame. Gail had arched an eyebrow at him and smirked.

"You're cute. You lost?" she'd asked. Margot had come up behind her, giving him a rueful smile and mouthing, "Sorry!" when she'd spotted him.

Luckily, Cole ordered enough food for all of them, and he'd been amused while listening to Gail lecture Margot as they ate about the importance of "communication" and how "communication" should happen in a timely manner.

"*Not* a week after the fact, Miss Thang!" Gail had said, squeezing Margot's shoulders affectionately. "I'm never too busy to be there for you, girl!"

Margot had merely hugged her in response, too moved and touched to say anything.

Cole could see why the two women were friends; they balanced each other out perfectly. Gail was an attractive woman as well and very smart—a chemist for a pharmaceutical company—and had more of the edge Margot only showed every now and again. They were as close as sisters, Margot saying her parents would've *preferred* having Gail as a daughter because at least *she* was doing something with her life.

"Your parents don't know what a wonderful daughter they have. I wouldn't wish your parents on my worst enemy!" Gail had responded and hugged her friend close again.

Their fathers were both professors at the University of Richmond. Gail's father, Edwin, was a chemistry professor and Margot's father was a professor in business administration. Their mothers had been stay-at-home moms, though Gail's mother, Sasha, was an heiress to a chain of ice cream shops in her hometown of Detroit. Faye did substitute teaching at the neighborhood elementary school when she wasn't writing columns for local papers and magazines. Both sets of parents had high expectations for their children, but only Gail had managed to meet them all to their liking.

Except for the whole finding a husband thing. Gail was still working on that one.

And was apparently working on that for Margot, too, for whenever Margot left the two alone, Gail would drill him with questions upon questions about his family, job security, past relationships, and hopes for future ones. He'd blushed throughout her one-sided interview, especially when she ignored his insistence they were "just friends."

"I was born during the day, but not *yesterday*," Gail had said, shaking her head slightly. "You sweet on her."

"Sweet on her?"

Gail had rolled her eyes. "You like her. More than just a friend. It's as plain as the broadside of a barn! Though you may be a little younger and paler than someone I would've chosen for Mar, I like you. You obviously treat her well enough that she was comfortable not to call me until two days ago!"

Cole had blushed even more and his mind had gone back to the last night he'd slept over, when Margot had kissed him. Though it had been fleeting and little more than a whisper of lips, Cole had never been so emotionally affected by a kiss. It was then he'd realized how much she'd loved her husband, and had gained an inkling of understanding as to why Marcus had fallen in love with her. There was something about Margot that made a person want to be the best he could be.

"Girl, quit botherin' him!" Margot would hiss whenever she came back into the room from her brief exits. "You're makin' him blush!"

It had also made him step back a little. Taking advantage of Margot was the last thing he wanted to be accused of doing, so he'd trimmed his visits and phone conversations, pleading "swamped at work" because he knew Margot would understand. It wasn't until she'd stopped calling altogether that he realized his stupidity.

After a week had passed since their last conversation, Cole had grown uneasy and concerned. In the month since their first meeting, Cole and Margot had never gone for more than a day without speaking to each other, even just a quick phone conversation. Perhaps he'd grown too comfortable in the fact that Gail, someone she'd known for far longer than he, was with her now and could probably comfort her far better than he could; or the fact Gail's words had spooked him into avoidance. Margot had sounded very surprised when she'd received his call and had even admitted she thought he'd finally grown tired of her.

"Impossible," he'd said sincerely. Cole had discovered Gail had returned to New Jersey by this point; and though the two women had talked every night since her departure, both he and Margot knew it wasn't the same.

Ever since then, they'd taken to nightly phone calls and once-a-week dinners that usually took place at her house, though sometimes they ventured out to a restaurant. It'd gotten to the point that restaurants knew their orders and what time to bring them whenever he or Margot called.

"We're pathetic," she'd determined after one such occasion, manipulating the chopsticks he'd taught her how to use to pick up her Thai fried rice.

"I don't mind if you don't," Cole had said.

"Not at all."

The one thing Cole hadn't done since their renewed friendship was stay overnight. He drew the line there, especially after what had happened the last time. He didn't want to put either of them in such an awkward position again, so he left, no matter how late it was, and always called her the minute he got home because it made her nervous when he drove late at night...and because that was the time most drunk drivers took to the road.

"I don't want to have to turn on the news and hear your name as a crash victim," Margot had said during one of those late-night exits. "I don't think I'd be able to take it."

Cole had pressed a long kiss on her forehead and vowed she wouldn't, not if he had anything to say about it.

They both knew he didn't; they'd gotten effective reminders of that almost two months ago, but it still made both feel better to hear him say it.

Mother's Day was coming up soon. Usually, Cole's family would take Jill to the Mother's Day brunch at the Café Fleuri. Cole wanted to invite Margot, especially since she would be a mother in five months. He didn't want to make her uncomfortable, however, and brunch with his family might seem a little like the "meeting the folks" stage of a relationship, even if they were just friends.

He had to remind himself of that with more and more frequency as the weeks passed, even going so far as to flip through his black book and date other women. While he'd had enjoyable times with them, they didn't compare to sitting on Margot's couch watching television with her snoozing on his shoulder.

What in the world was wrong with him? Dating women had never been a problem before—in fact, it was one of his favorite pastimes—but recently, he couldn't be bothered. Cole knew he couldn't blame it on his brother's passing; though it still caused a twinge in his heart, his grief had dulled enough for him to have a good time. Unfortunately, Jacob had been the only person with whom he felt comfortable talking about such dilemmas. Since Margot was indirectly the source of his current confusion, he could only think of one more person who might be able to help him.

"My...I didn't know if you still remembered the way home, as long as it's been since you've last been here!"

Cole grinned and entered the house, hugging his mother tight and kissing her tenderly on the cheek. "I'm sorry, Mom."

"It's all right, dear," Jill assured him, pulling him further into the house and walking with him to the kitchen. "I was just about to make tea."

"Is Dad here?" he asked, though he knew Frank shouldn't be. Cole had planned his visit when he thought Frank would be away from home. Jill had given him a look but said nothing, telling Cole she was onto his game. Cole gave a half-shrug, refusing to feel repentant about his timing.

He pulled down the teacups as she put on the kettle and pulled out cookies for them to snack on. They spoke idly as they waited for the water to boil, both wanting to save the meat of the conversation as they sipped their tea.

When it was ready, Jill filled their cups with water and put a jar of honey on the table for them to sweeten their tea, and Cole waited a few more minutes before finally broaching the subject.

"I think I'm ready for you to meet Margot," he said without preamble, eyeing his mother's reaction.

She arched an eyebrow as she put two tablespoons of honey into her tea before passing the jar to him. "Is she ready to meet us?"

"I'm honestly not sure. We don't talk about it much."

Jill frowned. "Why not?"

Cole shrugged. "Parents are not the easiest conversations for us to have."

"Cole..."

"I know," he said, squeezing Jill's hand. "But since Mother's Day is coming up, I want to treat Margot to something nice, but I don't want to miss out sharing the big day with you, either, so why not combine the two?"

Jill paled. "She's pregnant? Are you telling me I'm about to be a grandma!"

Cole would've laughed if Jill weren't so serious with her question. "No! No...no, it's not like that at all!"

Jill relaxed slightly but still looked at him askance. "But...?"

"She *is* pregnant, but not by me. She was to be the surrogate mother for her brother and brother-in-law," Cole explained.

Realization dawned on Jill and she gasped. "Oh my."

"Yeah. I don't want her to be alone on Sunday," Cole said, putting honey in his tea before taking a sip of it. "She deserves something positive after all that's happened to her."

He filled his mother on the details of the past month; and when he was finished, Jill was wiping tears from her cheeks with her napkin.

"That's so awful!"

"But I wanted to run it by you first before I invited Margot to the brunch—"

"Of course!" Jill said. "Of course she can join us! And if she doesn't, I'll understand if you want to spend the day with her—"

"I don't want to do that," Cole said, the field day his father would have with his absence notwithstanding. "I should be there for you, too, especially since..." Since the first reason she'd become a mother was now dead.

Jill left the table and hugged her son close. "If she'd like to meet me before the brunch, I'll be more than happy to, wherever she'd be comfortable. We don't even have to have brunch at the Langham; we can have it wherever she wants." Jill kissed the top of Cole's head. "Like you said, she shouldn't be alone, and I'm not so selfish a mother to make you choose, dear. Do whatever you think is best."

Cole returned his mother's hug just as strongly. Unfailing support, that was what his mother had always offered him, and this was why he had to be there with her on Mother's Day.

It was the least he could do to show how grateful he was that she was in his life.

-SJF-

Her skirt would *not* fit anymore. No matter how many times Margot did that awkward shimmy or sucked in her gut, the skirt would not zip or button, its sides gaping, mocking her.

Margot glared at her reflection in the mirror, taking in the way the strap of her bra slid down her left arm and how there seemed to be more cleavage than normal; the rolled-down elastic band of her hosiery at her waist as it peeked through the unzipped portion of her skirt; the sheen of sweat on her brow and upper lip from her efforts and hormones.

She was showing.

Margot had been in denial about it for a week, claiming the wash had suddenly shrunk her clothes instead of the baby inside her making her waistline grow. It was little more than a tiny bump, really, but it made her pregnancy suddenly very real and very tangible.

"Why now?" Margot moaned, dropping her face in her hands. Cole would be here soon and she couldn't fit into her clothes anymore! What kind of impression would she make on his parents if she couldn't meet them fully clothed?

Sighing, she stood and took a deep breath before emptying out her lungs and diaphragm and trying again.

"Up!" Margot willed as she inched the zipper northward. It passed the critical point where it had always gotten stuck. Only a few more centimeters to go.

"Whoa!"

Rip!

Margot closed her eyes and counted slowly, trying desperately not to cry. She'd been so close...

"Mar?"

She couldn't look at Cole, too embarrassed to do anything but wish she were somewhere, anywhere, but in her room half-dressed with him staring at her with what she knew was concern.

It was then she thought perhaps giving Gail and Cole keys to her apartment hadn't been the best idea.

"Are you all right?"

"My skirt tore," Margot said pathetically. "I have nothing to wear."

She sat down on her bed, tired. Perhaps this brunch wasn't meant to be. When Cole had presented the idea to her, she'd been wary, especially since she felt like an interloper on his mother's special day. While she was *going* to be a mother, she wasn't one yet; and she could use the day working on the illustrations for Oscar's book.

Never mind the fact her own parents had yet to return her phone calls—not the one before about Georgie being in a coma, the one a few days later to tell them he'd passed, or the one earlier when she'd called and wished her mother a Happy Mother's Day.

Just because they hurt and ignored her didn't mean she didn't love her mother, her parents, still.

Speaking of... "You should call your parents and tell them I can't come—"

"Oh, you're coming, Margot Elise Butler Reed! Even if I have to drag you out myself!"

Margot arched an eyebrow at him. "No you did *not* trot my full name out like that! You ain't my daddy!"

He smirked at her, coming further into the room. "Anything to get that fire in those deep, brown eyes of yours."

"Cole..."

He knelt before her, squeezing her knees. "You *have* to come. I want you to meet my parents, especially my mother. You need someone who's had experience being a mother, you know, since..."

He let the thought trail and Margot nodded absently. Since her own mother was stubbornly, stupidly, unavailable; and as wonderful as Nan was on the medical side of things, she didn't know the intangibles of motherhood because she wasn't a mother.

"It's *because* of my job I realized that this whole pregnancy thing is not for me," Nan had said, "but that doesn't mean I don't deeply respect and admire the women who do have children. Not every woman is supposed to be a mother, after all."

Margot had thought she'd be one of those women after her miscarriage and Marcus's death; now she was four months along into being proven wrong.

"I'm pregnant, Cole."

"I believe that fact's been established, yes."

"My clothes fit a Margot who's *not* pregnant."

His brows furrowed. "*Nothing* fits?"

"Nothing for me to meet your parents in!" Margot stood and went to her closet again. She hadn't been this on edge when she met Marcus's uncle!

She shoved hanger after hanger of clothes aside as she prayed something suitable would turn up, and it wasn't until Cole's warm hands enclosed around hers that she took pause.

"Relax, Mar," he whispered in her ear. "Everything will be okay."

"My own parents don't like me, Cole," Margot said just as softly. "How can I think yours will?"

Cole kissed her temple and slid his arms around her waist. Margot leaned into him, needing his strength and security right then. His fingers were soft as they trailed along the bare skin of her small bump, and he dropped his chin on her shoulder.

"They will like you, Margot, because you are a wonderful, talented, beautiful person. Your parents can't see that because they're too fixated on the fact you're not the specific type of wonderful, talented, beautiful person they wanted you to be. But Gail knows you are and *I* know you are; and soon, my parents will too."

She pressed her hand against his that was on her stomach, very grateful for his perspective and assurance in her moment of doubt. "Are you sure you're only twenty-five? That was some serious wisdom just now!"

He chuckled in her ear and kissed her cheek. "As soon as we find you something to wear, you can meet and thank the woman who passed it on to me!"

In the end, they found a sleeveless lavender sheath dress that, while a little snug, fit her well enough for brunch. Margot had half a mind to make him leave, but considering he'd found her in just her underwear, and the fact she needed his help, she tamped down her modesty. Besides, she was sure he'd seen women in far less clothing.

"There we are," he murmured as he zipped up her dress, and, surprising her, kissed her bare shoulder. "You look nice."

Margot turned to him, unaware he hadn't moved his face yet, so they were little more than a breath apart. Cole's eyes were kind and so blue. Margot stepped away from him quickly, suddenly very unsure of herself.

"Thanks," she whispered, going to the foot of the bed and slipping on her flats. She was clearly losing her mind. Looking into Cole's eyes had made her feel a way she only had with Marcus, but they were friends...just friends...right?

They spoke little on the drive into Boston, though Margot did her best to ignore the glances he threw her way. She'd analyze her weird feelings after she had this brunch with his folks.

It wasn't long until they reached the hotel, and she was amazed by the beautiful décor of the building. She'd never been inside of the Langham, though this hotel would have been right up her parents' alley. It had the air of wealth and sophistication to it, everything Robert and Faye Butler strived to achieve and maintain.

"I see them," Cole said, dropping his mouth to her ear so she could hear him. There was a jazz band playing amid the clanking of dishes and the murmuring of brunch patrons. There were numerous stations around the dining area—one for waffles, one for freshly carved roast, one for fruits, one for hot breakfast items, one for dessert, one for hot dinner items, one for cold items, and a chocolate fountain.

Her stomach growled, clearly anticipating the feast.

"Come on."

Her feet refused to move, and it wasn't until Cole linked their hands together that she could walk. Her grip tightened as they got closer to the table, and the very attractive auburn-haired woman smiled brightly when she saw them arrive.

"Cole!"

He went to her happily, hugging her tightly and wishing her a Happy Mother's Day. Margot clasped her hands before her but didn't move closer, watching their reunion wistfully. She wished she had this type of relationship with her own mother.

"Mom, this is Margot. Margot, this is my mother Jill."

Jill's blue eyes were as kind as her son's, and she approached, cupping Margot's face tenderly with both hands. "It's very nice to finally meet you, Margot."

"You too," Margot said, giving Jill a small smile. Her affection was entirely unexpected, and she blinked quickly to keep tears from forming in her eyes.

Jill saw this and hugged her close, her hands running up and down Margot's back soothingly. Cole was right; much of his empathy and compassion clearly came from this woman, and Margot was thankful.

"Is this Margot?"

The women pulled apart and a tall, broad man with brown hair and blue eyes that were just like his son's greeted Margot. She held out a hand to him. "Yes, Mr. Patterson, sir. Nice to meet you."

"Nice to meet you too," he said, shaking her hand. He gave her an appraising look, then glanced at Cole. "She's pretty."

There was something about Mr. Patterson's tone that rubbed Margot the wrong way, but Jill linked her arm through Margot's and patted Margot's hand. "Very pretty. I see why my son's taken with you."

"Jill, now, really," Mr. Patterson admonished gently and gave Margot a long-suffering look. "She's always ready to play the matchmaker." Mr. Patterson pulled out the seat for Jill while Cole did the same for Margot. She thanked him quietly and Cole gave her a reassuring smile.

"What do you do, Ms....?"

"Mrs. Reed," Cole answered for her.

Mr. Patterson was surprised by that. "You're carrying on with a married woman?"

"We're just friends, Dad—" Mr. Patterson's snort cut off Cole's explanation and Margot frowned.

"I'm widowed," Margot continued for Cole, "and we are just friends. He's been very helpful to me."

"I understand," Jill said, glaring at her husband. "And you...are you all right? How's the baby doing—?"

"*Baby?*"

Jill ignored her husband's outburst. "I can give you some tips on how to fight fatigue, morning sickness if you still get it, the best creams for aches and pains....Though it's been about twenty-six years since I last was pregnant, I still remember a few things!"

"Her first pregnancy was infinitely better than her second, though," Mr. Patterson said, squeezing his wife's shoulder. "Cole made Jill get on bed rest he was so active and difficult, but Jacob…Jacob had been a breeze."

"You want me to start making your plate, Mom? Margot?" Cole said, giving his father a dirty look before throwing his napkin on the table and leaving. Margot got up and followed, shooting Jill an apologetic look but not giving Mr. Patterson any, too afraid her disgust would show. Cole was at the fruit table, spearing the slices of honeydew far too roughly.

"Hey," Margot said, linking her arm through his. Cole barely spared her a glance. "The pineapples look good too."

"You know, if he had to choose which son had to die two months ago, he would've said me with no hesitation," Cole said, putting pineapples on his plate. "You should get some fruit too. For the baby."

"You two are pregnant?" a woman behind Margot asked, a smile blossoming on her face. "*Congratulations!* When is it due?"

"Ah—"

"October," Cole answered, ignoring Margot's look of disbelief.

"Oh! That is *wonderful!* I'd go for some strawberries and apples and oranges—can't go wrong, dear."

"Thank you," Margot said, then looked at Cole as if he were crazy when he proceeded to load up her plate with the fruits. "*Ever* so much."

"Just want you to deliver a healthy baby, *dear*," Cole said, winking at her as he finished preparing his mother's fruit plate.

"You two have a Happy…well…'Soon-to-Be' Mother's Day!" the woman called, and Margot gave her a little wave as she and Cole went back to their table.

"You are so bad," Margot said, chuckling a little at Cole's behavior.

"What, exactly, was bad about what I just did?" Cole challenged, a wicked, superior gleam in his eye because he knew he was right. Margot rolled hers, wondering why she wasn't nearly as irritated as she pretended to be. Cole had merely stated the facts; so what that he'd let the woman interpret *he* was the father of her baby?

"All my favorite fruits," Jill had gushed when they returned to the table. Mr. Patterson looked more subdued than earlier and didn't say anything to them. It was just as well; Margot didn't like the vibe she got from him at all.

"So, Margot," Jill said as she took a bite of pineapple. "Cole says you're an artist?"

"She's fantastic, Mom! She—"

"I'm sorry; I don't think I named you Margot, sweetheart," Jill said sweetly. Both Margot and Mr. Patterson had to chuckle at that.

"Right now I'm an illustrator," Margot said, patting Cole's knee under the table. "I also do portraits, still life, landscapes...anything that strikes a fancy."

Jill pursed her lips, cutting into the honeydew slice with her fork. "If I...gave you a family picture, could you paint it for me?"

Margot nodded. "Of course I can, Mrs. Patterson—"

"Jill, please, call me Jill."

"Yes, ma'am."

Jill smiled at her, chuckling slightly. "You're not originally from Boston, are you?"

Margot laughed also. She hadn't gotten that question in years. "Richmond, Virginia. Seems I still have a little of my accent."

"When you say certain words," Cole confirmed. "And when Gail was here, my goodness! I thought I would need a translation book to understand you two!"

Margot shot him a playful side-eye. "Got jokes, huh?"

"Plenty," Jill said, smiling softly at her son. "He always has; part of his charm, isn't it?"

"He could stand to be more serious more often," Mr. Patterson said. "Too many jokes make you seem incompetent. Jacob knew the proper places and times for such behavior; why Cole never learned the same, I'll never know."

"In the weeks that I've known him, Cole's been perfect," Margot said, getting upset by Mr. Patterson's constant dismissal of his son. "It's almost as if you have to stretch to find the things you don't like about him!"

Mr. Patterson's eyes narrowed. "You don't know me or my son well enough to make a judgment like that."

"I've seen him at his most vulnerable, Mr. Patterson," Margot refuted. "That's as well as anyone needs to know a person to make a judgment call. He's a good man, a good person. How many people do you know would make sure the sister of the couple his *brother* had killed was all right for more than a day? A week? That is compassion, Mr. Patterson. That is the marking of a good person. You and Mrs. Patterson raised *two* good sons; please don't devalue one for the sake of the other. It's not fair for anyone."

The table was deathly quiet after her speech. Margot looked at the remaining fruit on her plate, wanting nothing more than the floor to open up and swallow her. She'd just met Mr. Patterson and she was lecturing *him* about *his* son? He'd known Cole for twenty-five years! Her two months really did have nothing on that! Yet, perhaps it was the opportunity to say to Mr. Patterson what she wanted to say to her parents, couldn't say to her parents, that allowed Margot to drop her sense of propriety and speak her mind. She only hoped she didn't make the relationship between Cole and Mr. Patterson any worse.

The tender kiss on her cheek made her look up and Cole's soft blue eyes greeted hers. "Thank you for that," he said to her. Margot nodded.

"I couldn't have said it any better myself," Jill agreed.

Mr. Patterson stood, not looking at anyone. "I'll get started on your waffle, Jill."

The rest of the brunch went by much easier, though that was mainly because Mr. Patterson kept his conversations strictly with Jill. By the end of it, Jill had hugged her and invited her to tea whenever she wanted, and Margot promised she'd bring her sketchbook and portfolio so Jill could view her work.

"I'd like that," Jill had said, and kissed both her and Cole's cheeks. "It was wonderful to meet you, Margot."

"You, too, Mrs. Patterson—"

"Jill," she corrected gently.

Margot laughed. "Jill."

Mr. Patterson nodded at them both and ushered his wife out the building. Cole slinked his hand down to tangle his fingers with hers.

"She likes you," he said, squeezing her hand.

"You father…"

"I don't really care what he thinks."

"You do," Margot insisted. "We always do."

Cole kissed her temple and they walked out the building as well, waiting for the valet to bring his car to the front. Margot took a quick nap on the drive back to her apartment, and a soft sensation on her cheek roused her. Cole grinned at her and she returned a sheepish one.

"That waffle knocked me out cold."

"So, the first one was for you, and the second was for the baby, hmm?"

Margot rolled her eyes and chuckled. "Boy, get away from me with that mess!"

Cole laughed and caressed her cheek again before unbuckling her seatbelt for her. They left the car and went inside, Margot's moves lethargic as she really had enjoyed the food too much.

"Need me to carry you?" he asked once they entered the apartment's lobby,

"Boy, please!"

"All right."

She yelped as she was suddenly weightless, her arms clamping around his neck. He waggled his eyebrows at her and stepped on the elevator.

"Put me down!"

"You said please."

"I'll break your back!"

"You're not all that heavy, Margot. Relax. Enjoy. It's your day, after all."

Margot was embarrassed and a little thrilled at Cole carrying her to the apartment. He let her unlock the door, laughing in her ear as she had difficulty fitting the key in the lock at her angle.

"Shut up."

"You're adorable."

"I'm warning you, Cole!"

Finally, she got the door unlocked and Cole set her down gently on the couch. "Enjoy the ride?"

Margot plopped back on the couch in her answer, moaning a little as he slipped her shoes off her feet. "Marcus used to do that for me."

"Hmm." Cole began kneading her left foot.

"That too."

"It's your day to be pampered."

"Friends don't generally pamper friends."

Cole didn't stop but met her eyes. "We're not 'general' friends."

Margot inhaled deeply and let it out slowly. "No, we're not." She licked her lips. "The woman you marry will be very lucky."

That did make him pause. "What?"

Margot shrugged. "If you treat your friends like this, your woman will be *very* happy."

Cole blushed and took her other foot in his hand. "If you had met me earlier, you would've thought I was the worst kind of jerk."

"People change, gain perspective, grow. I didn't meet you earlier for a reason."

"My brother—"

"No, not your brother," Margot insisted. "We weren't meant to meet until when we did. Not meant to be friends before now. I may not go to church regularly, but I'm a spiritual person; and I believe God never makes mistakes when it comes to things like this. How else do you explain our friendship?"

"Why would you want to?" They smiled at each other. "Are you napping here or should I carry you to your room?"

"You've done enough of that," Margot joked dryly. "I'll just lie here for a minute."

She curled her body onto the couch, her eyes already growing heavy. A blanket draped over her, and Cole nuzzled her ear.

"I'm going to head out, get some work done. Want me to bring back something for dinner?"

"No. I don't think I can eat anything else for the rest of the day!"

He chuckled. "All right. I'll call you later tonight, okay?"

"Yes, Dad."

He laughed and kissed her temple. "Happy Mother's Day, Margot."

She smiled as she let sleep overcome her, thinking this day certainly was better than she thought it could've been.

Chapter Eight

It was a mild, late-May afternoon in New England with spring finally deciding to feel like spring. To celebrate, Jill and Margot decided to have their chat/consultation on the screened-in porch at the back of the Patterson house. Cole had dropped her off earlier that morning before going downtown for his meetings, promising to be back in the afternoon. Though Margot and Jill had gotten along during the brunch two weeks earlier, Margot was still nervous about spending the day alone with Cole's mother. Jill, however, put those nerves at ease when, after preparing tea for them, she broke out old baby albums of Jacob and Cole and shared them with her.

Aside from Jacob's black hair and Cole's blond tresses, and the fact they were two years apart, they could've easily been twins. Margot could tell from the photos the boys had been precocious charmers, especially little Cole, who always gave the biggest smiles even with his mother's lipstick, mascara, and blush smeared all over his face and torso; or with an entire five pounds of flour all over him, his brother, and the kitchen floor. Jacob had a more serious air about him, clearly taking his role as firstborn and older brother very seriously, and was hardly the same hands-on child Cole had been. They'd loved each other, though, as evidenced by one particularly touching photo of the two boys watching lightning bugs in a jar, one of Jacob's arms holding his brother while the other pointed out the insects.

"As different as they seemed to be, they really were each other's best friend," Jill said as they stared at the picture. "It's one of my favorites of them."

"I see why."

"Frank had said I was a bit overzealous with the pictures when they were younger, but childhood is so fleeting and I wanted to capture as many moments as possible."

Her parents hadn't been as enthusiastic as Jill, taking her and her brother to Sears for Easter and Christmas family portraits or paying for the basic photo packages when school picture days rolled around. All the candid, fun shots of her and Georgie were ones Gail and her parents took; and when she was in college, there were few pressures of the Butler household keeping her stifled. Marcus, however, was a camera fiend, catching her at all hours of the day—even when she didn't think she was picture-worthy—but he always managed to make her seem as beautiful as he thought she was.

"This is the picture I'd like as a painting," Jill said, pulling it out the photo album. It was a recent photo of the entire family and they were wearing formal attire. It seemed to be some sort of party or wedding, and they were outside in a beautifully sculpted garden full butterflies dancing around them and an explosion of yellows, pinks, reds, and violets.

"We were attending my girlfriend's daughter's wedding in St. Louis last spring; they had the wedding at The Conservatory down there—gorgeous gardens and landscaping. My girlfriend Susie insisted on a photo, and we took it. Frank has a secret soft spot for weddings."

Everyone was smiling in the photograph. Frank had his arms around the shoulders of his two sons and Jill stood in front of Frank with Jacob and Cole grasping each of her shoulders.

"You are a handsome family," Margot murmured.

"Yes; I'm just glad I have a photograph that proves it," Jill muttered. "The last few months had been anything but."

Margot cleared her throat, growing uncomfortable with the talk. "Do you have a scanner or a way to get this photocopied? I don't know when I actually start painting, but I can do preliminary sketches."

"You can keep it if it would be better for you. I trust you."

That surprised Margot. "You do?"

"I like you, Margot. I think you're good for my son."

Margot chuckled nervously. "We're just friends."

"An excellent foundation to a relationship, I think," Jill said, her lips quirking slightly.

"Mrs. Patterson—"

"*Jill.*"

"Jill," Margot repeated. "I don't...I mean...we're..." How could she explain? The possibility of her and Cole was ludicrous, wasn't it? They were in two different stages of their lives: she'd been married and was about to be a mother in five months; he was just hitting his stride and a family was probably the furthest thing from his mind! Then the whole racial aspect of it....Though Cole being white didn't bother her, and it seemed she being black didn't bother Cole or Jill, they would still have to think about it and discuss it should—

What are you thinking *Margot!*

"Attracted to each other," Jill finished for her, an amused expression on her face. "Though I've never seen Cole so attracted to anyone before."

Jill *really* shouldn't say things like that. It complicated matters. "He feels responsible for me."

Jill laughed. "Perhaps, but that's not all he feels!"

"Mrs.—Jill—surely, I...I must fascinate him on some level, right? I doubt he's brought many women who look like me for you to meet!"

Jill scrunched up her nose. "He rarely introduces me to any of his 'friends.'"

Margot grinned, grateful for the opening Jill had unwittingly given her. "He introduced me *because* we don't have that type of…'friendship.'"

That knowing look, however, never wavered from Jill. "It's all right, Margot."

"What's all right?"

"To have feelings for my son. And it's all right for him to have feelings for you."

Margot shook her head, unable to believe that. It couldn't be okay to open up her heart again, not when it had been slammed shut repeatedly over the years: first her parents, then Marcus, now Oscar and Georgie. She couldn't make herself vulnerable again, especially to someone who had entered her life so unexpectedly and accidentally. God might have intended for them to become friends out of this entire ordeal, but *not* for her to have these incredibly inappropriate feelings for her young companion.

Jill squeezed Margot's hand supportively. "It takes time to consider this with all the other things, duties you may have. I have friends; and one of my best friends, even though it may not seem that way, is Frank."

Jill was right; the last thing Margot would've thought was Frank being her best friend. Then again, Marcus had been her best friend— the first person she wanted to tell about her day; the first person who would hear about her fears about an upcoming project; the one person she would allow to see her preliminary sketches and drafts. Oscar and Georgie had filled that void, but only to a certain degree. It helped that she and Oscar had worked together and that Georgie had needed her for advice. But in terms of a best friend, Georgie and Oscar were each other's best friend; she was their mutual sister. Gail was different because she was female and lived seven hours away; there was only so much closeness and sharing they could do over the phone. They were not in each other's daily lives; and no matter how hard they tried, Gail could never understand the intense frustration that came when there was no more charcoal at the art supply store; and Margot would never understand the complete gridlock that could happen if someone didn't label a calculation properly, even if nothing had changed from the first time it was done to the most recent.

"You haven't seen my portfolio," Margot mumbled, then slapped her head and groaned. She'd left it in Cole's car. "And you won't see it until Cole comes back!"

Jill laughed and squeezed Margot's shoulder. "That's all right, dear. I'd much rather talk more with you, anyway!"

Margot laughed with her and relaxed. At first, they started talking about the weather, and then that turned into a discussion of her hometown's milder climate. Margot told Jill of how beautiful Richmond was in the spring, with everything an explosion of color and the very essence of renewal. Then Margot spoke of how she would walk along the banks of the Potomac River when she'd lived in DC and how she and Marcus would always make a point to see the cherry blossoms in bloom.

"Marcus?"

"My husband. My late husband."

Though there was a wistful twinge as she said his name, the fond, loving memories of their time together flooded her, and she smiled as she told Jill stories about him and their life together. Marcus had always had a habit of cupping her face whenever he kissed her, and he'd also had a habit of not washing his hands whenever he finished working on cars. That had led to one particularly embarrassing, yet in hindsight, humorous incident where Margot had given a presentation with two oily Marcus thumbprints on her cheeks as a result of him giving her a good-luck kiss when she'd stopped by the auto shop to drop off the lunch he'd left at home.

"My colleague kept wiping at his face, but I had no idea what he meant!" Margot giggled. Jill was laughing so hard her face was red. "I should've checked a mirror, but Marcus had said I looked fine and I believed him. The biased bastard!"

"Oh Margot!"

"I think he did that on purpose. He had a habit of playing practical jokes on me; said I was too serious and needed to loosen up!"

"Was he right?"

Margot threw her a sheepish grin. "Yeah, he allowed me to have fun. Said it was all right to let my guard down. He made it safe for me to do so."

"Do you have a picture of him?"

Margot took out her wallet and flipped it to the wedding photo she still carried of them. She was kissing Marcus's cheek in the photo. He was holding her gently and tenderly, a content expression on his face.

"You were a very lovely couple," Jill murmured. "You two were very happy."

"Very," Margot repeated, her smile widening.

Neither had dressed up for the occasion, as it had been done quite impulsively after they'd spent a day having a picnic on the Mall with Gail, Oscar, and Georgie, who'd been in town visiting. They'd gotten a license and the good fortune of being the recipients of a canceled appointment with the justice of the peace.

"How long ago did he pass away?"

"It'll be four years in August."

She couldn't believe it; time had gone so quickly these past few months, and with good reason. Margot couldn't help but feel a little guilty about not thinking of Marcus as often as she had in the past, but she was sure Marcus understood. Maybe before she got too big she'd go to DC to visit his grave.

"Have you seen anyone romantically since his death?"

Margot shook her head. "Not at all. I hadn't had an interest, even when Oscar kept trying to introduce me to his friends. I couldn't do it."

Jill nodded. "I can understand that."

"You can?"

"A loss is a loss, whether death, a breakup, or a friendship falling apart. There is no correct 'timing' about these things, Margot. It's okay, dear. Marcus probably wouldn't want a wonderful woman like you not to enjoy yourself and a second chance, right?"

"Everything okay?"

Cole walked in, his hands holding her portfolio and his eyes looking at her with concern. Margot offered him a small smile as he sat next to her and grasped her hand. "I'm fine, Cole."

"Did she eat, Mom? She's not had an appetite recently—"

"Proof you are over my house *way* too often!"

"I like your house," Cole said, waggling his eyebrows. Margot rolled his eyes and shoved him gently with her shoulder.

"We had some tea and cookies not too long ago, so she did eat," Jill said amusedly.

"And I already have a father; I don't need another one!" Margot muttered.

"Not for *you*," Cole said and touched his hand to her more-pronounced belly. "For *you*."

Margot felt Jill's knowing look but refused to meet it. How could a woman *not* melt at this? Cole talking to her belly was one of the sexiest things he could do, and it wasn't even his baby! Margot was still very surprised at how excited Cole was about her impending motherhood, though he really had nothing to do with it at all.

"We'll be fine," Margot assured him. She was talking with Nan for advice, and Gail had said she would try to take some time off from work during the first few weeks after the birth—the benefits of having saved up vacation days over the year.

"I know you will; I'll be there every step of the way," Cole vowed.

"You've already done more than enough for me and her," Margot said, unable to prevent herself from holding her hand over his. He was going above and beyond for her and the baby, but she wanted him to know he wasn't beholden to her in any way. Whatever phantom debt he thought he owed, he'd paid it tenfold.

"You're having a little girl?" Jill cooed.

Margot chuckled. "I'm not sure. Just a feeling. I have another appointment in about a week, but Oscar and Georgie wanted a daughter, so...I'm willing it for them."

"A little Margot," Cole said, his eyes twinkling and his smile bright. "She'll be adorable."

"The world doesn't need another one of me, that's for sure!" Margot said, trying to steer the conversation to safer ground, especially with Jill's sharp eyes observing them.

"I disagree," Jill said. "Don't you, Cole?"

"Completely," Cole said, rubbing her tummy. "Then again, you are one in a million."

Margot snorted. "That was too corny coming from you!"

"You wound me, Margot!" Cole gasped and whined to his mother. "She called me corny!"

Jill laughed. "It was a little hokey, honey, you have to admit."

Cole gave a mock pout to both of them and dropped his mouth to Margot's belly. "You don't think I'm corny, do you, baby?"

Margot gave a faux, long-suffering sigh, yet secretly relished the attention Cole gave her. He was making it very hard to stop the feelings that were burgeoning for him and making her wonder why she even tried.

It was dark by the time Cole and Margot decided to leave his parents' home. The trio had gone through Margot's portfolio, the quality of her work amazing mother and son, and Cole was even more amazed by Margot's discomfort with the praise. Eventually, Jill had commissioned two other paintings and bought a sketch, something that had surprised Margot immensely. Toward the end of the business portion of the visit, Margot's tummy started growling with gusto, and Jill suggested they stay for dinner. Though Cole had cut up apple wedges for Margot, all three decided to share in dinner-making duties. They settled on spaghetti with homemade meat sauce and garlic bread. Frank had entered the home as they prepared dinner, but only tossed them an absent greeting and said he wasn't hungry when Jill told him what they were cooking.

Margot, who had been open and laughing before his father's appearance, became very subdued.

"Ignore him," Cole had said, kissing her temple. "He rarely ate with the family when we were growing up."

"Cole," Jill had admonished half-heartedly. "I'll prepare him a plate, anyway."

"If it would be more comfortable for me to leave—"

"No," Cole had said firmly. "You'll stay."

Cole honestly hadn't known what his father's deal was, but Margot would not be made to feel uncomfortable because of it. Jill, thankfully, had gotten them back to their earlier jovial spirit; and by the time they'd finished eating, they'd all been happily full of good food and cheer.

Margot was currently in the bathroom and Jill and Cole were waiting in the foyer for her return. He noticed his mother's attention on him and he chuckled slightly. "What?"

"Margot is a special person, Cole," Jill said seriously, and it made Cole turn serious as well.

"I know she is, Mom. Sometimes I don't think she knows just how special she is."

"I mean, you need to be very clear about what your intentions are. You can't wing it with this one."

Cole frowned. "Wing it?"

"There's a reason you introduced her to me, Cole, even if you don't know it, and it's not because Jacob and her brothers were involved in an accident. If it were, you wouldn't have waited until Mother's Day Brunch to do it. You be very clear about the promises you make and be very prepared to follow up on them too."

"Mom—"

"Cole," Jill said quietly, framing her son's face in her hands. "Just be careful with her, okay? Make her know it's okay."

Cole pretended he didn't understand what she meant. Margot returned to the foyer, eyeing them with tender eyes. "If I could be half the parent you are, Jill, I know I've done good."

"You'll be ten times the parent I am," Jill promised, going to Margot and framing her face as she had Cole's. "Of that, I have no doubt."

Margot's eyes had skipped to him as if for confirmation, and she smiled when he winked at her. "Thank you, Jill."

The two women hugged tightly, and after one final kiss to his mother's forehead, he and Margot left.

He surprised her and himself when, instead of going to her apartment, they went to his condo. Margot looked at him oddly.

"You've never been here," Cole said sheepishly. "I'm always at your place, but you've never been to mine."

"Did that bother you?"

"We're friends. You should feel free to come visit me."

Margot shrugged. "It's two different circumstances, isn't it? Besides, it's a bachelor pad. Wouldn't a woman wreck its...mojo?"

Cole unbuckled his seatbelt and leaned over to whisper in her ear. "I think it's impossible for you to do such a thing, Mar."

She gasped as he left the car and he hurried around to help her out as well. "What are you playing at, Mr. Patterson?"

Cole didn't answer her as they began walking into his building, mainly because he didn't fully know or want to admit it to himself. The advice his mother had given him had made him own up to the feelings that had been growing from the moment he'd met Margot, feelings he'd denied because of her loss and her widowed status and the fact that they hadn't known each other very long for him to be comfortable with them.

They knew each other now. The past few weeks had been full of disclosure, secret confessions, and ardent encouragement. The instant attraction he'd felt for her had turned into something more substantive, rooted, and powerful. He'd been tempering himself, however, because there was no way this attractive, confident, talented, grounded, black, Amazonian of a woman would ever be interested in a rich white boy like himself. She'd been married and very much in love with her husband, and Cole was almost the complete antithesis of him.

Wasn't he?

They reached his floor and he led them to the apartment, taking a second to unlock his door before letting her inside first. It was clean, full of sharp angles and contemporary leather furniture—definitely a bachelor pad.

"What do you think?"

Margot nodded. "It's very you. I like the red, blue, black color scheme. It's blunt, yet spicy, not boring, and yet contemporarily classic. Very nice."

"Something like you?"

She gave him a look. "Like me?"

"You're all those things—except for the red and blue part, of course."

Margot chuckled and rolled her eyes. "You are somethin' else!"

"Take off your jacket, Mar," Cole said, coming behind her and slipping the garment from her shoulders. "Get comfortable."

She tossed him a smile over her shoulder but continued to look around instead of sitting down. Cole stood there and watched her, enthralled. Though she was advancing in her pregnancy, she still maintained the grace from when he first met her, and her growing bump only added to her allure. Cole never thought he would think a pregnant woman could be attractive, but Margot was. It enhanced her femininity.

"Cole?"

He shook out of his musings. "Yeah."

She eyed her coat; though by the way she was averting her eyes, he knew she'd caught him staring. "Did you change your mind about me being here?"

Cole quickly hung up the coat and approached her.

"Definitely not."

Her eyelids fluttered. "Oh."

There was apprehension in her eyes. Cole cupped her cheek. "Do you want to leave?"

She didn't answer him immediately, and he took that opportunity to bring her closer to him, wrapping his arms around her waist. "Cole."

"I don't want you to leave," he admitted softly, resting his forehead against hers.

"Cole..."

He kissed the tip of her nose. "I'd like for you to stay."

"Stay how?"

"However you like," Cole said honestly. "I'm...you...I..." He framed her face again. "You make me crazy."

"Crazy?"

"Crazy," he reiterated, his thumbs caressing the swells of her cheeks. "And thoughtful, and responsible, and considerate, and smug, and humbled, and overwhelmed, and peaceful, and—"

"Cole—!" she exclaimed with a surprised laugh.

"And amazed, and inadequate, and useful, and capable, and inept, and ignorant, and jealous, and honored, and...crazy."

She was breathing deeply when he finished, though her eyes never left his. "I'm sorry?"

"I'm not," Cole said, smiling a little at her apology. "It's the best feeling in the world."

"Is it?"

"I've been with plenty of girls before," Cole admitted. "Nothing serious because, well, I didn't want to be bogged down by it. I always chose women who I knew weren't interested in the diamond ring and the picket fence and the two-point-five kids with a station wagon. I'm twenty-five, too young and immature even to entertain things like that. And then I meet you."

Margot started to pull away. "I told you I would understand if you left—"

"But that's the thing, Margot," Cole said, bending so they were eye to eye. "I don't *want* to leave. I don't want *you* to leave. I want you to stay."

Margot shook her head. "I'm not going to do that to you."

"Do what to me, Margot? I've already said you make me crazy. What else can you do!"

"Saddle you with responsibilities you never signed up to have! You've been a great friend—"

"I wanna be more than your friend, Margot."

She looked slightly uncomfortable and a little shy. "Cole."

He kissed her forehead gently. "I know...I know you've been married before and you loved Marcus, and I'm not trying to compete with him or the place he has in your heart—"

Margot squeezed his sides, drawing his attention to her. "I couldn't take it if you suddenly got bored or irritated with me and you left, Cole," she whispered. "I'm too old for flings. I...I can't..."

"We have to start somewhere, right?" Cole whispered in return. "And I don't think I could ever get bored with you. Irritated, yes!" He chuckled to take the potential sting out his words. "But not to the point I'd leave. Never that. I'd be a fool to do so."

Margot still looked cautious. "Are you sure this isn't misplaced affection or you making that leap because of some weird obligation you think you have toward me? I mean what I said: The baby and I will be fine. You don't need to put your life on hold for me. I'm resourceful!"

"I'm not putting anything on hold, Margot," Cole assured her. "If anything, I think you've helped me get it on track, given me perspective, a goal, motivation. I'd just been bobbing with the current. Now suddenly, I have a rudder and a motor, and it's you."

Cole took her hand and guided her to the couch, sitting and pulling her so she'd sit in his lap. She looked at him as if he were insane, but he didn't relent, and she finally submitted.

"That first night we met," Cole began, wrapping his arms securely around her waist. "I wanted to hold you like this, to know how you would feel, instinctively knowing you'd feel wonderful."

"Really?"

"I felt like a little boy around you," he admitted. "I was in awe of you. I still am."

"There's no reason to be," Margot insisted, drifting the backs of her fingers against his jaw line. "And you're definitely not a little boy to me. You're all man."

He cupped her jaw and kissed her chin. "Margot..."

"Never once have I thought of you as less than that," Margot continued, her eyes closing as his mouth went to her cheek. "You've been more than a friend to me."

"Margot—"

"It scares me," she revealed, opening her eyes to meet his again. "I'm afraid of what I feel for you."

He drifted his nose along hers. "Don't be, Mar. I'm right here."

"For how long?"

"For as long as you want me and let me," Cole said, his free hand cradling her belly. "I'm not going anywhere."

They sat together like that for a while, his thumb stroking her belly above her navel and she sliding her fingers through his hair. Neither spoke, just getting used to the feel of each other, this new level of intimacy they were allowing each other to experience.

"It's been so long since I've been held like this," Margot whispered after a few moments.

"Is it different?"

"Of course. But it's not bad, either. It's...nice."

"I'm a nice guy."

Margot laughed. "This is a very true point."

Cole smiled and kissed the underside of her jaw. "I think this is nice too. I've never held a woman like this, either."

"I find that hard to believe."

"Okay, I have, just not recently."

"Why not? You're handsome, wealthy, intelligent, kind…"

"Immature," Cole admitted, tipping her chin down so he could look into her gorgeous brown eyes. "I know you don't think it, but I really was. It's part of the reason Dad and I don't get along. Especially during college. The more I could party and drink and fuck the better off I was." He noticed her wince at his expletive, and he blushed a little. "I'm not like that anymore."

"You probably charmed all the girls you met."

"You think?"

"You're very charming, Cole," Margot said, looking at him shyly. "I'm older than you are and yet I feel like a little girl. I feel…"

"You're the most womanly woman I've ever met," Cole said. "I could be the Cole I really am; I think you're the first woman other than my mother who actually knows the real Cole—the Cole who blushes and can be shy and likes quiet nights at home curled on the couch with a good movie instead of going out every night like I used to. Jacob liked doing that and I went because I knew I'd get action if I did. There was no use in doing that when he died and…I met you."

Margot hugged him and kissed his temple. He held her tightly, his body trembling at feeling her soft curves against his hard planes. He wanted to hold her while they slept, as he had that last time when she'd kissed him.

Not him. Marcus. She'd thought he was Marcus. And though Cole had understood, he'd wished at that moment Margot had known whom she'd kissed all along. That one, tiny kiss from her had shaken him more than anything he'd ever experienced, her tenderness more powerful than any mutual lust he'd had with any other woman.

"Perhaps I should take you home now," Cole murmured against her cheek.

"That would probably be best," Margot agreed, standing. Cole didn't let her go far, however, keeping their fingers intertwined and stepping close to her once they both were standing. "Ah..."

Cole kissed the back of her hand and winked at her. "We're still friends, Margot."

She smiled. "That's a relief."

He tugged on her hand and they left his building. He didn't hide his glances to her this time. Margot didn't return them, but her small smile let him know she noticed them. Once they reached her apartment, Cole took her portfolio in one hand and her hand in his other, and they walked to the entrance. She bypassed her mailbox and he looked at her curiously.

"Not going to check?"

"Tomorrow. It's too late to do anything about anything today."

They remained silent again until they entered her apartment, and Cole thought it felt different for some reason, lived in. Though he still slept at his apartment more often than not, he felt truly comfortable in hers. It was very homey, comfy, a place where the intent was to live instead of impress.

"Are you staying over?"

The question took him by surprise, not because she'd never asked it before, but because she'd asked it the same way she always had, even before their earlier discussion.

They were still friends. She was holding him to that, it seemed.

"Would you like me to?"

She let out a breath and quirked her lips. "You shouldn't ask me a question like that."

"Why?" he asked, not moving closer to her though he wanted to, "afraid of the answer?"

This time, Margot did laugh and she shook her head. "It's not like I'm a virgin or I've never..."

"I want to hold you, Margot."

"Hold me?

"I like holding you."

"You do?"

"Yeah. You feel wonderful."

Margot dropped her eyes and frowned. He wished he knew what she was thinking, wished he didn't feel like a complete tool as he did at that moment. What kind of thing was that to say to someone clearly unsure and unused to such overtures, to someone who had lost so much and was afraid of losing again?

Suddenly she lifted her eyes to his and held out a hand. When he looked at her inquisitively, she grinned and wiggled her fingers.

He smiled, understanding dawning upon him. He took her hand and kissed her knuckles as she led them to the bedroom.

"I like this answer," he murmured against her skin, chuckling at Margot's snort in reply.

Chapter Nine

Margot tended to wake up early, but she was always very quiet when she did. Sometimes she'd merely sit with her back rested against the headboard while her hand rubbed her tummy in soothing strokes. Other times she'd have her sketchbook in her lap and the light scratches of graphite or charcoal against the heavy paper would rouse Cole.

This morning, she'd been doing a combination of the two with a very pleasant third element—humming. Everything she did was soft, just like she was, and many times Cole would lie there and watch her, content and feeling very lucky and humbled to witness her private, early-morning rituals.

"Morning," he murmured when there was a break in her hum. He sat up and kissed her shoulder, his hand joining hers at her belly. "How are you two doing?"

"The little one is particularly antsy today and I'm not quite sure why!" Margot chuckled, still sketching. "How did you sleep?"

He didn't answer her for a moment, his chin resting on her shoulder and his fingers drifting along the taut skin of her belly as he watched her convert off-white canvas into a graphite reproduction of a brick wall with crawling vines and ivy.

"Wonderfully. Thanks for asking."

Every night for the past two weeks they'd shared a bed together, doing little more than falling asleep and waking up, and Cole had never thought something as simple as that would be so refreshing and fulfilling. The first night they'd done this Margot had been stiff, too stiff for Cole to attempt to touch. Her bravado had failed her once he'd slipped into bed beside her, and it wasn't until the third night that she'd relaxed enough to let him hold her.

Sleep had been infinitely better since then.

"What are you sketching?" he asked, watching her use her thumb to remove a stray mark she made.

"Background for one of the pages I'm illustrating for the book," Margot murmured, frowning as she concentrated. "The Baby Chick needs to be on the other side of it and at this point in Oscar's story, she doesn't know how to do it."

"What's the story about?"

Margot frowned more, the graphite hovering over the sketchbook. "A little chick who wants to go to the pond with her duckling friend, but the Mama Hen won't let her, so she decides to go off by herself; but when she does, Mama Hen panics because Baby Chick is gone and Papa Rooster and Uncle Goat search for her. The problem with all of this, however, is Baby Chick never makes it to the pond because she gets lost, and there's a storm brewing and they need to find Baby Chick so she isn't caught out there alone. Of course, since it is a children's book, all resolves itself in the end."

"Who came up with that idea?"

"The Powers That Be," Margot said, starting to sketch again. "When Oscar and I got the idea from our agent, we weren't crazy about it, but our agent was and so was the publisher, and we needed to put out something new to keep our readers interested. I'm trying to finish by Labor Day just in case something goes wrong with the pregnancy—"

"Nothing will go wrong," Cole said, kissing Margot underneath her earlobe. "I won't let it."

Margot smiled slightly, then laced her fingers with his as they rested on her belly. "Your optimism is inspiring, Cole."

Cole stared at her as she went back to her sketchbook, a corner of his mouth raised. They were certainly more affectionate than they had been before they visited his mother, but they hadn't progressed their relationship any further. They hadn't kissed on the lips, and they certainly hadn't made love, but Cole made sure Margot knew he felt more for her than friendship. When they'd gone to her last check up a few days ago, Nan had noticed their new closeness and had pulled him aside in warning. She'd seen too many men do the right thing up until the baby's birth; and if Cole did that with Margot, she'd make sure he could never have children on his own.

"Duly noted," Cole had replied, knowing instinctively the tall Korean woman meant it.

Besides, he couldn't fathom not being there for Margot, whether romantically or not. They were too connected for that to happen, brought together by a common tragedy that they helped each other get through. At first it had been his repentance, his way of atoning on his brother's behalf; but now, it was for him, for her, and for the baby he was considering his more and more. He wondered if Margot noticed how his language would shift from "the baby" to "your baby" to "our baby" sometimes. If she had, she hadn't approached him outright about it. How ironic. The last thing Cole had wanted was a child and always made sure he had a pack of condoms whenever he decided to be intimate with a woman, but now he was excited about the birth of a child that wasn't even biologically his, all because of Margot.

"Are you hungry?" Cole asked, returning to the here and now.

Margot paused her sketching and drew her bottom lip between her teeth. "I should eat, shouldn't I?"

"A bowl of cereal with strawberries on top?" Cole suggested.

Margot laughed slightly. "You spoil me."

Cole turned her face to his and dropped a light kiss to her nose. "You deserve to be spoiled, honey." Her eyes grew soft as his endearment, and at that moment Cole wanted nothing more than to kiss her.

However, he backed away when he realized his body had other ideas beyond a kiss and padded into her kitchen.

He cut the strawberries first, then took a full one from the plastic carton and snacked on it as he poured the bowls full of milk and cereal. He was just garnishing the cereals with the strawberries when Margot came out, stretching her arms overhead as she did so. Her face was free of makeup and her camisole couldn't completely cover her pregnancy's swell. Cole had never seen a woman so feminine and naturally beautiful. Margot's changing body was fascinating and a little arousing, growing ever softer yet stronger as she carried and protected the little life inside her. How the stereotype women were weak started Cole never knew; but from watching Margot, he was certain that one was definitely false.

"You're staring," she murmured, not looking at him as she did.

"I can't help it," Cole confessed. "I've never not stared at a beautiful woman."

Margot gave him an incredulous look. "I'm bloated, swollen, sore, sleepy, and the size of a garage. Beautiful doesn't fit in that equation."

"It fits mine," Cole said quietly and set the cereal in front of her. "Eat up. You need to look like Hearst Castle by the time the baby's ready to be born!"

Margot quirked her lips, taking the spoon he offered her. "I don't think your future wife would appreciate that comment!"

"You're mad?"

Margot shrugged and ate a spoonful of cereal before answering.

"No. In its own way, what you said was sweet."

Cole nodded but didn't say anything else. Part of him didn't think Margot fully understood just how deeply his feelings went, and much of that was his fault. Admitting feelings was one thing; admitting those feelings were of the love variety was something else entirely. He didn't doubt that was what he felt because he'd never felt this way before, and his closest point of reference was the love he had for his mother. As he'd told Margot, however, he could never think of her as *his* mother; but as his *children's* mother...

"You're awfully quiet this morning, Nat King Cole," Margot said after another spoonful of cereal. "Are you sure you're all right?"

When he didn't answer immediately, Margot put down her spoon and looked at him intently. "Cole?"

"How did you know Marcus was in love with you?"

Margot visibly started, the question clearly taking her off guard. Cole cursed himself, wondering if the query were too personal. Though Margot was generally an open woman, they rarely spoke about Marcus in a way they probably should, especially now that Cole felt for her what Marcus obviously had.

"Oh...wow..." Margot sagged a little, her hand going to her abdomen. She smiled a little after a moment. "I knew before he told me verbally."

Cole began blushing, his mind somewhere he didn't want to go as it involved Margot, a bed, and another man—even if that man was her late husband.

"We'd gone ice skating, of all things," Margot said, looking off at a faraway spot. "I'd wanted to go because it'd been years since I'd gone, and he'd teased me about how black people didn't do ice very well." Margot chuckled. "If he were basing that conclusion on his skating skills alone, then he would've been absolutely right! He spent more time crawling than skating, and he'd grumbled the entire time! Though I'd laughed in the beginning, I quickly grew irritated and sad toward the end because he wasn't having any fun, and I couldn't because he couldn't."

She winced and shook her head quickly. "That came out petty and it shouldn't have. I wanted him to enjoy something I enjoyed so we could share in it, and the fact I made him do something he didn't, I felt bad. Anyway, we left and I was apologizing—really borderline groveling—and he pulled me in his arms, gave me the lightest kiss, and told me to shut up. That's when I knew."

"Just like that?"

"Yes. I don't think he knew then, either. But I knew. It wasn't even the 'best kiss' we ever shared, but it was memorable for me because that's when I knew he loved me. I can't explain it. It's just something you know, I guess."

"When did you know you loved him?"

"After I knew he loved me," Margot admitted. "He'd never said anything, so I didn't; but I had allowed myself to drop whatever other defenses I'd had up and fully commit to him."

"Why?"

"My own parents, who were supposed to love me unconditionally, clearly didn't. No way was I going to be caught up in a man who could leave me at any point for someone else. But Marcus...he was loyal, and he loved me, so I made myself give him the proper shot. I knew I'd fallen when I started bringing him lunch because he'd told me once, on a whim and at the beginning of our relationship, that often he worked through lunch and he'd go hours without eating. Sometimes his first meal would be dinner. Yeah, the auto shop had a vending machine but really—Marcus was a big man and peanut butter crackers couldn't cut it.

"I'd been on my way back from a consulting job in Prince George's County and stopped by a delicatessen on my way back to DC. I picked up a sandwich for him. I wasn't even hungry and I didn't buy myself anything. That's when I knew, right when the cashier was giving me change for the salami and pepperoni sub, heavy on the mustard and pickles, no mayo."

Cole leaned over the counter and began eating his cereal, deep in thought. There hadn't been any grand gestures or declarations between her and Marcus. In fact, they'd been mundane, everyday things that had highlighted each other's affection. His father would give his mother some ornate piece of jewelry and his mother would...actually, Cole didn't know what his mother would do, though Cole was sure his father wouldn't appreciate a sandwich as an appropriate show of affection.

"Why did you want to know?"

Cole shrugged, scooping cereal on his spoon with a little too much focus. "Curious."

"Have you ever been in love, Cole?"

He kept his attention on the bowl. "Yes."

"Did she love you?"

He cleared his throat. "I'm not sure."

"Cole—"

"Are you done?" he interrupted, taking her bowl to the sink without waiting for a reply. The conversation was getting a little too personal, and he didn't think he could be as forthright as Margot had been with this discussion. How had he thought she wouldn't want to know about his past relationships, if one could call a series of one-, two-, and three-night stands "relationships?" Though fairly sure he had more sexual experience than Margot, he knew she had more love experience than he did, and that was just as daunting.

Her warm hand crept over his shoulder and squeezed. "Did she hurt you?"

"She'd never intentionally hurt me," Cole evaded.

Margot sighed, wrapping her arms around his waist from behind and resting her cheek against his back. "She's a fool, then, if she couldn't see how wonderful you are."

"Mar..."

"You are, Cole," she insisted, breathing deeply. Her breasts pressing against his back made him swallow a moan of longing. "You've been amazing to me, with me, for me and the baby—from the moment we first met. If you can be that way with me, then surely your woman could've seen you'd treat her right."

"I'd treat her the best," Cole said, linking their fingers together. "I'd make sure every day she knows I love her."

She tensed, and when she would've moved away he held her tightly. "I..." He didn't know what else to say, not ready to tell her because he knew she wasn't ready to hear it. Cole turned in the circle of her arms so they faced each other, his hands cupping her face. She closed her eyes and two tears trailed down her cheeks. He kissed them away with a murmur of her name.

"Take your time, Margot," he whispered against her cheek. "Or if you don't need it and know that you don't 'know', or know that you 'know' and it's not...what I feel, don't be afraid to tell me. I feel independently from you; there's no need for quid pro quo, I just—"

Her lips were soft and salty from her tears, and Cole moaned when she deepened her kiss. Her mouth tasted like whole grains, milk, strawberries, and her own unique flavor. He moved his hands from her face to lift her in his arms, forcing her to wrap her legs around his hips. He never wanted to stop kissing her, which was why he'd been so reluctant to initiate one in the first place.

He'd never get enough her.

Nevertheless, Cole ended the kiss so they could breathe properly and control their racing hearts. She buried her face in his neck and he held her closer as he walked them to her couch. He ran his hand along her back, smiled slightly as he felt tiny flutters from her abdomen, and kissed her temple softly.

"I knew," she whispered after a moment.

His heart swelled. "You knew what?"

"I knew it would be as intense as before."

Cole shushed her when she would've continued, not wanting her to do so. He needed to deal with that confession just as much as she did.

-SJF-

"I knew it."

Margot groaned and shook her head. Gail thought she was right all the time, and then gloated while doing so. Gail gloating about how she'd seen her and Cole entering a relationship made Margot a little skeptical, a little irritated, and a little curious.

"You can't be serious!"

"Yes, I can! Have you slept with him?"

"And by sleeping you mean...?"

"*Not* sleeping! Is he any good? I hear white boys like to do things..."

Margot rolled her eyes again, glancing over her shoulder at Cole putting clothes in his suitcase. They were both preparing for a long, holiday week to celebrate Independence Day in New Hampshire's White Mountains. They could use the time to relax and enjoy each other. It was also when Margot would spread Oscar and Georgie's ashes, and she couldn't think of a better time than sunset on the Fourth. Gail was coming to join them as well, but they'd be alone for the most of the time.

Margot's body hummed in anticipation of it, though she tried to act unaffected. They'd been sharing a bed for a month; and though the kissing had started two weeks ago, after their breakthrough in the kitchen, it hadn't gone much further. She'd been feeling frustrated about it, too; and Gail, being her best friend and an undercover freak, could hear it in her voice.

"I haven't had the opportunity to find out whatever you've heard," Margot muttered. "And you know I don't pay attention to stuff like that!"

Gail sobered a little. "I know you don't, girl. I'm just teasing, but I do find it funny you've gone from big, black man Marcus to big, white guy Cole!"

"Not so funny. They're very similar."

"Yes, they both loved you. And you love them."

Margot, who'd been slowly packing her suitcase while talking to Gail, stopped completely. "Gail—!"

"Yeah, girl, way back when I saw you last. I remember thinking you two reminded me of you and Marcus except...I dunno. It was different. Not different in a bad way, just distinct. I kept my mouth shut because you weren't ready to hear it, but homeboy was sprung on you long before now, and vice versa."

Margot breathed deeply. "Do you think I'm—?"

"Impossible," Gail said, and Margot could hear the smile in her voice. "Marcus would like Cole, I think. If Marcus were alive and Cole wasn't in love with you, I could see them being good friends."

"Even despite—"

"Oh, *yeah*, girl!" Gail said, chuckling slightly. "Cole may be young, but he can go with the flow for real!"

Margot snickered. She never thought about Cole like that. Cole was Cole and he was wonderful. "So, do you think—?"

"I think you should be honest and enjoy," Gail said seriously. "A woman is blessed when she can find love once. You are doubly blessed, sweetie. Don't ever feel guilty about that."

Margot took a deep breath. Though amused Gail had seemed to anticipate her questions before she could ask them, Gail's sincerity and her hormones caused her to tear up a little. "I love you."

"Right back at you, Mar. You call me when you get there before y'all get all *sookie-sookie*, and tell my godbaby hello for me!"

Margot snickered and said goodbye to Gail goodbye, ending the call and finishing her packing. She felt eyes upon her, and she tensed in shyness.

"Yes?"

Two strong arms encircled her waist and lips grazed her pulse point in her neck. "Gail's still coming?"

"She is." Margot sighed, leaning against him as Gail's advice echoed in her ears and heart. "You feel good."

"So do you," he murmured, nipping the curve of her ear. "You and the little one ready to go?" He rubbed her belly for emphasis.

"Yeah. The urns..."

"In a box with padding and on the floor of the back seat. I took extra precautions, Mar."

"Okay. Okay."

Cole loaded up the car and soon they were on the highway north. It was a long enough ride that Margot slept almost the entire way there, and she made a beeline to the bathroom upon reaching their destination. The cottage had two bedrooms in it, a spacious living room, a hot tub, and a host of other amenities they would enjoy.

When Margot left the bathroom, Cole was setting the suitcase down on the luggage rack at the foot of the bed. He grinned when he turned to her.

"I would've stopped at rest stops along the way if you had to go, baby."

Margot blushed slightly at his endearment, still trying to get used to them after a few weeks of Cole's use. She'd never pegged him as the type to use them, but she liked it.

"I'll be going to the bathroom more often now that the baby's getting bigger," she explained. "All that pressure on my bladder, how can I not!"

"I would've stopped, though," Cole said, sitting on the edge of the bed. "I wouldn't have minded."

Margot went to him, his legs opening to accommodate her, and she kissed his forehead. "You're always so thoughtful."

"You're always on my mind," Cole admitted, kissing her burgeoning belly. "I can't wait until she's born."

Margot smiled slightly, her fingers drifting through his hair. "You seem so glad it's a girl."

"I am."

During Margot's last checkup a week before, Dr. Dennison had determined the sex of the child. It seemed fitting, considering Oscar and Georgie had wanted a girl too.

"Why did you want it to be a girl so bad?" Margot asked, sighing softly as he pulled up her top and kissed the bare skin of her stomach.

"The prospect of a tiny Margot makes me happy," he whispered.

"Technically, it would be a tiny Oscar or George," Margot said, her belly clenching when Cole dragged his tongue along the taut skin beside her navel. "I want this child to know who the parents are. I'm just aunt Margot."

"Really?"

"I was never the parent, just the surrogate, and I want to keep it that way."

"You can't, though," Cole said gently. "You'll be this child's mother. It's all right to be that now."

It was a daily struggle for Margot to reconcile that fact, especially when that hadn't been the initial plan. She didn't want to do Oscar and Georgie's memories a disservice, didn't want them or the universe to think she'd just step in with no heed to them. Practically, it would be best to accept the responsibilities that were naturally hers; but personally, it was an entirely different matter.

Cole brought his hands to her sides, bringing her ever closer. "Did you ever want kids?"

"Yes," Margot said, yet averted her eyes and looked at her belly instead. If she did have more children, she'd do her best not to make this child feel less than or an outcast. She would love Oscar and Georgie's child as if it were her own, but she wouldn't keep the secret of the intended familial arrangement, either.

Cole kissed her belly again, then rested his cheek against it. "I am in awe of you, Margot."

Her breath hissed out as she continued sliding her fingers through his hair. "The feeling is mutual, honey."

He pulled back, his hands framing either side of her swell, and stared intently as he moved those hands up and pushed her shirt up until he cupped her breasts. It was the first overtly sexual move he'd ever made, and she sucked in a breath. Her breasts felt so heavy, and her nipples were more sensitive than she could remember. Her eyes dragged closed as his thumbs worried the peaks gently.

"All woman," he murmured. "So fucking beautiful."

He rarely cursed around her; but at that moment, it turned Margot on more than she ever thought possible and she moaned.

"God, baby, that's the sexiest sound I ever heard," Cole murmured, kissing the spot underneath the front clasp of her bra.

"Did you come with me to the White Mountains to get your freak on?" Margot asked, needing to inject a joke to keep from passing out from the overwhelming sensations he made her feel.

"No, I didn't," Cole said honestly, pulling back, but keeping his hands on her. "But you have no idea how hard it is for me not to touch or kiss you, regardless of the circumstances."

She believed him, but she was still blown away by it. "I can't believe you find me attractive like this!"

"Why wouldn't I?" Cole asked, genuinely baffled, "this is you in your full femininity. You can't get more beautiful than this."

It was a comment Marcus would've made, too, but purely all Cole as well. Margot stepped closer, hugging Cole's head to her belly as she kissed his hair. "You..."

He slid his hand up her back underneath her bra. "I...?"

"Heaven sent," Margot murmured. That was the only way she could figure it. Either God or Marcus or both allowed Cole to enter her life because she doubted she would've met this wonderful man on her own. Divine intervention had done its part, but it was up to Margot to allow herself to go that next step.

Cole shook his head, rising to kiss her. "You are," he whispered against her lips before deepening his kiss.

Her body was on fire. Everywhere he touched her ignited. She couldn't get enough, and somewhere along the way both ended up nude and underneath the covers on the bed. Cole was so patient with her, almost reverent, and his unhurried caresses and kisses made her deliciously restless.

"So soft and lovely, Mar," Cole whispered against her collarbone before pressing a kiss to it.

"So hard and strong," she returned, kissing his temple. She felt his heavy length against her thigh, and she moved her leg to let it drag along her skin. He sucked in a breath and gripped her hips.

"Baby."

"Sweetheart."

He chuckled and kissed the valley between her breasts. "I want to worship you a little while longer before I defile you."

A shiver of lust and anticipation shot throughout her body, and she opened her legs to accommodate him more comfortably. "It's been three long years with nothing but my hands, Cole."

He groaned and took said hands, kissing her palms. "Show me the places where you want me to touch you, then. Kiss you."

Margot whimpered, breathless at the thought this was actually happening. Unable to speak, she curled her fingers around his in a hard grip, trying to root herself to the present.

"Let me make love with you, honey," Cole said, smiling softly. "Let me show you how much I love you."

Tears fell on Margot's cheeks, happy and moved by his confession, and she pressed her palms against her face to hide them from him. He pulled those hands away from her face and kissed her eyes and cheeks before cupping her jaw.

"Anywhere else, baby?" he rumbled, his blue eyes dark with desire.

Chapter Ten

Margot never thought "Anywhere else, baby?" could be such a sexy question. It held Cole's bravado, confidence, consideration, and challenge in those three words. Margot could only answer head-on.

Looking deeply into his eyes, she held her hand to her mouth, smirking underneath it when his blue eyes darkened even more as he moved her hand to replace it with his fingertips drifting along her lips. Then his mouth captured hers slowly and completely. His tongue swirled with hers, his breath from his nostrils tickling her nose and upper lip, his body pressing hers deeply and securely into the bed. He kissed her with his entire body, not just his mouth, and Margot sighed brokenly.

"Jesus, Margot," he murmured once he ended the kiss, his skin flushed and hot. She smiled at him and sucked on his earlobe.

"Are you making an introduction, baby?"

He chuckled. "I get the feeling you two have already met."

Margot grinned and moved her hand from her chin down the column of her neck before drifting it from one shoulder to the other. Cole wasted no time, his fingers and hands following her path and his mouth bringing up the caboose. The way he used his tongue had Margot afraid, yet excited about how he'd make her feel when he moved on to *other* places.

"You taste like cinnamon," he murmured against her shoulder.

"Really?"

"Yeah. Weird. I like."

She pressed her hand to her mouth again and his eyes glinted. Cole understood her silent command and he kissed her hungrily, making sure to slide his tongue along hers.

"Actually, I say graham cracker."

Cole chuckled and kissed her more gently this time. "I'm sure you and Marcus had fun doing this."

"You're bringing up my late husband at a time like this?"

He pulled back. "Are you offended?"

"No, I'm just surprised."

He framed her face and pressed his nose against hers. "I'm not so naïve or jealous to completely ignore what he meant to you. If anything, I get it. I just don't understand why other men didn't."

Margot shrugged. "I wouldn't let them."

Cole's frown deepened. "Why not."

Margot trailed her hands along the muscles of his back, her body trembling at the feel of his strong, lean form. Marcus had felt similar, though there was more muscle, but both bodies were very pleasant to touch, to support with hers as they lay together.

"Margot?"

"I knew I wouldn't..." Margot trailed off, kissing the crook of his neck. His sharp intake of breath made her smile and she kissed her way up his neck to his ear. "I knew I wouldn't love them like I loved him. Like I love you."

Suddenly his arms banded around her and he turned them so he was on his back and she was on top. She straddled his waist to get more comfortable and remove her large belly from him. He followed her, however, still holding her close as their breaths mingled together.

"Say it again," he breathed.

Margot laughed and cupped his cheek. "I love you, Cole Patterson."

"Say it again..."

She kissed him softly, not minding how tightly he squeezed her, instantly understanding why he needed the confirmation. "I love you, Cole. I love you."

"I love you," he whispered against her mouth. "I love you."

They clung to each other, feeling each other's heartbeat and breath. She was dazed, humbled, and a little overwhelmed. It'd been so long since Margot had felt the body of a man, had been held as such by a man, had been loved by a man; but something told her Cole had never felt this way before with anyone.

"Someone loves you, baby," Margot whispered against his cheek.

He held her tighter. "Someone loves you too," Cole returned, thrusting his hips slightly. "*Something* too."

Margot giggled and kissed him. "You only love me for my body, hmm?"

"If that were the case I would've slept with you long before now," Cole answered frankly. "Even now..." His eyes drifted down her body to her breasts. Margot, remembering his earlier request, cupped them, wanting to feel his hands and mouth on them just as much as he did.

"Now," Margot encouraged, sucking in a breath when he palmed her breasts, his hands warm and firm against them.

"I want to wait."

That surprised her. "You do?"

Cole nodded, his thumbs thrumming her nipples gently. "I want to touch you, hold you, kiss you, but I think I'll need a minute before I make love to you. I want it to be good for you, Margot, but I'm too emotional right now to be of any use to anyone, and I don't want to hurt the baby."

Margot understood, but her breath shuddered out when he tongued her nipple. "You're making yourself very useful right now."

Cole snickered. "I know. I can feel you wet against me."

"Cole!" She gasped, both at his comment and at his tender bite on her breast. "Nan said I'd be."

"Blame it on the pregnancy," Cole teased.

"I blame it on *you!* The pregnancy just exacerbates it."

Cole sucked hard one last time before moving to her other breast. "I'd apologize for that if I weren't happy about it."

Margot moaned, her breathing becoming more labored as she ground herself against his hair-roughened thigh. "And you can't hurt the baby, baby."

"No?"

"Aside from the fact I know you'd never, you couldn't," Margot reassured. "Just for future reference."

"That right?" he murmured into her cleavage. "Thanks for the info."

His hands squeezed her breasts and pinched her nipples. Margot groaned. "I'd never been attracted to blonds before," she revealed randomly.

"Really?"

"The darker the better."

"I've been told I'm handsome," Cole said, his hands moving lower to cup her behind as he tongued her nipples again.

"Never said you weren't, baby," Margot said. "But maybe I just never thought blond men would be interested in me, so I never allowed myself to be attracted to them."

Cole released her nipple and rested his chin between her breasts, looking at her with dark, blue eyes. "I can guarantee you'd make any color-haired man attracted to you. You're a goddess among women."

Margot flushed prettily as her fingers danced over his mouth. "Have you been with a black woman before?"

"No. I've been with girls before, of all colors, but never a woman. You're a woman, Margot."

"A woman?" She felt like a woman with him, and she undulated her hips. "And you like older women?"

"I love you," Cole said, groaning and squeezing her buttocks. "Damn, girl, you feel so good."

"Girl? I thought I was a woman?"

"You're both," Cole amended, kissing her lips lightly. "You're a woman who can take care of herself and yet all I want to do is take care of you...protect you. You're my woman and my girl."

"You're my man," Margot said, kissing him deeply. She then laughed and let out a whoop of joy. "It feels so good to say it!"

His laughter joined hers; and when her hands dragged down her body to the juncture between her thighs, he moaned. "Baby..."

"We went from woman to girl to baby in three seconds flat—Cole!" Margot squealed, then giggled. He'd flipped them over again, his mouth pressing warm, open-mouthed kisses on her distended belly.

"I wish she were mine," Cole murmured against her skin. He rubbed his nose around her navel, then moved his mouth lower. "I can't wait until she's born. I can't wait until you're pregnant with my child."

Margot tried to focus on the feelings he evoked from her with his hands and lips instead of his insinuation of permanence, of the wish he had that echoed some of her deepest secrets. His fingers were gentle and evocative as they danced on her hot, sensitive flesh, and she couldn't have stopped her moans and whimpers if she tried.

"You did this to yourself for the past three years, Mar?" Cole whispered against her inner thigh. "Only you touched this secret, beautiful place? That's selfish, Margot."

"Cole..."

"Then again, you're letting me in, aren't you, Mar?" he continued murmuring, using his thumbs to spread her apart. "You're letting me love you."

"Yes..." Margot cried brokenly. "Yes!"

He took her to ecstasy with his slow, deliberate ministrations. No matter how much she bucked, threatened, clawed, scratched, or squeezed, Cole refused to break the pace he'd set. He loved her good and thoroughly; and by the time he was finished, she'd had three explosive climaxes.

She was still crying when he climbed up to her. He tucked her in his arms and kissed the crown of her head. "You all right?"

Margot could only nod.

"Rest, Margot," Cole said, pulling the coverlet over them and extinguishing the lamp on his nightstand. "I'll be here all night holding you."

Her answer was to snuggle into him, intent to make sure he kept that promise.

Cole's arms were empty and cold when he awoke the next morning, and he shot up in bed. There was an indentation of the body he'd been holding next to him; and after a moment, the smell of bacon, coffee, and buttermilk wafted into the room. Cole's stomach growled mightily and he slipped on his boxers before padding into the main living area.

Margot made a far too tempting picture darting from stove to sink to oven, her feet in fuzzy pink slippers and her body draped with his button-down shirt. She was pouring batter onto a griddle and humming, her head bobbing with her private melody.

It was so very domestic and simple, yet Cole had never experienced such a thrill in his life. The women he bedded usually left after they'd finished or early in the morning; and if they *did* stay the night, they certainly didn't cook breakfast! Then again, those women hadn't loved him, and he hadn't loved them.

He still couldn't believe it. When Margot had said she loved him, he'd felt as if he could've pushed Mount Everest off its very foundation. Despite all his experience, wealth, and good looks, he'd never thought he could gain Margot's interest as a man; and even if he could, he'd never be able to compare to Marcus. But Margot had never asked him to; moreover, she'd always made sure Cole knew she was focused on him alone whenever they shared moments together. Perhaps it was better they'd started as friends. Marcus had never been taboo between them, and it made the transition from friends to lovers go much more smoothly because of it.

They were lucky men that they could say they'd experienced Margot's love.

Cole watched her flip over the cakes and his mouth watered, though he honestly didn't know if it were because of the food or the curve of her neck and shoulders as she worked her head from side to side, apparently to alleviate tension. When she removed the now golden cakes from the griddle he struck, sliding his hands around her to cup her breasts, and his mouth captured the pulse point at her neck. She sucked in a sharp breath. Cole smiled against her skin, laughing a little when she hit his hand with the spatula.

"A little warning would be nice!"

"Would it?" Cole asked, moving his mouth up to grasp her earlobe with his teeth. "I'll remember that next time."

Margot pressed against him with her back and bum, and Cole moaned lowly. "Are you hungry, honey?"

"*Mmm*," Cole intoned, his fingers undoing the top few buttons on his shirt so he could slide his hands inside and palm her bare breasts. "Were these pre-pregnancy?"

Margot snorted but leaned into his hands. "What's it to you?"

He squeezed her nipples. "Curious."

Margot dropped her head and gripped the countertop, a tiny moan slipping from her lips. Cole grinned and slid his hands lower, the rest of the top becoming unbuttoned as his hands now glided along her belly. "Some of that was pre-pregnancy," Margot answered seriously.

Cole spun her around, dropping a gentle kiss to her lips before moving his mouth in nips and soothing caresses down her body. He spent some time at her nipples because her dark, large areolas fascinated him and her nipples were perfect for sucking—perhaps in preparation for the baby—but Cole rarely passed up opportunities when he saw them.

Margot was demonstrative about her wants and pleasures, sometimes holding his head so he could get the maximum suck, sometimes pushing him away because she was sensitive and he was intense. Nevertheless, he eventually moved lower, worshipping her belly as he knelt before her. He felt the baby shift and Cole smiled, his finger trailing over where he'd feel the movements.

"You're gonna be like your mommy-aunt," Cole predicted. "Strong and amazing. It'll be an honor to meet and know you, little one."

Margot, who had been running fingers through his hair, tugged a little so he'd look at her. "The feeling will be very mutual, honey."

Cole grinned and kissed her above the navel, his hands sliding from the swell of her belly to the swell of her hips. His fingers dipped underneath the elastic of the panties she wore and he smirked against her skin. They danced along the crisp hairs underneath, then lower still, and he relished in her audible intake of breath and the sudden rictus of her body.

"Cole—"

"I'm *ravenous*," Cole said, his blue eyes looking into hers mischievously before sliding down her underwear.

"You are being very bad," Margot said, yet stepped out of her panties for him and shuddered as his hands moved up the outside of her legs to her hips.

"Are you going to spank me?" Cole asked, his eyes glinting while he nipped and kissed up the inside of her thighs. Margot's hands tightened on his shoulders, and he moaned at the pressure.

"You'd enjoy it too much," Margot snickered, then gasped when his mouth touched the core of her. "Baby…"

She tasted so good. He would never get enough of her. He guided her movements as he took his fill; and when she reached her pinnacle of pleasure, he stood quickly and kissed her hard, wanting her to enjoy her taste as he had.

"The food," Margot panted, groaning as his lips moved to the column of her neck.

"Can be reheated," Cole said, picking her up and putting her legs around his waist. "I want you."

She bit her lip and tightened her arms around his neck. "I want you too," she whispered.

He grasped her chin between his thumb and forefinger and looked deeply into her eyes. "I love you."

She smiled. "I love you too."

He kissed her lightly, his hand sweeping along her back. "If you're not ready to go further, Margot, we won't. I can wait. I want you to be happy and pleasured and loved, not pressured—"

"I want that for you, too, Cole," Margot whispered, nuzzling her nose against his. "This is a two-way street, dear. And I think it's time I return the favor."

Though his body hummed and pulsed from her words, Cole shook his head. "This is not tit-for-tat, Margot. I don't want you to think I'm doing this because I expect something in return—"

"You should, though," Margot insisted, frowning slightly. "When two people love each other there are certain expectations; it's naïve and really stupid to think otherwise. What we have to do is learn what they are and strive to meet them. If we can't, we'll discuss them."

Amazed by her once more, Cole kissed her deeply, bringing her body ever closer to his. "Are you finished here?"

Margot pulled back and looked over her shoulder, then clenched her legs tighter around him as she leaned back to turn off the eyes on the electric stove and the exhaust fan above it. As she did so, the shirt draped open, revealing her ebony body to him, and Cole felt himself harden even more. Unable to ignore the call, he pulled her right nipple into his mouth and sucked hard, grinding his hips into hers as he feasted upon her.

"Are you gonna...Jesus, Cole...you gonna take me in the kitchen?" Margot wheezed, grinding just as actively as he did.

"Though the thought had crossed my mind," Cole admitted around her breast, "I want our first time to be in a bed so I can adore and love you properly."

"You already do, honey," Margot assured him with a kiss. "You already do."

They continued kissing as he ambled back into their room and he laid her gently on the bed. He kissed his way up her body, making sure not to leave any part of her skin unloved by his mouth, until he reached hers. Their tongues dueled, both Margot and Cole struggling to get her out of his shirt. He undulated his body against hers, trembling as he felt her power and love beneath him.

"I'm terrified," Cole confessed.

Margot frowned, touching her fingers to his cheeks. "Why?"

He kissed her forehead. "I've never made love before."

Her frown deepened. "What? I thought you said..." It dawned on her what he meant and she smiled, drawing the backs of her fingers along his cheek. "You have nothing to worry about."

"But what—?"

Margot kissed him, and he brought her body flush with his. "Nothing to worry about."

Cole trusted her prediction and kissed her lightly one last time before leaving the bed and finding his pants that were heaped on the side of the bed. He fished through the pockets for his wallet, then pulled out a foil package. Though Margot was pregnant and he knew he was clean, he didn't want her to think he didn't respect her enough to wear a condom.

He nuzzled her neck as he slipped it on. Once he was set, he stroked himself against her heat.

"Are you ready?" he shuddered out, wondering if he himself were a little *too* ready.

Margot nodded, sinking her fingers in his blond hair. "Make me yours, baby."

He kissed her as he entered her, groaning at how tight and hot and wet she was. Margot sucked in a harsh breath, her fingers gripping his hair, and he cooed to help relax her body.

"I won't move until you want me to," he murmured once he reached the hilt. Margot nodded and held him closer, her breath fanning against his shoulder.

Suddenly a piece of advice his brother had given when he was a teenager entered his mind, and he tightened his arms around her before sitting up and scooting to the edge of the bed. Margot yelped slightly, surprised by the move, but her body relaxed against his.

"More comfortable for you?" he asked, smoothing his hand along her short, soft, natural hair to her back.

She shifted, causing him to leave her body, then she settled back onto his length with a soft groan. "You feel so good."

Cole thought about every unpleasant thing he could so he didn't completely lose it. He was an experienced, twenty-five-year-old adult, not a green adolescent; but he might as well be a virgin with Margot. She brought him to the edge so quickly.

"I love you," he whispered, their mouths hovering, their lips brushing each other, their breaths melding into one. He began thrusting counterpoint to her and his eyes rolled in the back of his head. These were the most intense and overwhelming sensations he'd ever felt.

"Stay with me, baby," Margot murmured, her lips dancing along his and the planes of his face. "I'm right here."

"I feel you," he said, bringing her closer. His hand cradled her belly. "Margot..."

"Cole...Nat King Cole...my Cole..." She nipped his jaw, then soothed it with her tongue. They started moving faster, the temperature in the room borderline unbearable. He moved even further on the edge of the bed to gain more purchase as if it would prevent him from toppling over from pleasure.

"Are you close, love?" Margot whispered, leaning her head back as he bit at the column of her throat.

"Too close."

"Never too close."

Her arms tightened around him and he buried his face into her neck, their movements frenzied and erratic until she suddenly froze, let out a choked gasp, and exploded. Her name was wrenched from his mouth in reaction as he met his release. Their bodies shuddered as they came down from their mutual highs.

Her mouth moved along his face. "You're crying."

He was? He touched his fingers to his cheeks and he felt moisture. It wasn't sweat.

"I'm sorry," he whispered. She probably thought him completely unsophisticated!

"Don't be." Margot put his hand to her face and he felt her tears too. "Oh, Cole..."

She didn't need to say it; he knew. She'd never experienced anything like that before, either, and that only humbled him more.

Wordlessly, he kept her close as he maneuvered their bodies until they were under the covers again. They didn't sleep and they didn't speak, hands moving along each other's bodies as if to confirm they were actually there.

The pancakes, bacon, and coffee remained in the kitchen forgotten.

Chapter Eleven

Though it was supposed to be a vacation, Cole and Margot found themselves in the living room of the cottage doing work. Margot was curled in the easy chair with her sketchpad balanced on the armrest and part of her knee, her brows furrowed in concentration as the gentle scrape of graphite pencil added to the comfort of the birds chirping and wind rustling through the trees outside. Cole's typing and mouse clicking on his laptop created another layer of sound; yet, he couldn't completely focus on his work as he kept glancing in Margot's direction.

They'd spent the better part of their time together in bed, sometimes making love, but mostly chatting and getting to know each other even more. Cole remembered she was very ticklish and had exploited that fact ever so often, for he'd discovered a dimple in her right cheek that only appeared when she truly laughed.

He'd revealed he'd loved baking with his mother when he was younger; but when his father had given him disapproving looks and his brother had teased him about it, he'd stopped.

"I think I hurt my mother's feelings when I did that," he'd murmured, bringing Margot closer because he couldn't stop touching her.

"Probably," Margot had agreed, humming from his caresses. "But there's nothing stopping you from going home and baking with her now. You're a grown man, Cole. If you want to bake, bake!"

That comment had led to kissing and then another round of lovemaking.

Right now, Cole was trying not to stare at the adorable picture she made and had spent much of his time typing, deleting, and retyping the same sentence in the e-mail he was trying to send. His eyes also kept straying to her abdomen, where her little girl rested, and he felt his gut clench. He wondered how Margot would feel if he told her he wanted to adopt the baby. Margot didn't know how often he'd wake up in the middle of the night and whisper to her belly; how, when the baby would start to move, he'd tell stories and answer each fetal tap with one of his own. Cole already thought of the baby as his, regardless of the fact she wasn't biologically. Part of him was a little scared at how quickly he'd grown attached, but he also felt a contentment he hadn't thought he'd feel for a long time after Jacob's death.

Sighing, Cole forced himself to focus on the e-mail as it was time-sensitive. Stock markets overseas didn't close just because it was Independence Day in the United States, and some of his clients needed advice pronto.

"You all right, baby?" Margot muttered absently, kissing her teeth a moment later. Cole glanced at her and saw her erase energetically on her pad.

"Should I be asking you that?"

"I can't get this the way I want it to be," Margot said, sighing herself. "I should be patient and let the image come to me instead of the other way around."

Cole wished he could help her with that, but all he could do was give her an encouraging smile. "I know it'll come. Who could resist you?"

Margot snorted and shook her head, though a corner of her mouth lifted. "You're a charmer."

"I try."

"You succeed," Margot said, and Cole knew she blushed by the way she ducked her head.

He wanted to kiss her badly. The boyish feelings he'd had when they first met were still there, but now he felt more like a man around her. *She* made him feel that way. He'd had no idea he could make this fierce woman moan, beg, curse, or whimper as she did when in the throes of passion—he'd never felt so virile. Everything about her was purely feminine; and though he'd read about pregnant women's voracious sexual drives during the second trimester, something told Cole she'd react the same way even when not pregnant.

Margot began squirming. "You can't look at me like that right now."

He blinked. "Look at you like what?"

She grinned but kept her focus on her sketchpad. "Like you wanna sop me up with a biscuit."

His grinned matched hers. He loved her Southern expressions. He quickly finished the e-mail, not caring if it was accurate or not, and pressed the send button before standing. Cole grinned at the way her breathing became more shallow, and she didn't seem at all surprised when he framed her face in his hands and tilted it up to kiss her firmly on the mouth.

"Hmm. Maybe I should go on back to the front desk and get my own cottage with the way you two carryin' on!"

Margot inhaled sharply but Cole chuckled breathlessly, kissing her one last time before pulling away.

"Hi, Gail," he said, winking at Margot.

"Hey, yourself," Gail said, rolling her eyes good-naturedly when Cole came and kissed her cheek. "Mar."

"Gail," Margot mumbled, sinking further into the easy chair. "I'm glad you made it safely."

"Girl, I am too! This my room?" Gail asked, walking into the small hallway where doors were. She'd stopped to the first one on the right.

"Yes," Cole said. "You have any more luggage I can help with?"

"I have one more bag in the car," Gail said, flashing him a smile. Cole returned it and went to get the suitcase. It was a larger bag than the rolling one Gail had, though it wasn't that heavy. He carried it inside, looking over at Margot. She was sketching again, her brows furrowed once more and her bottom lip between her teeth. He smiled again. She really was too adorable.

"You want me to get it?"

Cole snapped his attention to Gail, who was smirking at him. He blushed and shook his head. "No, I got it. Sorry about that."

"You'll get no complaints from me," Gail said seriously, looking at Margot as well. "I'm surprised she's working on vacation! She's sounded tired when I talk to her on the phone recently."

"The baby."

Gail snorted. "That's all it is?"

Cole blushed more. "Let's get this to your room."

Gail's husky chuckle followed him inside and he placed the suitcase on the luggage rack. "I'm glad you made it safely."

"I am too," Gail said. "The last thing that girl needs is another person dying in an accident!" Cole winced a little at that, and Gail squeezed his arm. "Sorry."

"Well, you're right. We're all she's got now." He sighed and sat on the bed, watching Gail remove the jacket of the dark-green cotton tracksuit she wore. The pale green tank she had on underneath offset the red tones of her skin and her ponytail whipped over her shoulder as she draped the jacket on her suitcase.

"How long you plan on staying around, Cole?"

He was taken aback by the question and the hard tone with which Gail had asked it. Her eyes were unforgiving as they stared at him, and Cole fought the urge to squirm.

"What kind of question is that?"

"A valid one," Gail said, putting her hands on her hips. "Like I said, she doesn't need to lose any more people, and she's very attached to you."

"And I'm very in love with her. So, what's your point?"

She quirked an eyebrow. "For real?"

"Very real."

It was Gail's turn to sigh and she sat next to him on the bed. "Glad to hear you mean it."

"Of course I do! Why wouldn't I?"

Gail shrugged, then chuckled dryly. "When a door closes, God opens a window. In Mar's case, the door closed, got dead-bolted, and a chair was shoved under the knob just in case when her parents had disowned her and her brother. Her window had been Marcus at that time, and never had I seen her happier or more alive. Then he died, and that window had been shut, but not completely because Georgie and Oscar had been there to help her. I would've been there, too, but my parents *and* Margot would've been *very* upset if I didn't handle my business on the job front—I'd just been offered the researcher position at my job when Marcus died—and Mar wouldn't let me come up here to 'babysit,' as she put it. She's always been fiercely independent."

This was a fact Cole was still learning; Margot loathed asking for any help, and sometimes Cole would have to force it upon her so she wouldn't put herself or the baby under any undue stress or danger.

"Then with this latest tragedy, I really became scared for her, especially because she hadn't called me immediately with the news. And then I came up and saw you there...I was relieved and wary at the same time."

"Because I was a stranger," Cole deduced.

"Not only that, but you're young and wealthy and white and Mar was growing very attached to you, and I don't think either of you noticed. You were different from Marcus and yet not. You were being who I couldn't be and no one had been for her in a long while."

"What?"

"Someone she could depend on. Someone she could love."

It surprised him more than a little to realize Gail had noticed the signs weeks ago. Then again, so had his mother, but he'd chalked it up to mothers always wanting to pair off their single children. Gail had been friendly, though a little uneasy, and now Cole knew why. The knowledge, however, made him nervous.

"I didn't plan on it," Cole said, more to himself than to her.

She chuckled genuinely this time. "Who does? I know many women who have a plan to be married by thirty or whatever, but planning to get married and planning to fall in love are really two different things."

"You think she'd get married again?"

Gail raised her eyebrows again. "Huh."

"Is that an answer?" Cole asked again, hearing concern and amusement in that response.

"Marriage?"

"Just a hypothetical."

"Well, hypothetically or no, don't ask her because you feel some sort of obligation to her. She'll sniff it out so fast you won't even be able to ask the question. Just enjoy your time with her for now. She's definitely set up to support a child by herself."

"She shouldn't."

"Millions of women do it every day—"

"She doesn't have to do it by herself. I *want* to do it for her. *With* her."

Gail was quiet, staring out the cracked-open door to where Margot was in the living room. "I honestly don't know if she'd get married again or not. I haven't asked, and she hasn't been in a position where marriage would be a possibility."

"I haven't, either."

"So why talk about it? You two haven't even known each other for half a year and she's about to have a baby. Instant family already, Cole. And what about your parents? What about your friends, colleagues? I know you don't care about the race thing, but you have to be prepared to handle people who do."

Cole scowled a little. "My father doesn't get a say and my mother loves Margot. She's the one who gave me the push I needed to approach her."

Gail smiled a little. "Mar likes your mother too."

"And her parents?"

"*Her* parents don't get a say, either," Gail said, her eyes darkening. "If they can't even call her back when she told them about Georgie, they don't *deserve* a say."

Cole definitely agreed. He was appalled and disgusted with Robert and Faye Butler; he didn't know whether to be relieved or saddened they wouldn't be there for their grandchild. He'd been with Margot when she'd called her parents. It'd been almost a week after Georgie's passing because she hadn't the courage to do so until then. After that first brush off, she hadn't known if she could handle another one. This time, the phone had rung and rung, nobody answering. Cole had wanted to punch something at Margot's devastated expression. Though he and his father didn't have the best relationship, Cole thought even Frank Patterson would give a damn whether or not he was alive. The callousness of the Butlers was unforgivable to him.

"I had to get my mother to tell Mr. and Mrs. Butler about Georgie when Margot told me her parents ain't listen, and even *she* had to fight to get the news out. Those bougie-ass people ain't said a word when Mama told them, either. It's killing Margot. I know it is. It's killing *me*! Her parents should be here, but they're so damn petty and caught up in appearances that they're forfeiting a relationship with their daughter and grandchild for people who don't give two damns about them, anyway!"

Cole squeezed Gail's shoulder, seeing how riled up she was getting. Gail took a few deep breaths to calm herself and muttered a thank you at his support.

"I've never seen a friend get so passionate about another friend's problems."

"That girl is more than my friend; she's my sister. I was an only child and she...she wasn't as snooty as a lot of the other girls were. I'd thought I was supposed to be like them, and we butted heads when we first met. *Boy*, we hated each other! I was popular; she wasn't—always gettin' in trouble for doodling and daydreaming. I would tease her, but she gave back as good as she got and that made me so mad! Then we were partnered for a project in sixth grade. We got to know each other then, and she drew some fabulous posters for our project too. Sharp as a whip and so humble, she was the one who made it all right for me to love science, though she'd said on numerous occasions it could die and she wouldn't miss it! To this day, I don't think she knows how fantastic she is. How much she means to me. That girl's my heart."

"I know the feeling," Cole said absently, squeezing Gail's hand again.

Gail laughed and shook her head. "Still can't believe someone like you would fall for her...a younger man. Men our age and *older* don't have the balls to approach her!"

"I took a chance," Cole said, smiling a little. "I didn't anticipate it becoming this. Some days I still wonder how it happened. I feel guilty that it did, especially considering the circumstances."

It was her turn to squeeze his shoulder. "The Lord works in mysterious ways, Cole Patterson. That's what my grandma would always say when she couldn't think of an answer herself. I think that's what this case is."

Cole nodded and a companionable silence fell upon the pair. It had to be divine intervention, Cole mused. There had been no reason for him to stay in the hospital that night and he'd surprised himself by doing so. Usually, he was not the go-to guy for accepting responsibility or for comforting, especially when it wasn't his fault; but he hadn't been able to leave. Then he'd seen Margot, and empathy and compassion had overwhelmed him. He'd known, instinctively, seeing this woman so broken was not right. She should've been as strong and proud and awesome as her aura had said she could be.

Everything was a work in progress for both of them still, and Cole thought perhaps that was why she couldn't finish the children's book illustrations. She was still searching for her center and she didn't feel right completing the book without Oscar's input.

"Maybe she should tell her editor she can't do it."

"Do what?"

Cole glimpsed at Gail, then sighed. "Do the illustrations. Her mind isn't on a chick, that's for sure. She has bigger fish to fry."

Gail made a disapproving sound. "Mar's not gonna go for that. The one thing she hates is bailing on responsibility."

"She's not bailing. She literally can't do it. It's Oscar's story and he's not here anymore. She feels lost and rightly so. The images aren't coming because they *can't*."

Gail didn't say anything, just shook her head to let him know she still disapproved. In a show of affection that was becoming more frequent, Cole stood and kissed her temple. "I'll let you get some rest; that's one hell of a drive from Jersey."

"Hmm, leave it to Mar to take all the good men," Gail said with a lazy smile.

"There's one out there for you," Cole said sincerely. Maybe he would need his mother to run interference on Gail's behalf too.

Cole closed the door behind him softly, his heart swelling at the sight of Margot curled in the easy chair taking a nap. She must've been more tired than he thought for her not to go to bed. He didn't mind, though; it gave him a chance to hold her.

Just as he got her settled in his arms, Margot eased one eye open. "What's goin' on?"

"You feel asleep," he whispered, kissing her forehead. "I'm taking you to bed."

"'Kay," Margot mumbled, burying her head in the crook of his neck as he walked them to the room. Cole smiled and slid her underneath the covers, noticing she settled right back into slumber. He started to walk away, but she looked so lovely, soft, and serene that he couldn't resist sharing in the rare freedom from stress.

Kicking off his shoes, he slid into bed behind her, pressing a kiss on the crown of her head before pulling her into his arms and falling asleep himself.

-SJF-

A fire roared in the grate despite it being a muggy, warm night. Margot wrapped the blanket tighter around her as she sat on the floor in front of the fireplace. She stared into the orange flames, breathing in the scent of burning wood, yet not even that was enough to warm her from the chill that had overcome her body. She wasn't sick—she'd been taking good care of herself during the pregnancy—but the coldness wouldn't go away.

"Here."

Margot looked up to see a steaming cup of chamomile tea in Cole's hand. She took it. "Thanks."

"You sure you don't wanna sit on the couch or something, Mar?" Gail asked, getting comfortable on one said couch.

"I'm fine where I am," Margot replied monotonously. She needed to get warm.

Cole sat behind her and cocooned her body with his. After a brief moment of tension, Margot relaxed her body against his and took a sip of tea.

"I don't think it's morbid or desperate. Waiting to spread Georgie's and Oscar's ashes until after the baby's born is very considerate. It gives their daughter a chance to say goodbye too."

She stared into the cup as Cole's words vibrated through her. They'd hiked a distance to get to the spot Georgie and Oscar had indicated in their will, only for Margot to get cold feet. She couldn't let them go. Not yet. Not now.

"And maybe by then, Mama and Dad could—"

"Don't even mention them," Gail said sharply. "They got no place here!"

Margot rubbed her forehead and sighed, glancing at the urns that sat on the mantle above her. "They're still Mama and Dad, Gail. Just because they forfeited the right to be our parents doesn't mean Georgie or I forfeited our rights to be their children."

She set the mug on the floor between her legs and touched her belly. What if this child did something Margot considered so completely abhorrent that she cut off all ties? Margot wondered if there were genuinely such a thing that could. The overwhelming love that grew day by day made it impossible for Margot to imagine. How had they determined their love would be so conditional? How had she and Georgie not been more assertive in making their parents accept them and their decisions, anyway? It'd been easier to leave for everyone; had given both sides excuses not to sit down and really hash out their issues. Now her parents and Georgie never would.

Another pair of strong hands joined hers. Their fingers linked. "They should know their grandchild," Margot whispered.

"According to them, they have no children. If they have no children, they can't have a grandchild," Cole said gently.

"They *do*," Margot insisted.

"Why do you want that baby to know those hateful people?" Gail asked.

"Because without those hateful people, I wouldn't be here, Georgie wouldn't be here, and this baby wouldn't be here," Margot said. "I know we were never the warmest family, but this baby deserves to know her legacy. If I could track down Oscar's family, I would do the same with them."

Oscar had never known his father, who had died before he was born. His mother had also died when he was young, leaving him in the care of his *abuela*. *Abuela* Graciela had been everything to Oscar; and when she'd died before the publication of his first children's book, Oscar had dedicated it to her. Nevertheless, Oscar never spoke about any other family members. He didn't know his paternal side and Oscar's mother had been an only child like him.

She closed her eyes when she felt Cole's lips against her temple. "It's a pipe dream, isn't it?"

His fingers untangled from hers to slide underneath her top and touch her bare skin. "It's a noble thing to try to do, but I don't want your heart broken again."

"Cole's right," Gail said. "Your parents didn't deserve children like you and they won't deserve this grandchild they're about to have."

"It's not about they deserve," Margot said. "It's about what is."

The trio spent the remainder of the night in thought, Gail turning on the television to have noise in the cottage. She'd eventually fallen asleep and Cole carried her into her room while Margot shuffled into theirs. When Cole entered, she was already changed and underneath the covers with the sketchpad in her lap.

"Did the image come?" he asked. Margot shook her head. "What are you working on?"

"I don't know," she said honestly, making random arcs along the paper. "Just a doodle."

Cole went into the bathroom to change. When he returned, she was still making random, geometric shapes.

"I should've brought my paints," she muttered.

"Really?"

"No."

Cole pulled the pencil and pad away from her and she let him. He held her hands and kissed her knuckles before rubbing his thumbs along them. "It's your coping mechanism, isn't it?"

"What is?" He eyed the sketchpad and Margot huffed a wry laugh. "If that were the case, I should've created masterpieces!"

"Your doodling, not your art, though I'm sure some of your doodles could probably be considered art."

Margot shifted into a cross-legged position in front of him, and he sat spread eagle around her, his hands at her waist. "I started because I was bored, and then…I guess, yes, it became a coping mechanism. Gail had said my work was good but I didn't believe her because they were just doodles. I'd never really thought about it until my college roommate had asked to use one of my doodles for the cover of the English department's literary magazine."

"What was it?"

She laughed slightly. "I don't even remember. But from that year on, I pretty much did all the covers, and then that turned into posters. I'd worked up a little business on the side and I'd saved that money so I could get my first apartment."

Her parents had demanded to know where she'd gotten her money and her mother had been livid when Margot had told them. Her father had seemed proud of her and had calmed her mother down, yet he'd also encouraged Margot to put down her paints and get serious about finding a "real" job.

"Do you regret becoming an illustrator?"

Another chuckle. "I never set out to be an illustrator. It was something Oscar had offered; and because I liked Oscar and trusted him, as well as Marcus encouraging me, I accepted."

"And now that's he's no longer here, you're lost?"

Margot shook her head. "I wouldn't say lost. I'd say uninspired. I'm not a children's book author—just an illustrator—but I can't be inspired by this project when neither of us had liked the topic in the first place. The publisher had suggested it to keep Oscar from doing what he'd really wanted: write a book about children from alternative families, ones like he and Georgie were trying to start. But because we all needed that check, Oscar had caved to their conservatism."

"You wish you hadn't," Cole guessed.

"The urge to say 'F-it' and write the book Oscar really wanted to write is *incredibly* overwhelming, but that'll have to wait. In the meantime, I have to figure out if I should I buy out my contract or let them fire me."

"What would *you* want to do? In general?"

Margot smiled a little, looking off far away. "Other than not completely lose my mind or this baby? Paint, draw, doodle, illustrate...whatever *I* want to do and not worry about all the political stuff. I just want to do what inspires me, not what pays me. Hopefully, though, one leads to the other regardless!"

Cole turned her hands over and kissed each palm. "I have every bit of faith you can do that."

Margot smiled, leaning over to kiss his lips. "And it's that faith that's kept me from completely breaking down and lose it. Thank you, honey."

He grinned against her lips, cupping the back of her head and kissing her deeper.

Any desire she had to half-work on the illustrations dissipated and she slid under the covers with Cole. Resting her head on his chest, she let his heartbeat lull her to sleep.

They all left the next morning. The two women hugged each other tightly and for a long time, neither saying anything because words were trite and unnecessary.

"I'll call when I get home," Gail promised.

"You better," Margot said.

Gail hugged Cole for a shorter amount of time yet with just as much meaning and extracted a promise Cole would look after Margot and her godchild with his life.

"I will, and the fact you frighten me has nothing to do with it," Cole deadpanned, earning snickers from the women.

Cole handled checkout and Margot did a sweep of the cottage to make sure no one had left anything. When both tasks were completed, they headed back to Boston.

Margot didn't sleep on the trip back, the sketchpad in hand as she mulled over the illustrations. It wasn't hard to draw a chick and a farm and all the other images required for the plot, but she didn't care enough to do her best. She couldn't let this children's book be the last in Oscar's name while knowing it wasn't the one he'd wanted to write.

In fact, he'd already written the one he'd intended for publication before the Powers That Be had urged him elsewhere.

"Can we make a pit stop to the studio?"

They hadn't even reached Boston city limits, but she wanted to ask before he'd committed to going into Cambridge.

"Sure. Want me to drop you off? I can put the luggage up and come back to get you."

"Okay."

"Are you hungry?"

Cole reached over and rubbed her tummy, causing Margot to grin. "You're spoiling her before she's even born!"

"She better get used to it. I plan on spoiling her rotten!"

"Do you?"

"Absolutely."

Cole glimpsed at her before turning his attention back on the highway and Margot's heart clenched. There was a wealth of meaning in that quick look, and she was unable to stop her mind from going down that all too enticing path. Their relationship whatever it was—should be taken one day at a time and with realistic expectations. Just because they'd admitted to loving each other didn't mean they were ready to be a family. Sure, Cole kept saying he couldn't wait for the baby to be born, but he always had the option of leaving if things got too tough. Margot didn't.

Once they were in Boston, Margot gave him directions to the studio, which was not far from the Roxbury section of town. Cole walked with her inside the building to make sure she got in okay and because he was curious. He whistled low when, upon entering, he saw canvases with partially finished and just-started works and storyboards.

"It's a big, colorful place," Cole muttered.

"Yes. And also where I can find the story we had started working on," Margot said, setting her bag down in her office seat. She stared at Oscar's empty space, feeling a slight pang in her heart. Cole came behind her and kissed her temple.

"Sometimes it hits you so hard, you know?"

"I do," Cole murmured against her skin.

Margot turned in his arms and hugged him, her face resting against in the curve of his neck and shoulders. He returned her embrace hard, his strong arms squeezing her shoulders. The contact was what she needed to get through this episode of mourning.

"I'll come back when I'm done, okay?" he murmured, his voice a balm to her soul. "No rush. I'll bring my laptop in or I'll just watch you."

"*That'll* be fun!"

"I watch you sleep, Margot," he admitted, framing her face. "I love watching you."

She smiled and shook her head. "How no woman was able to snap you up before now is astonishing!"

He kissed her softly. "I was waiting for my Amazonian woman to come for me."

Margot scrunched up her nose. "You really think of me like that?"

"Hell yeah. One Halloween we're gonna have to do that, you know."

Margot blushed even as she rolled her eyes. "We all know it won't be this one!"

"I can wait until next year; then again, you may be pregnant again."

"I am *not* doing in vitro again!"

He tightened his arms around her and pitched his voice low, looking deep into her eyes. "Who said anything about that?"

Her breath caught, her mind refusing to believe what he'd just said, just insinuated. Cole took mercy on her and kissed her one last time before whispering, "Later," against her lips and leaving the studio.

She rubbed her belly, knowing the flutters inside it had little to do with the baby she carried, and went to Oscar's desk. She turned on his computer and typed in the password (his and Georgie's initials plus the date they were married) and pulled up the rough draft of his story idea.

It was set in a first-grade classroom and the students gave reports about their families. There were traditional nuclear families, blended families, single-parent families, families with grandparents as the primary caregiver, families with aunts, uncles, cousins as the caregiver, interracial families, gay and lesbian families, foster families.

Margot honestly didn't understand why the publisher had shied away from this story; this was the reality of many families now. There were only so many cute animal stories one could do before it became stale. This was fresh, and the images for this story were so clear and bright she thought she might need shades.

She pulled the computer paper from the printer on his desk and began sketching away, so consumed by her task she didn't know how long she'd been there or when Cole had returned. He'd left her alone, going to her desk and doing work while she sketched furiously, and it wasn't until she could no longer keep her eyes open that she stopped.

Chapter Twelve

"You know it's a good idea. I just don't understand why you won't go forward."

Three pairs of eyes looked at each other before turning back to Margot. The mouse was sweaty in her hand and her back and feet were killing her, but she'd stand there until she could make her agent and editors see she was right to completely go over their heads with the concept. She'd worked nonstop for the past few weeks after the trip to New Hampshire, and if she were the type to gloat, Margot would deem this work the best she'd ever done.

"It's a much fresher idea, a much more *relevant* idea than a chick that gets lost on a farm," Margot said, making sure to keep the respect in her voice regardless of how uninspired she'd thought the idea. "And given this day and age, there's a market."

Dean Anthony, a short, pale balding man and one of the senior editors at Family Books Publishing, leaned forward and cleared his throat. "Margot, I understand you are still mourning the death of your brother and Oscar; he was a great author and a wonderful human being—"

"I didn't do this in a haze of grief, Dean," Margot interrupted, eyeing Dean's two cohorts briefly. "This is the book he really wanted to do—*we* really wanted to do—and I wouldn't have gone forward unless I thought there was a real story to tell and a market that would read it."

"I agree there is a story to tell," their editor Tawny Cutler said, her curly brunette hair tied into an elegant bun atop her head, "but why not make them fruit or…puppies or…cars even—"

"Because kids should be able to read a children's book and, for once, see images that look like them. To do anything less is a cop out. There are many children who have diverse families. What better way to reflect that than with *humans*?"

"This is still controversial, however," Nathan Gordon said, hers and Oscar's agent. Completely bald with sharp, wire-rimmed glasses, he leaned back in his seat. "Parents would be more likely to buy the book if there weren't humans involved."

"Which kind of parents are you talking about?" Margot asked quietly. "'Traditional' parents? Is that always going to be the people we sell these books to? And why do we think 'traditional' wouldn't buy this book? *Everyone* needs it. There will be classmates of these traditional parents' children who *have* these alternative families—the blended families, the interracial families, the *gay* families, the single-parent families. And think of the schools! Schools would buy this book to read to their young classrooms to teach about tolerance and diversity. There is a market."

"And what happens when these 'traditional' parents demand a boycott from the book because the teacher read it without their permission?" Dean asked, though his tone was more contemplative than accusatory.

"They're just mad they're being dragged into the twenty-first century. They'll get over it," Margot muttered, then shook her head and sighed, her hand unwittingly going to her belly. "I'm sorry that came out so harsh."

"Should you sit, Margot? Are you all right?"

Margot smiled at Tawny and nodded, understanding the woman would be particularly sensitive since she'd had her own baby ten months ago.

Nathan stood immediately and helped Margot into her seat, squeezing her shoulder before going back to his own chair.

"Well, if nothing else, you were definitely inspired by this topic," Dean said again, staring at the last PowerPoint slide that was still projected on the screen. It featured a little brown girl with her two brown daddies, all of them snuggled on the couch with a bowl of popcorn in the girl's lap. Margot had tried not to make the men look too much like Oscar and Georgie, but all who knew her recognized the gesture for what it was.

"I agree. This is the best illustrative work I've seen from you yet," Tawny said with a soft smile. "Oscar would've been proud."

Margot nodded, suddenly feeling tears sting her eyes. She looked down at her abdomen and its ever-growing swell. She'd have a baby in two months and she could hardly believe it. The bittersweetness over the fact Oscar and Georgie were no longer here hadn't gotten any easier to swallow.

She heard the scrape of chair's legs against the floor and then two warm hands enveloped her shoulders. She leaned against Nathan's strong form, glad for the comfort he offered. He'd known Oscar for longer than she or Georgie and had taken the death almost as hard as she had. They hadn't been able to talk about it at length because he had to settle things on the business side, and he wasn't much of a talker in general. He'd kept in contact with her through e-mail and little messages on her voice mail, however. Seeing him during this trip reaffirmed her decision not to spread Georgie and Oscar's ashes; Nathan should also be there for the final home-going.

"Are you prepared to stand by this book?" Nathan asked.

"I wouldn't be here fighting for it so hard if I weren't."

"Look, I know times have changed; and maybe things won't be so bad, but brace yourself. It *will* open up a firestorm. And especially given your circumstances now, I don't want you to be alone through it."

She looked at Nathan, then the other two sharply. "You'd abandon me at the first sign of trouble?"

The trio immediately shook their heads. "No!" Tawny said, exclaimed a little hurt by the assumption. "At least, *I* won't!"

Dean sighed. "You have us in your corner, Margot. We won't abandon you, but you could be a target."

"I know."

"We'll do a limited run and send it to the reviewers and to other organizations such as GLAAD, Planned Parenthood, that sort of thing."

"Besides, every company could use a healthy controversy every now and again," Tawny added and everyone laughed.

By the time the meeting officially ended, Margot felt much lighter. The baby poked her tiny foot against her ribcage as if to remind her it was time to eat. Nathan led her out of the Manhattan office building and into the hot, sunny streets of the city. Car horns blared, the chatter of many different languages saturated the air, and the smell of exhaust and fried foods fought for dominance in her nostrils. She felt her belly clench in retaliation, and though her stomach wanted nothing more than a hotdog with all the works, she knew she'd regret that later.

"Are you sure you want to go back to Boston tonight? I have no problem putting you up in my apartment," Nathan said, easing her in front of him to avoid two people who didn't care they were in the middle of a busy sidewalk as they made out enthusiastically.

"I should get back," Margot said, her mind going to Cole. He hadn't been thrilled with her making this trip to New York by herself. At first, she'd wanted to take the train because it was more convenient, but he'd said no quite firmly.

"I want you there and back as quickly as possible," he'd said as he helped her pack her briefcase. "The less time I have to worry about you, the better."

"Gee, thanks," Margot had said sarcastically, and had been very surprised when Cole had brought her into his arms with a force for which she hadn't been prepared.

"I *always* worry," he'd admitted, his breath fanning her nose, "I just hide it better when you're around."

She'd kissed him then, touched and a little thrilled by his ardent concern. It was almost as if they were a seasoned couple, the kind she and Marcus had been before his death. He'd always been nervous about her trips to New York, too, but she'd always had Oscar with her. This was her first time going alone, and she was pregnant on top of that. Of course Cole would be nervous!

"Be careful," she'd muttered against his lips. "You're starting to sound like a husband."

"I hope so," he'd replied, and his tone had made her breath catch. She'd meant it as a joke, but the fire in Cole's eyes had made her realize he didn't take it that way.

She still reeled from it.

"Is it that white boy Gail was telling me about?"

Pulled from her memories, Margot looked at Nathan in surprise, then rolled her eyes. Gail really could never keep her big mouth shut!

"He's a man, Nathan."

"He's twenty-five. Don't know many men at that age."

Margot had to grin a little at that. "You wish you were that age again, don't you?"

"Every day," he said with a tiny, mock sob. She chuckled.

At thirty-eight, he was older than all in their ragtag group and Georgie had looked up to him as an older brother, though she didn't think Nathan ever knew that. Nathan had tried to keep their relationships strictly professional; but as the only black agent in his literary agency, and she and Oscar being two of only a handful of clients of color, it had been easy to blur the lines.

"I should've contacted you better," Margot said as they entered a small deli. It was one of Nathan's favorite spots and the sandwiches would agree with Margot's stomach better.

"You should've," Nathan agreed, "but you wouldn't have been able to reach me, anyway. I was taking this loss just as hard as you, Mar."

"But Kelly's helping?"

Nathan smiled a little. "Yeah."

Kelly Chen, another agent at the agency, was Nathan's wife of two years. Georgie, Oscar, Gail, and Margot had all come down to New York for their wedding. Margot smiled at how happy everyone had been during that time.

"She'd love to see you," Nathan said, breaking through Margot's thoughts.

Margot bit her lip. It would be nice to visit, but she hadn't brought any clothes with her. "I don't know..."

"She will kill you *and* me if she found out you were in town and she didn't get a chance to see you!"

Margot chuckled, knowing he spoke truth. Sighing in surrender, she pulled out her phone. "I'll have to call the airline and change my flight." And call Cole.

"We'll take in a show," Nathan said, clapping his hands and rubbing them together. "Musical or play?"

Margot let him brainstorm as she first called the airline to change her flight from that night to an early-morning shuttle the next morning. She then called Cole and left a message on his voice mail. Maybe this night apart would be good for them. It was scary how domesticated they'd become and how much she relished it.

"All settled?"

Margot nodded, squeezing the cell phone in her hand before slipping it back into her briefcase. She hoped Cole would understand.

"So...what Broadway show did you decide for us to see?"

"It's not funny, Mom!"

Jill, however, only laughed harder at that announcement, patting the cushion next to her so Cole would sit. He gave a loud groan but complied, shoving his fingers through his hair as he rocked back and forth, restless.

"She's seven months pregnant, Mom. She can't just make impromptu changes like this on the fly!"

"Seems like she did," Jill said, then cooed when Cole scowled at her. "She's a grown woman—"

"She's *pregnant!*"

"That doesn't make her an invalid, Cole."

He rocked back into the couch, sulking. "I should've gone with her."

"Cole, really! The last time you were like this was when you were a child and Jacob would steal a toy you were playing with and wouldn't give it back."

He huffed. "She's with *Nathan!* Who the hell is Nathan!"

Jill didn't even bother to chastise him about his language, instead realizing the heart of his distress. "You're jealous."

He gaped at her briefly, then shook his head to deny it. "Mom—"

"You *are!*"

Cole rolled his eyes and returned to sulking. "I thought he was just her agent."

"And he *still* could be 'just her agent'! She had a life before you entered it, my love, and so did you. Do you think she'd be this insane if you wanted to spend time with one of your female friends?"

Cole glared at her. "It's not the same thing."

"It isn't?"

Of course, his mother was right, but Cole wouldn't admit that. What if something happened to her or the baby? He wouldn't be there, and that scared him more than he cared to admit.

"She will be fine," Jill said, grasping her son's hand. "Doesn't it mean something that she called you so you wouldn't worry."

"It didn't work," Cole muttered. "I'm worried."

Jill chuckled and rubbed his hand between both of hers. "You've got it *bad*."

"I'm *not* jealous—"

"Not jealousy. Love."

Cole didn't bother to deny that assertion and sighed, rubbing his eyes. "Talk about being blindsided!"

"At least you're not denying it. Your father fought it tooth and nail until I finally broke it off with him and started dating someone else. What a sight to see Frank Patterson grovel!"

"He *groveled*?" Cole asked.

"Oh yes," Jill said, chuckling slightly. "I was a plump, bookworm of a girl and he was so popular, like you and Jacob were. We ended up being class officers together our junior year and that was that."

Cole frowned. "I didn't think you started dating until after you graduated from college."

Jill chuckled breathlessly. "We did, but we had a fling the summer before we left for college—kind of stumbled into that one, really. We were each other's firsts, but I didn't press him for a relationship because we were going to two different schools and he really wasn't ready, so I let him go. I didn't tell him how I felt, but I think we both knew.

"Then we did the letter-writing thing, and we met up during all the school vacations, though we weren't intimate again. We actually formed a friendship through those letters. I still loved him, and he was still not ready, but I could wait. Then he surprised me with a visit during Valentine's Day freshman year and became infatuated with my roommate. Talk about awkward! We had been friends, and she was absolutely gorgeous with rich brown hair and a body that probably could've made Ann Margaret jealous! It hurt me to see them hit it off so well, but I bore it because what choice did I have?"

"He dated your roommate knowing how you felt about him?"

"He asked me if it was all right," Jill said, defending Frank. "I said it was. I lied through my teeth! But I had no claim over him, and it provided an excuse for me to see him more often than when I was at home. My roommate broke it off with Frank our junior year and he was really upset over it. He wanted me to help get her back and it was just...really hard for me. I finally asked him why was he chasing after someone who didn't want him when someone who *loved* him was standing right in front of him. After he picked his jaw off the floor—I don't think he ever expected me to call out the enormous elephant in our relationship—he first said he didn't want to lose our friendship. When that wouldn't wash, he accused me of being jealous.

"Of course I was jealous! That didn't mean I was wrong, but we had probably our worst fight ever, and we didn't speak for a long time afterward. Eventually, I decided to *really* let Frank go and let my mother set me up on a date with her coworker's neighbor. Alan Turner. What a guy *he* was. Very dreamy, but not Frank. He was everything I would've wanted had there not been a Frank Patterson in my life, and yet...I don't think spending the rest of my life with Alan would've been bad."

"Yes, it would have."

Jill and Cole snapped their attention to a newly arrived Frank, who stood at the threshold of the living room with his tie loose and his shirttails hanging outside his trousers.

"A bad thing for whom, dear?" Jill asked, though Cole saw the twinkle in her eyes.

"Me."

"And we can't have that, now can we?" Jill asked with an exaggerated pout.

Frank smirked at his wife as he pulled his tie from his shoulders. "Jill Corbett Patterson."

"I had wanted to keep my maiden name," Jill told Cole in a stage whisper.

"But I wanted everyone to know you were mine," Frank said. "Including that jackass Alan Turner—"

"He was a nice boy!" Jill defended.

"But you wanted a man," Frank said and winked at his wife.

Cole was surprised at his mother's blush and at the gentle teasing his parents had just given each other.

Jill cleared his throat, seemingly regaining her composure. "This 'man' ended up getting on the intercom of one of Boston's classiest restaurants and sang my favorite song over it—*while* I was on a date with Alan!"

It was Frank's turn to flush and he shook his head. "I was drunk—"

"On love," Jill said dreamily, giggling at Frank's eye roll. "He even did the backgrounds for 'I Hear a Symphony!' It was as hilarious as it was sweet."

Cole had to bite his lip to keep from laughing himself. His father was as tone deaf as they came; to know he'd sung a Supremes song in public in order to woo his mother made Cole see Frank in a new light.

"What brought on this unfortunate jaunt down memory lane?" Frank asked, sitting in the easy chair opposite them.

Jill glanced at Cole before saying happily, "Cole's in love!"

Frank frowned. "Is that possible?"

"How could you ask something like that!"

Frank shrugged at his wife's outburst. "I just mean he's either working or taking care of that woman. When would he have time to fall in love?"

"You just answered your own question, Frank!"

Frank's attention jerked to Cole then, and his eyes widened. "You can't be serious!"

"As a stroke," Cole said, his guard rising as it always did whenever he spoke to his father. Something told him he wouldn't like where this conversation was headed, but he'd rather have it now without Margot here to witness it than somewhere down the line.

"*Her*? Of all the women—*her*? Jesus, Cole! Sometimes I think you pull these stunts to piss me off!"

"Don't give yourself that much credit, Dad," Cole said, his eyes narrowing with banked anger. "You barely cross my mind."

"Coleman Henry Patterson!"

Frank, however, ignored his son's mean-spirited words with a scoff, pulling off his tie. "Love? Please! You two are too different, in two different places, and you're both clinging to something you need to be there! She lost everything, you're feeling guilty about Jacob, and she's your ticket to redemption, isn't she?"

"Frank!"

"You know *nothing* about *her* or *me* or *us!*" Cole said, standing. "You've never *cared* to know, either! You've treated her worse than a dog tracking in mud, and I don't get it. I've pegged you for a lot of things, but a racist wouldn't have been one—"

"Need I remind you Ryan Irving of Patterson, Irving, and Rouche is a *black* man?"

"Yeah, but I'm not thinking about marrying him anytime soon, either!"

Jill gave an indelicate snort at that and Cole allowed himself a small grin in response. Frank rolled his eyes and shook his head.

"You're missing the point—"

"Then find it for me," Cole snapped. "And it better be good because I don't want my daughter around you if you're going to treat her like shit!"

Jill stopped her giggles and Frank's eyes widened. Even Cole had to pause at his slip of the tongue. *His daughter.* It was the first time he'd voiced his private thoughts. Then again, why shouldn't he? He'd been there almost from the moment Margot herself had realized she was pregnant and had never left her side since. He and Margot's belly had bonded to the point that it didn't matter they didn't share the same DNA. That baby was as much his as it was hers.

"I thought she was already pregnant," Frank said flatly, the first to break the stunned silence.

"She was," Cole said. "But I love her and I love that baby. They're both mine."

"Are they?"

"Dad."

"You've never given any indication until this woman you were even remotely interested in getting married and starting a family, so why now? Did she convince you to do this? Is she trying to find a substitute for her dead husband and brothers? Maybe you shouldn't spend so much time with her anymore!"

"As usual, you give her too much credit and me not enough. I know what I feel for her and I know it's not because of grief. She makes me want to be a better person, Dad. She makes me think of other people, consider things I'd never even dreamed of considering. She's made me grow."

Frank shook his head, but it was more with resignation than anything else. "I'm just afraid you're conflating one emotion for another, Cole, and I don't want you hurt."

Cole blinked at that. "You actually sound like you *care*."

Hurt flashed in his father's eyes before he scowled and stood. "Yeah. God forbid, huh?"

Cole immediately felt guilty as he watched his father stalk from the room. He turned his attention to his mother, who was frowning.

"Mom—"

"Cut him some slack," Jill said. "I know you two don't have the best relationship, but never doubt that he loves you. *Never* doubt that."

"He's never said it," Cole mumbled.

"It doesn't mean he doesn't feel it. Jacob may have been his favorite, but that doesn't mean he didn't love you or wants to make sure you're happy and safe!"

"But what he said about Margot—"

"Is relevant, even if it's inapplicable," Jill said. "Part of me thinks you've *kept* her away."

"Dad couldn't even stand being in the same room with her!"

"Ever think that was because he couldn't handle knowing *his* son had destroyed *her* family?"

No, Cole had never thought of it that way. It was as if Margot was the walking manifestation of the guilt Frank harbored on behalf of and because of his son. Now here was his other son trying to make that guilt a permanent fixture in his life.

"Jesus."

Jill shook her head. "You two need to have a serious sit-down. The tension between you two is getting out of hand, and I don't want to lose another son because of pride and stupidity!"

Cole nodded and sighed. "You're right, Mom. This chat's long overdue."

"Yes."

"Later, though," he said. "We both need time to cool off and..."

"It won't be solved in a day, dear, but he loves you, Cole. Please never forget that."

Cole nodded again, kissing his mother's forehead and whispering his love before leaving the home, opting not to seek out his father to say goodbye. It would be far too awkward for either of them to consider it genuine.

He drove to Margot's apartment while in thought, hoping one day such courtesies wouldn't be so.

Chapter Thirteen

Cole sat on Margot's couch with a bowl of cereal in his hands and the remote control next to him on the cushion. The meeting scheduled for that morning had been canceled and the other work he had to do could be done outside the office, so he'd decided to stay home. He tried convincing himself it had nothing to do with the fact he wanted to be here when Margot arrived, but it did make him feel a little better that he would. As it was, it took everything within him not to drive to the airport and pick her up, remembering his mother's words from yesterday that Margot was a grown and capable woman even while pregnant, and the last thing he wanted to do was act as her surrogate father.

The *last* thing.

Nevertheless, he stopped his channel-changing when it flipped to a judge show. He'd always liked this particular one. The judge was in the middle of catching the plaintiff in a lie when the apartment's buzzer sounded.

Cole frowned. "Did she forget her keys?"

He shook his head and pressed the button to unlock the door, not bothering to ask who it was because he didn't know anyone else who would visit Margot. When the knock sounded on the door Cole grinned, a teasing comment ready on his tongue. He opened the door, mouth poised to demonstrate his rapier wit, but he gaped instead.

"You're not Margot," the man at the door said suspiciously.

"Neither are you!" Cole replied, scowling.

"Did she move? This was the address Sasha gave me..."

Cole didn't answer, blocking the entrance further. This man, older and distinguished looking wearing a black twill suit and a fedora, glared at him.

Cole returned the favor. "I'm sorry, sir, but I don't know who you are." Yet the longer he stared at the man, the more pieces fell together in his mental jigsaw puzzle.

"Robert Butler, Margot's father."

Cole's face darkened at the man's confirmation and he shook his head. "Margot doesn't have a father."

Mr. Butler scowled. "Is that what she's told you?"

"No, it's what *you* told *her*! Why are you here?"

"Is Margot here?" Mr. Butler asked again, trying to look over Cole's shoulder inside the apartment.

Cole refused to budge. "Does she know you're coming?"

Mr. Butler cleared his throat. "Not exactly."

Cole wanted to slam the door in this man's face. How dare he show up unannounced and uninvited as if he hadn't broken his children's hearts and completely ignored them?

"Sir—"

"Who are you?"

Cole clenched his jaw and held out his hand, almost sardonically. "Cole Patterson."

"Are you the help? You don't look like the help," Mr. Butler murmured, ignoring the hand and taking in Cole's breakaway pants and T-shirt.

Cole bit his tongue and the urge to tell this man he'd been more of a help to his daughter than he'd been. "Why are you here?" he asked instead, dropping his hand.

Mr. Butler stood straighter. "I came to see Margot."

"Why?"

"I don't have to answer to you! I don't even know who you *are!*"

He'd raised his voice, and Cole finally moved aside so the other man could enter. He didn't need the neighbors to be disturbed.

Mr. Butler looked around the space with an indiscernible expression. The judge show was still on but Cole didn't make a move to turn it off since he didn't plan on Mr. Butler staying very long.

"I am waiting for an answer, son," Mr. Butler said, turning his attention back to Cole.

Cole closed the door and leaned against it. "I am not your son." That didn't mean he hadn't been thinking of ways of how he could be by law.

Mr. Butler clenched his jaw, taking off his fedora to reveal a completely bald head. "Do you know when Margot will return?"

"Why do you care? For all these years, you couldn't be bothered and now all of a sudden you show up? What's going on, Mr. Butler?"

He cut his eyes at Cole before they fell on the bookcase where the urns sat. Mr. Butler's harsh features softened and his grip on the fedora tightened. Cole grew uncomfortable at Mr. Butler's change in demeanor but didn't move from the door as he watched the other man inch to the bookcase. His eyes, so much like Margot's, began getting glassy and his eyelids fluttered rapidly.

"George."

If Cole had ever wanted to know what regret sounded like, he learned it by the way Mr. Butler had said his son's name just then. Mr. Butler reached out a violently shaky hand and touched the solid forest-green urn that held his son's remains. How Mr. Butler had figured out which urn was Georgie's Cole didn't know. Maybe it had something to do with the connection between a father and his son, no matter how estranged they'd been.

Suddenly a loud wail drowned out the whooping studio audience of the judge show. Mr. Butler sank to his knees, succumbing to his grief. Cole's discomfort grew but he didn't dare approach. He was torn between feeling sorry and feeling self-righteous at Mr. Butler's predicament, and Cole didn't like it. Clearly this man hadn't hated his son as much as he'd led his children to believe; but where did that leave Margot, and where was Mrs. Butler?

"George…" Mr. Butler moaned, his hands gripping the shelves as his body heaved with his sobs. This was a far cry from the proud, erect man who'd stood at the door earlier. Cole wondered if his father had behaved this way when Jacob had died and was very glad he hadn't been around to see.

Mr. Butler completely slumped over, his hands sliding off the bookcase and clasping between his legs. His body rocked back and forth in sorrow. It was too much for Cole, and he started to go to him when he heard the tumble of locks from behind him.

Cole turned and went to block the entrance as the door opened. Margot looked at him in confusion and Cole kissed her before she could speak.

"I love you," he whispered against her mouth.

Margot frowned and pulled back immediately. "What's wrong?"

Cole gave her a look. "Why do you assume something's wrong?"

Margot snorted. "Are you serious? You're blocking the entrance to *my own house* and you kissed me and declared your love for me in a tone that says, 'Please forgive me!'" Margot stepped back and arched an eyebrow. "You got another woman in there?"

Cole didn't even dignify that with a response, especially since he knew she wasn't serious about the question. "Mar—"

"Baby, I'm tired, sore, and crave all the salt in the ocean! Let me in!"

Cole sighed, even less sure about letting her in the apartment. He glanced over his shoulder to see Mr. Butler sitting on the floor with one hand over his eyes and the other braced against the bookshelf.

"Your father is here," he said without preamble.

"That's not funny," Margot said, her face falling flat.

"I'm not laughing," Cole returned.

Margot stepped forward and Cole allowed her entrance this time. Mr. Butler didn't look up and Margot didn't say anything when her eyes fell on him. She swayed dangerously, forcing Cole to grasp her upper arms and step behind her for support.

"Mar—?"

"Daddy?"

Mr. Butler sniffed and looked up. His eyes moved slowly along Margot's person until it stopped at her middle. He shook his head and dropped his face in his hands, sobbing anew.

Margot pushed away from Cole and he didn't stop her, too stunned to see his woman drop awkwardly to her knees and gather her father in her arms.

"George—!"

"Shh," Margot said, rocking their bodies soothingly. "Shh..."

Cole felt like an intruder, but he couldn't turn away. Margot held her father close, comforting a man who hadn't been there for her or her brother for years. Cole turned off the television to give the moment the proper respect and reverence.

He went into the kitchen, prepared two glasses of water, and sliced an apple because Margot was hungry. He looked up from his tasks to see Mr. Butler help his daughter stand and then frame her face. Margot lowered her eyes, but Mr. Butler pressed his lips to her forehead, his body still wracking with his sobs. His tears were clearly visible from where Cole stood.

"You should sit," Cole heard the other man say, his voice hoarse and rough.

"So should you," Margot murmured. "Gail had said you've been ill. How are you feeling?" Mr. Butler couldn't handle the gentle inquiry, however, and sank to his knees again, his hands holding her sides as he cried into her belly. Cole saw Margot close her eyes and breathe deeply as if trying to bring herself together, then she sat on the couch because she couldn't support her weight, the baby's weight, and her father's.

Cole blinked back his own tears. This was the last thing he'd expected to witness. The ability Margot had to comfort someone who had hurt her so badly was astounding, and yet Cole couldn't be too surprised. All she'd wanted this entire ordeal were her parents, and now here was her father. Margot slid her hands over her father's head, humming a tune Cole often heard whenever the baby was particularly restless. To hear Margot use it with her father seemed to bring things full circle. Taking a deep breath, Cole put the glasses and sliced apple on a tray and went into the living area, setting it on the coffee table. When he was about to leave, a hand circled around his wrist.

"Stay."

He looked to Margot in disbelief at Mr. Butler's request. Margot nodded, holding out her hand to him. He took it and sat down with them, taking part in the healing. Watching them gave him hope about his own situation with his father. While he hadn't had the relationship Jacob had had, his mother had been right in saying Frank loved him. At the very least, Frank had never abandoned him.

A few moments had passed before anyone moved or said anything, then Margot announced she had to go to the bathroom. Once again, Mr. Butler stood and helped his daughter stand. Margot gave him a small smile, patted his hand, and then went down the hall. Mr. Butler remained standing, watching her go until she was hidden from his view.

Cole still didn't speak, not knowing what to say. Mr. Butler blew out a breath and sat in the seat Margot had vacated, swiping his hand along his head with a dazed expression.

"I am the *worst* kind of parent."

Cole's eyes snapped to Mr. Butler, but he didn't respond. There was no need considering Cole didn't disagree.

"She called Mother's Day. I'd answered the phone. I didn't say anything, but I let her talk. I put it on speaker so my wife could hear. Margot was just about finished when Faye silently walked up to the phone's base and disconnected the call."

Cole sucked in a breath. That was simply hateful.

"I couldn't even say anything to that," Mr. Butler admitted. "I couldn't believe I'd been complicit in all of this. It took me this long to get off my butt and try to make amends—it's hard to admit you're wrong...*especially* to your children."

He looked toward the bookcase where the urns were. "Child."

"If you'll forgive me for saying," Cole began, sitting straighter. "I don't think either of you deserves your children."

Mr. Butler swung his eyes to Cole, but his shoulders sagged and he nodded. "I'd think you're right. Parents don't disown their children for worse, and here we did because they wanted to be happy? God forbid! The cards Faye didn't get to first I kept. I still have them. Birthday cards, Christmas cards, Easter cards—I kept them. I missed my children, and one I'll miss for the rest of my life."

Mr. Butler tilted his head back and closed his eyes. "Faye doesn't even know I'm here."

They heard the bathroom door open and both men stood. When Cole would've approached Margot, she shook her head and came to them, giving both tremulous smiles. Cole took her hands and kissed her temple.

"Are you all right?"

"Not really," she admitted on a whisper, leaning against him. Cole wrapped his arms around her and kissed her temple again.

Mr. Butler picked up his fedora from the coffee table. "I should go—"

"Will I see you again?"

Mr. Butler appeared close to tears again at that question. Cole wasn't far off himself. The older man held out a hand to her and she took it, wincing slightly at the bone-crushing hug he gave her.

"I've been stewing in pride far too long, daughter," Mr. Butler said. "If you'd like, you can see me and talk to me as often as you like...or not at all."

"How long are you staying?"

"I have to leave Friday," Mr. Butler said apologetically.

That was two days away. "Would you like to have dinner? Where are you staying?"

"The Doubletree Inn off the highway, and I would be humbled to have dinner with you." He stepped back and looked at her. "You are so beautiful, daughter."

Margot ducked her head and shook it, touching her belly and breathing deeply.

"We will talk. Let me give you my phone number."

Cole began cleaning up as father and daughter exchanged contact information. When Mr. Butler finally left, Cole found Margot leaning against the door, forehead on the cool wood. She was taking measured breaths and Cole rubbed her back soothingly.

"Hold me?" she whispered.

Cole nodded, taking her hand and leading her to the bedroom where they both slid onto the bed fully clothed and snuggled until they fell into slumber.

-SJF-

She'd missed him so much.

Margot and her father tried very hard to pack years of stories into two days, but it was impossible to even hit all the main highlights of everything that had happened. Many of the stories Margot told her father he already knew and that had surprised her. It was then he admitted he'd kept as many letters and cards she and Georgie had sent as possible.

He'd also given her a new cell phone number—his private phone. Faye didn't know anything about it.

"I don't want to go through this again, daughter," Robert had admitted quietly. "I don't want to be the person I've been for the past seven years."

That person had been a cowardly zombie Robert went on to explain, going through the motions, too afraid to tell his wife they were wrong and too afraid his children wouldn't accept him and his forgiveness. He'd started to reconsider when Georgie and Margot had left for Boston; but by that point, Margot had been estranged for a year and Faye had been too angry over Georgie's homosexuality for Robert to do anything about it.

"Marcus loved you, though," Robert had said. "He loved you enough where I couldn't."

"Dad—"

"I told him to look out for you," Robert continued in that same low, broken voice. "Do what I had failed to do; love you as I had failed to love you. He was your husband now, your family now. You didn't need me anymore."

These were difficult conversations to have in such a public setting. The Thai restaurant was too small and intimate to go into detail, and to have her blubbering all over her food would no doubt cause the other patrons to lose their appetite. So both decided to keep the conversations as light and innocuous as possible. Robert spoke of his classes and how it appeared that the smarter the students were, the dumber they seemed. He'd never experienced so many bright individuals not use the sense God gave a gnat, and Margot laughed at the humorous stories he told.

They returned to her apartment to talk. It was within walking distance of the restaurant and the weather wasn't so sweltering to make it dangerous for Margot. There they had the privacy they required because Cole was at work that day, yet it still took a few more safe topics before either of them could broach the tough ones.

"Why?"

It was the best way she could start and keep her composure. He could pick any of the numerous layers to peel off the question too. Margot just needed *some* sort of explanation; and hopefully, they were better than the ones she'd fabricated on his behalf.

Robert shook his head. "Hurt. Anger. Pride. Disappointment. Failure." None of that made any sense to Margot, but she would wait patiently for more.

"All I could see was a mechanic, not the doctor or lawyer we had envisioned for you—"

"I didn't love Earl," Margot said quietly.

"I know. We thought Marcus was a stunt you were pulling so we'd drop the entire affair. Then you came and told us you were in love....We thought the ultimatum would break you."

It had, just not enough to give up Marcus. Though Margot didn't think she would have ever married Earl Winston, she'd been more than prepared to entertain other options or remain single until her parents backed down. Fortunately, Marcus had come into her life instead, presenting Margot with a beautiful third choice.

"We were so angry with you that we couldn't see how happy you were, how much you two loved each other. We were too prideful to take back that ultimatum, so we let you walk out our lives."

Margot couldn't look at her father right then, the memories of that Thanksgiving suddenly too raw. Her parents had barely treated Marcus with civility, and it had been irritating to hear them butter up Earl while tearing down Marcus. Faye's snide comments about Marcus's occupation and her outrage over Margot being the one to support them financially should they get married had almost been too much to bear. Of course, since Marcus had been there with her she did, but Margot had never been so ashamed of her parents.

"You challenged his masculinity, Daddy," Margot said quietly. "You challenged his intellect, his worth. I couldn't believe *my* father could be so cruel—the same father who would go out of his way to meet with students *whenever* they had difficulties, no matter how big or small."

"It definitely wasn't my proudest moment," Robert conceded, "but I was too hurt to lash out at you, so I chose him. I didn't have an emotional attachment to him."

"And what's Mama's excuse? She should know better than anyone about humble beginnings."

Faye's mother had been a laundress for white people and Faye had babysat their children as well as done some seamstress work. Faye had worked hard in school in addition to this; and between their two incomes and a scholarship she'd earned, Faye could afford to go to college. The fact Faye Hollis had caught the attention of the handsome and prominent Robert Butler while at school had apparently earned both their share of grief. They being so adamantly against her and Marcus had surprised Margot.

"It seemed you were laughing in her face by bringing him to our house," Robert said. "All that hard work she put in to make sure you'd have a husband worthy of you and you chose a *mechanic*? He didn't even have family—at least not a respected one—"

"Marcus and his family have treated me wonderfully, which is more than I can say for either of you."

Robert bent his head. "Yes."

"And then the way you treated *Georgie*! My goodness! Not even I expected it! Then again, I don't know why I was so naïve to think you'd stand by him." Margot scoffed. "Appearances mean more to you than your children."

"Margot—"

"Don't *even* think about telling me not to be mad! Don't *even* say it!"

Margot hadn't even realized how truly angry she was until her father had started talking. His explanations were just as paltry as she'd imagined they'd be and the confirmation hurt.

"We were good children, Daddy! *Good people*! Why couldn't *you* see that?"

Robert shook his head and hung it further. "If I could go back in time—"

"You can't," Margot said flatly. "None of us can. Believe me, I wish I could. Then I wouldn't feel what I'm feeling right now, a feeling I don't like at all because all I want to do is love you. For *seven years*, I tried. Yet housekeeper after housekeeper continually got on the phone to tell me 'The Butlers don't have a daughter.'"

Robert began weeping; but unlike yesterday, Margot didn't comfort him. She'd cried every night for at least four months after that exile from her home, and Marcus had been there to hold her and brush away every tear she'd shed. When Marcus had died, Georgie, Oscar, and Gail had helped, but too many nights had featured her clutching a pillow that gradually lost Marcus's scent until she could only smell the salt of her tears.

"My husband died four years ago next week. These have been four very trying, very difficult years, and I couldn't even go to my parents. They were two busy not giving a damn about what had happened to me—to their *grandchild!*"

Robert sniffled and nodded. "We knew."

"You knew," Margot ground out. "Gail."

"Not just Gail," Robert admitted quietly. "Georgie."

Margot reeled as if she'd been punched in the gut. *Georgie?* They talked to *Georgie!* Margot couldn't speak for a good five minutes, unable to comprehend her parents having contact with Georgie and none of them telling her. She put her face into shaky hands, taking deep breaths at the wave of hurt that crashed into her.

"Your mother doesn't even know I did," Robert admitted quietly. "And I told Georgie not to tell you because I knew it would hurt you too much."

"You...*knew.*"

"And I put flowers on Marcus's grave before I came up here."

"Flowers?"

"Yeah." He shook his head. "The first time I did it was right after Marcus's death. You had called and told us. I remember hearing the grief in your voice and feeling so helpless. That's when I first called Georgie—a few weeks later. After he lit into me like no one's business, he told me you'd lost the baby. So I went to Marcus's grave, put down some lilies, and cried. I cried for you, for Marcus, for the grandchild I'd never know...for me. I just...cried."

Margot's heart ached so badly, and yet she felt conflicted. Her father still cared, but why hadn't he contacted *her*? And her mother still was stubborn about everything. How could she bring a child into this world with this kind of family situation? She thanked God she was a grown woman and had the income to support the child herself, but she didn't know if she could—

"When you called the house and told us about Georgie and Oscar…when *Gail* and *Sasha* called us…your mother…she's still in denial, but she stares at pictures of you two when she thinks I'm asleep. I've caught her in the attic looking over pictures of you two. She misses you, Margot."

Margot didn't want to hear any more. "I need for you to leave."

"Margot—"

"For three, almost four years you—why are you even here? You do know this child I'm carrying is Georgie and Oscar's, right? You do realize *I'm* the mother of your gay son's child—the son you kicked out and yet brought back into the fold. You do realize I'm the daughter— the firstborn—you couldn't extend that same courtesy to. What did you think you'd accomplish by coming here?"

Robert sighed and stood. He took a deep breath and stared at the painting hanging on the wall in front of him. "You really are very talented Margot."

Margot didn't answer him, rubbing her belly as the baby suddenly became very active. She could feel her stress levels rising dangerously. She was too far along in her pregnancy to lose this child now.

"I don't want another seven years to go by, daughter," Robert said softly, still staring at the painting. "I miss my son, and I will always, *always*, miss him. He told me what he and Oscar had been trying to do. I helped finance some of the processes."

Margot looked up at him. "What?"

"And I referred them to Dr. Dennison because a colleague of mine...her daughter and son-in-law were having problems conceiving and Dr. Dennison had been the best in Maryland. When I learned she'd moved to Boston, I told Georgie to get in contact with her. Only the best for my children."

"*Child*," Margot all but spat.

"Daught—"

"Don't," Margot said, shaking her head. "I really need for you to go. You're upsetting me. I can't lose your *precious* grandchild, after all—*Georgie's* child."

"Margot, please—"

"I'm not going to ask you again. You need to leave. Now."

Her voice had remained calm but firm, but she couldn't look at this man before her. She felt his eyes on hers but she kept her focus on her middle, reminding herself she needed to remain composed for her baby...*Georgie's* baby...the baby.

"I understand, Margot," Robert said finally. He went to the door and opened it. "But this...all that's happened...I can't leave here without you knowing your mother, even if she won't admit it aloud, and I love you. We've done an incredibly poor job of showing that but...we'd like to start. Losing Georgie...I can't lose my daughter without her knowing her parents love her. Anything you need..."

He sighed. "I checkout at noon tomorrow. If you decide to call again, we'll answer. We want to be in your life and our grandchild's life. Though we don't deserve it, we're asking for your forgiveness and a second chance. Please."

He left then, the door clicking shut softly. Margot didn't move from her spot, her focus ever faithful on her belly.

Chapter Fourteen

Margot felt grimy, dirty. No matter how hot the shower's spray was or how hard she scrubbed the sudsy loofah over her body, she couldn't escape the uncleanliness she felt. Margot rested her forehead on the steamed tiles, her bottom lip held tightly between her teeth as harsh breaths exited through her nostrils. She didn't know how long she'd been in the shower, but it wasn't long enough. She needed to feel clean...acceptable...worthy.

Her father sure knew how to drop a doozy. The one thing that had kept her relatively sane during the estrangement was knowing she and Georgie had been in it together. Now her father was telling her it'd been only *she* out in the cold—at least for these last few years. They said they wanted to love her again, but part of Margot couldn't escape the thought her parents only wanted her back so they could be a part of *Georgie's* child's life. If she hadn't been pregnant, would her father have even bothered?

She wanted to slap Georgie for his deception. How had he been able to keep up the lie for so long? Had Oscar known about this too? Gail? Margot never remembered feeling so isolated.

The water was starting to get cold but Margot barely noticed. She sank down into the tub, crouching as best as she could with her belly in the way. This baby...Georgie and Oscar had left the baby in her care, despite the fact Georgie knew their parents would probably be more than happy to raise it. Why? Honestly, just because Georgie and their father had kept in contact it didn't mean it was cordial, did it? Maybe

Robert had to beg every single time he called Georgie for "just a minute." Georgie had seemed more than willing to cut off ties with his family, especially since he had his older sister with him. They'd always been close; this was why Georgie's secret hurt so much.

"Mar?"

Margot hid her face in her hands. Cole! *Cole!* He couldn't see her like this. She turned off the shower and huddled herself closer, hoping he'd just leave—

"Margot?"

He was at the bathroom door. Margot held her breath. She just wanted to be left alone.

"I should've never agreed to let you meet him without me," Cole said and she heard the door open.

"Cole! Please!"

He ignored her, and she saw his fuzzy form through the clear shower curtain. "Baby..."

She shook her head and began rocking. Cole couldn't see her like this! Cole couldn't—

The shower curtain slid open, revealing a fully dressed Cole and letting out the steam that had accumulated in her shower. Margot hid her face again and shook her head.

"Cole—"

"Shut up, Margot," he said firmly. A few moments later, she felt a fluffy towel surround her body and he helped her stand. He wrapped the towel around her as well as he could, then put another around her head. She didn't want him to see her tears, but they came regardless, streaming down her cheeks in steaming streaks.

"It's okay," he murmured, holding her close, clearly not caring she was wet and he was wearing a nice suit.

Margot was so tired, the emotional turmoil of the day hitting her at full force. She sagged against him. Cole held her in strong arms as they walked to her bedroom. He laid her down on the bed, the ends of her towel falling away to reveal her nude, swollen body to him. Suddenly she felt not only dirty, but slovenly as well, regardless of the fact she was pregnant. Her father hadn't been bothered to talk to her; her brother had lied to her; her husband had left her; Cole…

"Don't do this, Margot," Cole said, kneeling at the bed. His hands cupped her cheeks and his thumbs brushed away her tears. "Don't shut me out, baby."

"They wouldn't talk to me," Margot croaked.

"I know," Cole said sadly, pressing a long kiss on her forehead. "I know—"

"They talked to Georgie but they couldn't talk to *me*…wouldn't talk…"

"Mar?"

She heard his confusion, but her throat was too tight to reply. Cole shrugged out of his suit jacket before leaving the room briefly. He returned with yet another towel and a basketful of bottles and he spread the towel on the bed.

"Lie on it," he said softly. "On your side."

Margot frowned slightly but did as told. Cole rolled up the sleeves of his shirt and poured a bottle's contents in his hand. He sat behind her, the bed sinking under his weight, and soon she felt his warmed hands on her back.

"*Mmm…*" she moaned, his hands strong as the kneaded her muscles. He was efficient and true as he worked every single knot he could reach in her back. Her body felt like liquid. He brought her naked form to his and held her when he was done, his lips drifting along her temple.

"You don't have to tell me what happened, okay?" Cole began, his lips brushing her skin as he spoke, "but please don't shut me out. I can't help you if you do that, Margot. I want to help you. I love you too much for you to go through this alone."

She pressed her body closer to his and rubbed her nose against his jaw. "Cole..."

"Let me relax you, baby," Cole murmured, rolling her onto her back. His eyes and smile were soft. Margot pressed the backs of her fingers against his cheek. His smile widened and he pressed his lips against her fingers before moving down her body and rubbing her feet and legs. She was the clay to his sculptor, being molded into a serenity and peace that had left her earlier in the day. There was nothing sexual in his touch, his aim to heal, and his ministrations were doing more than repairing her achy, tired body. They were repairing her spirit as well.

Margot watched him pay very close attention to her abdomen, almost becoming breathless when he dropped on his knees on the floor by the side of her bed and pressed a long kiss to her tummy.

"It has been so amazing watching you these last few months, Mar," he murmured against the taut skin of her belly. "Watching you cradle and protect this little life inside you. She couldn't ask for a better mother."

"And what about a father?" Margot muttered, thinking about her own and Marcus and Georgie and Oscar. "Seems like Margot Elise Butler Reed and her spawn are to remain fatherless."

"That's not true," Cole said with a frown.

Margot nodded. "My father left."

"Margot—"

"Marcus left and so did his baby—"

"Honey—"

"Georgie and Oscar too—"

"Cole."

She looked at him, confused. "Cole?"

He shrugged. "I'm here."

Margot nodded. "For now, yes." Clearly it didn't matter if people loved her and she loved them, they always managed to find a way to leave. It seemed it didn't matter how hard she loved, she could only keep them in her life for an insignificant amount of time. She had to prepare herself for Cole's inevitable departure—whether voluntary or not.

"Forever," Cole said with a small frown. "I don't know what the hell happened or what your father said to you, but you need to get out of whatever funk it's got you in."

Margot pouted. "My daddy loves me and he won't talk to me."

"He has a funny way of showing it."

"Georgie loved me and he lied to me. Marcus loved me and he left me. Me and 'forever' don't have the greatest track record."

"What about *us* and forever?" Cole asked quietly, his hands rubbing her stomach idly.

Margot took a deep breath, her eyes frozen on his earnest face. "Cole?"

"I want to be a father to Margot Elise Butler Reed's baby," he revealed. "I already think of her as mine," Cole confessed. "I want to make it permanent. Legal."

"Legal?" Margot slipped her hand to cover his, stilling his hands' movements. "You're young—"

"Not so young that I don't know what I want. I want this baby to have a name—*my* name—and I want her mother to have my name too."

Margot sat up as quickly as she could, considering her condition, and Cole helped her, still kneeling, still looking earnest as he held her hands. "Cole—"

"I've been thinking about this," he began, dropping his eyes to stare at her hands. His thumb ran over the ring finger of her left hand, "for so long. Wondering if I was overstepping my bounds, rushing things…forcing things because they seemed neat and logical."

Margot didn't say anything, still in disbelief over what he was revealing to her. He moved closer and she spread her legs so he could get as close as possible. He nuzzled her belly and she slid her fingers through his hair. His hands drifted along her skin.

"I love you," Cole whispered against her skin. "Wow, do I love you." He laughed. "You came in and completely changed my life, and sometimes I don't even think you realize how loved you are, how much you deserve it. I want to spend the rest of my life showing you."

"Cole…"

Margot kissed the top of his head and he hugged her so tightly. He snuggled his head into her bosom and she allowed it. She needed this intimacy as much as Cole did.

"You deserve love too," Margot whispered. He lifted his head and she cupped his face. She smiled at him and he returned it. "You beautiful man." She kissed his forehead. "You're so beautiful."

"I have to keep up with you, you know," he said, caressing the outside of her thighs.

"You're the last person I ever expected to come into my life," she confessed, leaning her forehead against his. "You…" Tears filled her eyes again, overwhelmed by him and the love he felt for her, the love she felt for him. "You want me to marry you."

"Yes," he said, kissing the back of her hand.

"Do I have to answer you right now?"

He looked at her and shook his head. "No. I know I dropped this on you; and after the day you've had, I don't think I *want* an answer. But I do want you to know I want to marry you. I love you. My mother loves you. You have a family, baby. I want to make us a family."

She kissed him then. There was nothing else she could do, his words removing all the self-doubt and dirtiness she'd felt not hours before. She began unbuttoning his shirt and he helped, shrugging out of it and smiling against her lips when her hands drifted along his chest. His mouth moved down to her neck but she giggled when he had to move away from her and stand. He was breathing hard and his blue eyes were so intense on her. She kissed the space over his heart and began unbuckling his belt and trousers. His hand caressed her neck and the back of her head, and he began moaning as her mouth traveled south. She squeezed his bare behind before shoving down his pants and boxers. He stepped out of them and her hands moved back up his flanks. Their breathing was deep and labored.

He cupped her face and kissed her. "Baby."

"I love you," she said against his mouth, her hand gripping his hard length. He sucked in a gasp and she grinned. "Big boy."

He laughed. "So 'size' is all that matters to you."

"It certainly helps."

"Margot!"

She giggled against his throat before placing an open-mouth kiss upon it. "I love you for your soul more."

"Yeah?" he asked breathlessly.

Her mouth reached his chin, then his mouth. "Yeah."

He pulled her up to her feet and kissed her harder, his hands moving down her body to her behind, then her belly, then the apex of her thighs.

"Cole…" she moaned.

"You're the beautiful one," he said, slipping a finger inside of her. "You're having my baby, aren't you?"

Margot nodded, hugging him tightly and working her hips on his finger. She kissed his shoulder and the crook of his neck.

"My baby…my woman's having my baby," he murmured against her temple. "Mine."

"Yes," Margot said, whimpering when he removed his hand from her then stepped away. He sat down on the bed and pulled her between his legs. "Yours."

He reared up and kissed her, wrapping his arms around her waist and bringing her to straddle him. She felt his erection brush against her center, and she gasped when he entered her slowly.

They didn't say much during this lovemaking session, but his eyes were so vocal, so full of love and awe that she couldn't take it. Margot kissed his forehead, his cheeks, his nose, his lips, overwhelmed and humbled that he was in her life. Cole was promising himself to her, to her baby, a baby that wasn't his and yet…was. He'd been there for every obstetrician appointment, every birthing class, every craving and cramp and cranky moment. Even now, his hands couldn't stop touching her belly, her back, her bottom. And though they were as close as they could get given her pregnancy's swell, it wasn't close enough for him.

"Damn, baby, you love me so good," he groaned against her shoulder.

"How good?" she asked seductively, nipping at his ear and holding him close.

"The best," Cole muttered, his hands sliding up to cup her breasts. They were so sensitive. He'd barely drifted his thumbs over her nipples before they tightened and swelled. "You're a goddess."

The reverence in his eyes overwhelmed Margot and she kissed him softly. "Yes, I'll consider your proposal."

He seemed to sense she wasn't talking about his goddess comment and he pulled back, his eyes wide. "Yes?"

She'd accepted he wanted to marry her, to make himself the legal father of her baby. At first, she'd thought it was his way of making her feel better, his way to heal the pain in her heart after what her father had revealed, but now she knew differently. She wasn't ready to say yes to *the* question, but she was ready to accept it was genuine, from the heart.

"You love me," Margot whispered, rubbing her nose against his.

"Very much."

"You love my baby."

"*Our* baby."

She smiled and kissed him. They remained kissing throughout their climaxes and the ride down from them, and he held her so close. "Our baby."

He slid back into bed, his strong arms managing to take her with him, and they snuggled atop the covers, his hands cradling her and the baby she carried protectively. She didn't fall asleep, and she knew he didn't either by his consistent, comforting strokes, but she didn't mind.

She was already imagining falling asleep like this for the rest of their lives.

-SJF-

Frank was watching him stare at her, but Cole didn't care. Margot and his mother were laughing at something while on the porch, and the light in Margot's eyes was a welcome comeback after her father's visit almost a week ago. Tomorrow would be the four-year anniversary of her husband's death, but Margot had insisted on spending the day with Jill. She had preliminary sketches to show the older woman, and it had been far too long since the two had been able to sit and chat.

"You really do love her, don't you?"

There was mild disbelief in the question, but also acceptance. Cole looked at his father and nodded. "I asked her to marry me."

Frank blinked, clearly not expecting that. "What?"

Cole nodded and looked back at the two women he loved the most in the world. "I want to marry her, so I asked."

"And what did she say?"

"She can answer whenever. She loves me. She's told me so. I kind of sprung it on her, and she's been going through a lot. I just wanted her to know I would always be there for her—"

"But marriage?"

Cole bristled and glared at his father. "What's wrong with that? You told me I should be more responsible, think ahead about my future, and when I finally do you get upset!"

"But with *her*?"

"I love *her*. Sorry if you don't like it but I really don't care. Mom likes her!"

"I never said I didn't like her," Frank mumbled.

"Then is this about the campaign?"

Cole honestly didn't know why his father was worried. He was up double-digits in the polls, and whether he'd wanted it to happen or not, Jacob's death had earned him more voters. It wasn't as if Cole didn't think his father could be a competent attorney general. He was fair in terms of legality and justice. It seemed only with Cole he held prejudices.

"No." Frank looked out onto the porch where the women were still laughing and he sighed. "I'll admit that her color and her age do leave me wary. I can't help it. When I envisioned my daughters-in-law, they didn't look like Margot."

Cole nodded, prickling at his father's honesty, but was glad Frank was coming out and saying it. "Would it make you feel better if I thought the same thing?"

Frank smiled slightly. "A little, but what really bothered me was I thought you were shoving her in my face, using her to get back at me for…" He shrugged and bowed his head. "I was too blinded by my own grief and anger to see what was really going on."

"You thought I was making you relive the worst night of your life," Cole finished softly. "Mom got on me about that. I thought you were being racist."

"And I was a little jealous."

"Jealous?"

"I love my wife," Frank said. "I think she's the most beautiful woman in the world, but you have *Margot*. I kept wondering how in the world you pulled *that* off!"

Cole chuckled a little. "And you think I don't?"

"I can tell you do," Frank said, giving his son a small smile. "You always look at her with wonder, amazement. I couldn't believe my son had finally fallen in love and it was with the woman whose life my other son destroyed. I couldn't believe I would have to stare at the evidence of my poor parenting skills for the rest of my days."

Cole winced at his father's choice of words, but then he felt bad. The fact his mother had already told him this didn't dampen the complete revelation that had come upon him at his father's admission. Cole squeezed his father's shoulder.

"You can only do so much for us, Dad," Cole said quietly. "I know we've never gotten along the way you got along with Jacob—"

"You were your mother's," Frank shrugged. "Jacob was mine."

"Why couldn't we belong to both of you? I may not have been interested in law or all the dry reading, but I like going to Patriots' games or Red Sox games or Bruins games. I like skiing…you were so busy trying to groom Jacob to be the perfect son I had to carve out a niche for myself. Mom helped, but every son needs his father."

They sat quietly for a moment, letting Cole's words sink in. This was the first heart-to-heart he'd had with his father for years, and Cole figured he had to thank Mr. Butler for that, at least indirectly. Though he was still unhappy about Margot's breakdown after speaking with her father, both knew it was the first step of the healing process. Margot hadn't spoken to her father in the days since his visit, but Cole knew he was on her mind. She kept staring at the business card that held her father's information, would visit her father's Web site about the classes he taught, would even go to online bookstores and browse the books he'd published. Cole had to admit Robert Butler was impressive, but he was also not the greatest father in the world. The hopeful part was, however, one didn't have to continue being a lousy father—just as one didn't have to continue being a lousy son.

"I never thought you needed me," Frank said after a moment, and the comment surprised Cole so much all he could do was stare at his father incredulously.

"Dad—"

"You were always so self-reliant," Frank said. "Made me proud, but...you never really came to me for advice. You either went to your mother or figured it out on your own. Sure, a lot of that is my own doing. I did spend a lot of attention on Jacob at the expense of you; but by the time I was ready to focus on you, you'd already figured out how to go on without me."

It hurt Cole a little to hear Frank say that, especially because it was true. He'd been told, "Not now, Cole" and "In a minute, Cole" so often he'd just stopped asking for his father's time. His mother had done the best she could, but Cole had long accepted his place as the spare to Jacob's heir.

"So I nitpicked at you to make myself feel like I'd done *something* other than help create you," Frank said with a dry chuckle. "Petty, I know, and I never felt good about it, either. This isn't to say you haven't given me much fuel over the years, however."

Both men chuckled at that, knowing his father spoke truth. Cole had decided to be the anti-Jacob for a few years, thinking why not live up to the expectations, or lack thereof, of his father. At least he'd notice him some way.

"You were the one who kicked my butt into gear, though," Cole revealed. "At that point, not even Mom could have said anything to me. But you...you said, 'It would really break your mother's heart if we had to pick you up in a morgue one of these days.'"

Frank let out a breath. "Cole—"

"But it was the fact you couldn't look at me as you said it that really brought it home," Cole continued, ignoring his father. "Every time we went at it, you were always able to look me square in the eye; but that time, it scared me."

"It scared *me*," Frank said after a moment of silence. "No parent wants to bury his child, no matter how awful a relationship they had. We may not have gotten along, Cole, but I love you. I guess I was frustrated and confused that my boy had suddenly decided to make bad decision after bad decision, and knowing there was really nothing I could say to make you do right just..."

"So you focused on Jacob," Cole murmured, squeezing his father's shoulder. "You put a lot of pressure on him."

Frank nodded. "I put the pressure of two sons on one." He buried his face in his hands. "I might as well have killed that boy myself—!"

"No, Dad," Cole said, his heart clenching in his chest. It broke Cole's heart to see Frank so beaten down. "Jacob had problems. He'd always been a heavy drinker. Yeah, maybe you put a lot of pressure on him...but he had his own demons that had nothing to do with you. We all go through dark periods. The trick is to find a way to get out on the other side. He was so ashamed of disappointing you, Dad, so he'd rather sink further into the darkness than trust you'd love him regardless."

"I do," Frank said, breathing deeply. "I do."

Cole remained quiet, and then he let out a little sigh. "So these past few months have been about Jacob, but since…I…" He couldn't finish the sentence, not liking the trajectory it was going.

"I failed," Frank said quietly, looking ahead, but Cole didn't think he saw anything before him.

The look in his father's eyes told Cole he meant more than just Jacob. In a rare move, he pulled his father into a hug. Tears stung his eyes at his father's tight embrace, and he thought of all the missed opportunities by both of them, and the humility he felt at having the chance to start anew. They still had things to work out; but with his mom and Margot to help them, Cole knew this would be a new era in the Patterson household.

They pulled apart but Frank framed his son's face in his hands. Cole saw the tears in his eyes and sobbed a little when his father wiped his away with his thumbs. "I am proud of you."

Cole closed his eyes and more tears fell, prompting Frank to wipe those away as well. "Dad…"

"I send my clients to you if they ever need financial advice," Frank said. "I admit I've been too proud to do the same, and part of me didn't think you'd even take me on as a client."

Cole dropped his head, ashamed that his father was right. "I'm sor—"

"My self-reliant boy," Frank said, kissing Cole's forehead. "I understand. Now, anyway. Jacob's death has helped me put things in perspective."

Cole nodded and hugged him again. "I do too. We'll do better."

Frank kissed his son's forehead again and they separated. When Cole looked back at the porch, he saw Margot and Jill bent over something, more than likely Margot's portfolio. His heart pinched a little. Here he was on the way to repairing his relationship with his father and yet Margot still couldn't breach the void with her parents. He wanted to help her but had no idea how to go about it.

"She's an incredible woman," Frank said, bringing Cole from his thoughts.

"Mom?"

"Mrs. Reed. She shows incredible strength, and she isn't afraid to tell someone what she thinks of him!"

The men laughed, remembering Margot's ardent defense of Cole during the Mother's Day brunch.

"I just want to love her," Cole said, staring at Margot as she smiled at something his mother was saying. "I want to spend the rest of my life loving and adoring her."

"And she'd be a fool not to let you," Frank said, squeezing his son's shoulder in support. "Anything you need me to do, let me know. Besides, I think Jill wants her to be her daughter-in-law maybe more than you want her to be your wife!"

The men shared a laugh and the women returned from the porch. Jill gave her husband and son an appraising look, then glanced at Margot. "They're up to something."

"Why do you say that?" Frank asked, standing and approaching his wife. He gave her a soft, lingering kiss on her lips and Jill quirked an eyebrow.

"There are no ugly, surly looks; or bitter, hurt language....Who are you and what have you done with my husband and son!"

Cole shook his head, bemused, and stood, helping Margot sit and putting a protective hand on her belly. "It's us, Mom. We're just trying something new."

"Speaking of new," Jill began excitedly, "Margot just finished showing me the preliminary sketches and they are *amazing*! I cannot wait until the final product!"

"I want to finish before Labor Day but—"

"You just worry about you and that baby inside of you, Mrs. Reed," Frank interrupted gently. "That's the most important thing."

Margot blinked, clearly surprised by Frank's concern, then smiled a little. "I'm doing the best I can."

"We're here to help, too, dear. You do know that?" Jill asked seriously, allowing Frank to wrap his arms around her waist from behind her.

"Oh, you don't—"

"It would be our honor," Frank said, looking between Margot and Cole.

Cole leaned his mouth to her ear. "Even if you say no to my proposal, that doesn't mean we remove ourselves from your life. First and foremost, you are a friend, a very dear, wonderful friend. You and Little One will always have a place here, sweetheart. We promise you that."

Margot pressed her palm against his cheek and her forehead against his. "You're too good for me."

"No," Cole said, taking her hand and kissing her palm, well aware of his parents watching. "I can never be good enough, but I promise to try every day. That's a guarantee."

Chapter Fifteen

Cole must have a sixth sense when it came to her, for there was no other reason to explain what had made him wake up in the middle of the night. Instinctively, he'd known she was no longer in the bed, and it took him a few moments to realize what day it was.

The fourth anniversary of Marcus's death.

He slipped out of bed, not worrying about putting on a shirt in favor of worrying about her. She hadn't spoken about the day since her father's visit; and though she'd been happy and personable at his parents' house, Cole had kept waiting for her to acknowledge the significance of today in some way.

He hoped she was all right.

Cole stepped out into the hallway and saw soft light pouring into it from a doorway on the left. He went inside to see Margot sitting in the rocking chair in the spare bedroom-turned-nursery, her cheeks wet with tears.

"Mar?"

She didn't look at him. Her arms went tighter around the stuffed yellow teddy bear she was holding and she sniffled.

His heart breaking for her, he approached her slowly. "Honey?"

Margot sniffled again, shaking her head. "I'm an awful person."

He frowned, not understanding what made her come to that conclusion, especially when it was so incredibly wrong. "No, Mar, don't say that—"

"I am," she insisted, nodding her head and holding the teddy bear even tighter. "Four years after Marcus's death and here I am struggling with..." She trailed off and shook her head. "I'm not a very good widow."

Cole knelt before her, placing gentle hands on her bare knees, her nightshirt only reaching mid-thigh thanks to her distended belly. "That's not fair, Margot."

"Fair? You wanna talk about *fair*?" Margot asked. She gave a short, sarcastic laugh. "If life was fair I would be pregnant with *Marcus's* baby, and this would've been our second or even our third! Oscar and Georgie would be smothering me and going crazy with baby showers and buying things for the nursery, and my parents would be happy for me—us!"

"Mar—"

"But then I wouldn't know you," Margot added, her voice growing soft as she finally set her eyes upon him. "I wouldn't have ever known you existed, and I don't think that's very fair, either."

Cole swallowed but said nothing, her words very true and sobering. Four years ago, there had been no Margot Elise Butler Reed and he hadn't known he'd ever want to meet her. Now he couldn't fathom his life without her.

"So," Margot continued, averting her eyes to a faraway spot in time, "now I'm struggling with whether or not Marcus was a pit stop, a detour to you, because what I feel for you..." She stopped talking and put her face atop the teddy bear's head. "I loved Marcus."

Cole nodded and kissed her knee. "Do you need some space? I can go back to my apartment." Though he didn't feel comfortable leaving her alone at this late stage of her pregnancy, and the fact he worried less while with her, he didn't want his presence upsetting her, especially not now. Though he could never fully understand what she was going through, he could empathize. It was hard to reconcile his brother's death with Margot's entrance into his life, and Cole often wondered if that were the only way they could have ever met. It was also hard to fathom Margot had belonged to someone else before him; and had that someone else not died, Cole might not be as happy and content as he was today.

"I've never been alone during Marcus's anniversary," Margot admitted, turning red, watery eyes back to him. "Oscar and Georgie have always spent the day with me. I still haven't gone back to his grave since the burial; I haven't been ready to handle it. Now I know my father's been going—ain't that a bitch? He hadn't liked the boy when he was alive, and now he has the gall to put some flowers on the damn grave! He's doing what *I* should be doing! I loved him! I do! God..."

Cole reared up and cupped her face, his thumbs brushing away tear after tear as he pressed soft lips to her forehead and temple. He was truly at a loss of how to help her, but he murmured nonsensical words, hoping his voice would calm her down. She shouldn't get too upset.

"You think he knows I love him, Cole?" Margot asked, pulling back to look into his eyes. "I can love him and love you, too, can't I?"

"Of course you can," he replied, dropping his forehead to hers. "I'm not trying to take his place, Margot."

"I know," she whispered, "but it's scary. What I feel for you...what I felt for him—I just don't want him to think I didn't love him. I did, Cole. I loved him so much, and yet the thought of never loving you, of being loved by you, that's scary too."

It was downright terrifying, but Cole merely nodded. Margot was a woman he was supposed to love. Had he met her while she was married to Marcus, Cole didn't know if he would've had the moral compass not to go after her. Of course, it would've been a futile effort because Margot was a very loyal woman, and he wouldn't have been good enough for her. Some days he wondered if he even were now.

"And I don't want you feeling awkward," Margot breathed, her hands grasping his at her cheeks. "I don't want you to feel bad, or think I don't love you, either, because I do. But Marcus..."

"He was your first love," Cole finished for her, his eyes looking deeply into hers. "I understand, baby."

"I miss him," Margot admitted. "I wish he was here, but not at the expense of you! I'm selfish."

She'd dropped her face and he tucked it into his shoulder. He rubbed her back and kissed the side of her head. He wished Margot wasn't in this position. She was feeling guilt she shouldn't feel, and part of him wondered if he rushed things with her. Between her father's visit, his proposal, this anniversary, and her pregnancy, he was afraid Margot was at a breaking point emotionally.

"Whatever you want me to do Margot, I'll do," Cole said after a few moments. "If you need some time to yourself I can give you that. Do you want to visit his grave? I can arrange a trip to DC for you."

Margot pulled back and cupped his cheek. She didn't say anything immediately, but her eyes were intent upon his face. "What are you doing in love with me, Cole?"

He was taken aback by the question. "What?"

She frowned. "You are too gorgeous for words! Wealthy. Kind. Considerate. Younger...white, and yet you love me?"

From the way Margot peered at him, Cole knew the question was rhetorical. She looked as if she was trying to solve a very hard philosophical dilemma, and no answer she'd find would fully encapsulate the why of it all. Then again, Cole thought the better question was why she was in love with *him*.

"How could you even ask that?"

He blinked, unaware he'd spoken aloud. Cole then shrugged. "Some days I'm still amazed you're with me; that you love me. I know I've said it before, but I can't help it. I'd never been with an older woman; and though I have been with black girls before, I'll be honest enough to say I didn't think I'd fall in love with one—not because I didn't want to, but..." He shrugged.

"Same here," Margot said, smiling slightly. "Though you're the first white man I've ever been intimate with—"

"And the last," Cole said, his tone teasing, but his intent serious.

Margot sighed. "I thought Marcus would be the last."

Life was so fragile and apt to change with split-second speed, and her comment made him confront that fact yet again.

"One day at a time, Margot," he said, resting his head in her lap. He touched her belly lightly. "One day."

"One day..."

"I'm going to love you with everything I have for each day I'm given," Cole promised, and it was one he knew he could keep.

"Cole."

"I probably rushed things with you," he continued, pushing up her shirt to look at her bare tummy. His finger traced the darkened line that went through her belly button. "In my excitement of finding you, loving you, things have happened so fast for the both of us, especially for you. I probably should've given you time to breathe. Call me young and impulsive."

Her fingers tangled in his hair and he closed his eyes at her ministrations. Even in her sorrow, she had time to comfort him. And she wondered why he loved her so much.

"I know Marcus was your first love, Margot, but you know what? You're mine. From the first moment I saw you, I was blown away. Something knocked over in me and I didn't know what it was, but that something recognized you for who you were, would be to me, even though I thought no way a woman like you could ever give two shits about me like that."

He paused when she kissed the top of his head. "You were the woman meant to be my wife and have my babies, Margot. I know that may sound callous, especially considering what today is, but I can't help it. I feel it in my gut, in my soul, and we've always been honest with each other, so I thought I should let you know that."

Neither spoke after a long moment. Cole was afraid he'd overstepped some invisible boundaries. He'd forever be grateful to Marcus for taking care of her before he entered her life, but as wrong as it was, Cole couldn't shake the feeling Margot always had been meant for him and he for her.

"I give more than two shits, baby," Margot said brokenly, and she let out a breathless chuckle.

Cole smiled and kissed her stomach, relieved she wasn't offended. "Thank goodness! I've never had to pine unrequitedly before."

"And you never will."

They met eyes. Cole stood and helped Margot to her feet before pulling her into a hug. "Thank you. For giving me a chance. *Us* a chance."

"There's not a man on this earth like you, Cole Patterson," Margot said softly with a faint smile. "I took a chance with Marcus and that led to seven beautiful years. If I only get seven years with you, I can say I've had fourteen years of being loved and loving two wonderful men. Of course I'd take a chance with you."

"Baby I plan on tacking at least fifty more years to that seven!" he said with a grin, pulling her tighter to him.

"Boy! That's what—almost sixty years! I'mma be old and not able to move by then!"

"Nonsense. Ninety will be the new sixty!"

"That means I'll still have to beat all those young girls away with my overstuffed purse?"

He quirked an eyebrow. "You do that now?"

"No. Don't mean I don't wanna. I'm gonna have to invest in an overstuffed purse soon."

He chuckled and kissed away the pout that had formed on her pretty face. "I like that I'm not the only one who gets jealous."

She scowled slightly. "It's not that. I just don't like some of the stares we get. I didn't have to worry about those with Marcus."

Cole had noticed the stares, some of them not kind to be sure, but they rolled off his back. He was too busy strutting like a peacock because Margot was on his arm. He'd give people who stared large smiles and bring Margot closer to him. He wanted everyone to know she was his woman, he was her man, and that baby she carried was his—even if they were the only ones who knew the particulars. Luckily, the news of his brother's accident had fallen off the front page, so reporters weren't so interested in him and his love life. Besides, his father had been doing an excellent job in keeping his own name in the papers for positive things and gains in his attorney general race while his opponent was too busy putting out fires for their relationship to be newsworthy. And gratefully for both him and his dad, the major state political race was for governor, and it was so dirty that sometimes Cole wanted to take a shower after watching the political ads!

Then again, he couldn't blame people for staring. Margot was stunning with her pregnancy glow.

"They're probably wondering how much I had to bribe you for you to go out with me," he murmured against her mouth.

She grinned slowly. "Like you could afford me."

He laughed and kissed her. "I adore you so much."

Margot pulled back to look into his eyes, and her smile was soft and contemplative. "I'd prepared for a life as a single woman after Marcus died. Preemptive? Maybe. I never thought I'd meet someone who could make me feel the way he did, love me the way he did. And then here you come." She grasped his chin between her thumb and forefinger and nodded. "He sent you to me. He had to have. He and God....That's the only way I can square it away in my head and my heart, and so for that I thank them. I thank them very much."

He breathed her name and kissed her softly, joining her in expressing the gratitude of being in each other's lives.

-SJF-

Margot hit a creativity boon this past week, so much so she was afraid she'd be depleted of it for the rest of the year. She managed to finish the illustrations for the book and sent it to the editors for review, then she finished the family portrait Jill had commissioned. She was proud of both works, though she did feel a twinge that she couldn't call Georgie and Oscar so they could see the fruits of her labor. Cole had been busy with work since Labor Day was coming up soon. He'd be going down to DC with her to visit Marcus's grave. During that trip, she planned to meet Marcus's uncle and *maybe* visit her parents.

That plan still hadn't been finalized. She hadn't spoken to her father since he left, but he'd left her messages on her voice mail and e-mail. Margot heard the remorse in his voice, the pleading; and while part of her was still very angry, she wanted to move on. Margot was scared to trust her heart to her parents again, however, and that was the saddest part of all.

Sitting in her studio, Margot took a deep breath as she stared at her canvas. The pencil markings outlined the image she was supposed to be painting—watercolors because it was the safest bet—but a new idea entered her mind. She carefully took down the canvas and set up a new one, not even bothering to make a draft first.

At first, the canvas was nothing but oranges, reds, and yellows, with dots of black and brown peppered upon it. It was starting to look like a desert, and Margot frowned. This wasn't turning out the way she'd anticipated.

The little one started becoming active as she painted, so she rested her left hand on her belly, then pulled up a chair and placed the palette on it for easier access. She dipped her paintbrush in the water, and then hovered it over the paints, wondering what else she could do. She was determined not to waste the canvas. In a split-second decision, she dipped the brush into the blue paint and drew it along the paper, then added white and gray to give it more definition.

A cerulean pool appeared in the center of the canvas, still, yet refreshing. Some of the paint colored her sable finger. At its bank, a tall tree with plentiful green leaves and clusters of white buds appeared. The bark was dark, almost black, and the trunk was a little narrow, yet sturdy. She decided to add mountains in the far background to fill out the scene, and she painted the sky in marigolds, pinks, and purples. The sun peaked over the smallest mountain in the range, leaving it was unclear if it was rising or setting.

"Rising," Margot murmured aloud, putting down her paintbrushes at last. "Definitely rising." Though she doubted such a deciduous tree would last in the desert, it fit the scene. It would be a resilient tree; one that could take the harsh conditions and still survive, *thrive*, despite them.

The baby moved energetically and Margot cooed. "You like Mommy's drawing?" There was a slight pressure in response. "I'll take that as a yes!"

She took her phone from her desk and took a picture of the image. She sent it to Gail and Nathan, thinking they would like it. Gail replied immediately, asking her what made her paint this scene.

"The spirit moved me," Margot texted back.

It also moved her to stop for the day. She cleaned up her workspace but kept the painting on the easel. Margot looked around the room a bit wistfully. The lease would be up soon and she didn't think it made sense to keep it when she was the only one using it now. Perhaps she'd dip into her savings to rent a smaller studio just for her. In the meantime, she'd have to find a place to store her other work, though she had a niggling suspicion Jill wouldn't mind holding it for her.

Margot took a taxi home, feeling too tired to ride the T and then walk to her apartment. When she arrived she immediately kicked off her shoes and drew a bath, needing to soak. Her ankles and back were killing her, and she wondered if this baby would weigh eighty pounds by the time she gave birth!

Margot didn't know how long she stayed in the tub, falling asleep; but by the time she awoke the water was cold, her fingertips and toes were wrinkled, and there was a fluffy blue towel on the lid of the toilet seat she hadn't put there. Smiling, she stretched and let out the stopper before easing her body out the tub. She wrapped the towel around her body as much as it could go given her tummy, and she padded into the hallway.

"Cole?"

"Kitchen!"

She heard clanging and sizzling. Her stomach rumbled at the tomato and oregano aroma tickling her nose. She'd had her lunch almost five hours ago and she'd been too busy painting to snack as she normally would have. Margot went into her room and changed into one of Cole's dress shirts and a pair of Marcus's old boxer shorts before going into the kitchen.

"Hey," she greeted, leaning against the breakfast bar. "What are you doing?"

Cole laughed and approached her, kissing her lips. "Dinner!"

"What kind of dinner?"

He made a face at her incredulous tone. "Spaghetti!"

"When did you suddenly know how to cook spaghetti?"

"I can read, Margot. I can also boil water, *and* I can dump noodles into a pot of boiling water. On top of that, I can tell time! Aren't those all the steps necessary for making spaghetti?"

She laughed and nodded. "Yes, it is. I'm sure you'll do a wonderful job, but you do realize that pot is too small to hold all the spaghetti you're trying to make?"

Cole cursed softly, dumping the water into a bigger pot and added more to it. Chuckling under her breath, Margot went into the living area and turned on the television. The evening news was on but she barely watched it. The correspondent was giving his report from the White House, and she felt a phantom nudge. Her trip to DC was the right thing at the right time; she had much to tell Marcus and his uncle.

"I think I should see my parents too," Margot said aloud to herself.

"What?"

There was another bang and Margot started, twisting her head to look at him. "Are you all right in there?"

"I will not be bested by a colander!" Cole announced.

Margot smiled. "You got it, baby!"

"You mock me!"

Margot laughed and shook her head, drifting a hand along her belly and turning back to the television. "I support you, dear. Do I find some humor in all of this? Yes, but I know you can do it."

She giggled silently at Cole's mutterings behind her. He was such a breath of fresh air into her life. She could easily see him in it for the rest of it.

"He may not be the daddy planned for you, but he'll do, yeah?" she murmured to her belly. "Then again, I'm not the mommy planned for you, either, but I promise we'll love you, baby. We'll love you so much and I'll tell you about your daddies all the time. They love you too. They're looking down on us, baby."

Her nose twitched as the scents from the kitchen reached her. Something was smelling good, garlicky, and something else—

"Cole, are you burning something?"

"Aw, hell!"

She heard the oven door bounce open and the slam of something followed by more cursing. "What happened?"

"Remind me to use oven mitts when reaching for hot things in the oven, yeah?"

Margot stood as quickly as her girth would allow. "You all right?"

"Yeah, a real quick touch to snap sense back into me," he mumbled. "This is proof I was right to abandon baking."

"I'll get some Vaseline," Margot said, hurrying into the bathroom. She brought out the tub and went to Cole who was scowling at three fingers on his right hand.

"Oh, let Mama look at it," Margot cajoled, taking the injured hand in hers. She dabbed the jelly onto the fingers, looking at him apologetically when he winced. She felt lips on her forehead and grinned.

"Cole."

"You're going to be *such* an awesome mom."

"Less than two months' time too," she whispered.

Cole nodded. "I've begun clearing my schedule to prepare."

She blinked at him. "Cole!"

"What? I want to be there every step of the way. It's not as if I can't work from home, anyway. I just moved meetings around and the ones that couldn't be avoided I made sure they were here in Boston."

She kissed the back of his injured fingers, and then placed them on her cheek. He hugged her close, and they stood there for a few moments, enjoying being in each other's arms.

When her stomach rumbled once more, he chuckled and kissed the top of her head. "Let's get you and the little one fed."

They took their meal at the dining table since Margot's belly couldn't accommodate her at the breakfast bar. Cole's movements were slower as he favored the burned fingers, but he refused any help she offered because he wanted her to relax.

"Not bad," Margot said after eating the first bite of the spaghetti. It was simple—just noodles and tomato sauce—and the frozen garlic bread was a little dark, but she didn't care. The fact he prepared it made it excellent to her.

"I don't think I'll be buying a chef's hat anytime soon, though!"

Margot laughed. "After the baby's born I'll start teaching you some basics, okay?"

He stared at her for a moment. "Really?"

"Of course! Why wouldn't I?"

He shook his head and smiled slightly. "It's just refreshing to hear you say things like that, talking about an 'us' after she's born."

Doubt crept in her voice. "You still want that, right?"

"I want it all," Cole said quietly. "I want you and that baby to have my last name, but as I said before I won't pressure you. I know you have things to work out and—"

"I want that too."

Both heads snapped up, eyes wide with that admission. Her heart beat double against her ribcage, and her breathing accelerated almost dangerously. Neither moved nor spoke for a good while. Why was she so nervous? It wasn't as if he didn't want to marry her—he'd asked *her*. Besides, *she* was the one who had suggested to Marcus that they get married. Of course, she'd been kidding, asking off-handedly; but when he'd called her bluff, Margot couldn't get to the courthouse fast enough.

The circumstances had been different then. She'd known Marcus for a long time before the proposal. She hadn't been pregnant, and the fact he'd stood by her after her parents had disowned her let her know Marcus would always be there for her. Hadn't Cole proven the same? He had, multiple times. That early morning on Marcus's anniversary had sealed it for her.

"You want what?" Cole asked softly as if giving more voice to it would change Margot's answer.

Margot tried to be nonchalant, shrugging as she tore off a piece of bread. "If that proposal's still good, I'd like to accept it now."

Cole didn't move. "What proposal?"

She chewed the bread and swallowed. "The marriage one?"

Cole remained still for a moment more before standing and going down the hall toward the bedrooms. Margot looked at her plate in disbelief. What in the world was going on in that head of his? Why didn't he seem happy she all but said she'd marry him? She wasn't hungry anymore. Margot pushed her plate from her and dropped her head in her hands. He couldn't have changed his mind because he *just said* he wanted her and the baby to have his last name!

Right?

A kiss to her shoulder had Margot lifting her head and greeting the sight of a platinum ring with tiny diamonds studded in the band traveling to a brilliant-cut solitaire diamond in the center.

"Huh," Margot grunted, unable to express anything else. This was the last thing she expected. She and Marcus hadn't even given each other rings when they married. Marcus had said only the best would go on her finger, so they'd been saving up for a spectacular, no-holds-barred, fifth-anniversary wedding complete with rings instead.

"You don't like it?"

Margot let out a harsh breath and turned incredulous eyes to him. "What's not to like?"

"You're really quiet," he said with a shrug.

"I forgot you could afford something like this," Margot said honestly. "I never realized I could own something like this."

"This isn't even the least you deserve," he said softly, seriously. He took her left hand and kissed its ring finger. "Something told me you wouldn't want anything too ostentatious, though. I thought this was a happy medium."

She closed her eyes against the familiar sting of tears, except these would be happy ones. "When did you get this?"

He cleared his throat. "The day you spent with your dad. I hadn't even intended to buy a ring, but I passed Shreve, Crump & Low, and something told me to go inside."

She touched her forehead to his and cradled his cheek with her left hand. She smiled. "Yeah...now more than ever I want to be your wife."

"You know this is a binding contract of at least fifty-seven years? My dad's a lawyer and about to be attorney general. I have connections."

Margot laughed even as tears fell down her cheeks. "Will there be a prenup I have to sign?"

"There's no need for a prenup when we're not ever getting a divorce. You're not that type."

"No."

"And I'm too selfish to let you go," he murmured, brushing away her tears. "And fifty-seven years, remember? Don't think I'm not gonna hold you to that!"

She laughed again and hugged him tightly. He held her just as tightly, even more so, his face buried in the crook of her neck. Unable to remain in her precarious position, Margot eased from the chair to her knees on the floor. After a while, Cole pulled back slightly and took her left hand in his again. Both were breathless as he slipped the ring on her finger, amazed at how perfectly it fit.

"You do realize the fifty-seven years starts now, right?"

Margot kissed him in response.

Chapter Sixteen

Victor Reed, or Uncle Vic as Margot affectionately called him, stared at them with an appraising eye. Cole squirmed next to her. She patted his knee and smiled at her uncle-in-law.

"Say something. You're making him nervous," she said in a stage whisper to the older man.

"Good! He should be!"

Margot rolled her eyes but couldn't stop her grin at Cole's blush. He hadn't been this nervous when her own father had visited. Then again, Victor Reed was not a man one wanted to cross. Tall and broad like most of the Reed men, he had a head full of completely white hair despite his age of sixty. He still was as handsome as he must have been in his youth, and Margot remembered the numerous times she and Marcus had teased him when women would approach him wanting more than an oil change.

The fact Margot hadn't been down to see Uncle Vic recently was atrocious, which was why he was her first visit on their DC trip. Cole and Margot had driven down yesterday and were staying in a hotel in Alexandria. They'd arrived at Uncle Vic's house in Anacostia earlier that morning. He lived next door to his auto shop; and since today was Sunday, the shop was closed.

"Girl, stop apologizin'! You here now, ain't you?"

He'd said he understood her avoidance and she believed him. Marcus's death had hit him very hard as well, and he'd always tell her to "take your time" whenever he brought up visiting DC. They had kept regular contact on the phone after Marcus's death, although these past few months hadn't been so normal because of all the changes that had been happening.

"You're beautiful, Margot. Then again, that ain't new, either."

It was Margot's turn to blush. "What did Marcus tell you about flirting with me?"

Uncle Vic let out a whoop and slapped his hand on his knee. "He was just afraid I'd take you away from him!"

Margot laughed as well. "You're awful!"

"No, but I am mighty glad to see you. All of you…" His eyes had dropped to her belly. "You was tellin' me about that in vitro? It took or is it Casper's?"

Cole coughed. She glared mildly at Uncle Vic. "His name is *Cole*."

"Cole? Like Nat King Cole?"

Cole's coughing gave way to laughter and Margot giggled. "That's what I said when he first told me his name!"

"Ain't nobody in the world could sang like Nat King Cole. You sing, Cole?"

"Awfully."

"Least you honest about it!"

The trio shared another laugh and Margot instantly felt lighter. She could tell Uncle Vic was starting to like her young fiancé and she was glad. He was the first person they'd told about their engagement other than Cole's parents. In fact, Cole hadn't even been able to get out the words. Jill had seemed to sense what the news was, weeping and mumbling over the speakerphone that she was so happy for them before Cole could make the big reveal. Mr. Patterson had had to take the phone from Jill and speak for the both of them, and his congratulations had sounded sincere.

"Thanks, Dad," Cole had said genuinely, and Margot realized the healing between the two had begun. It also reaffirmed her decision to go see her parents, particularly her mother. If Cole and Frank could begin to mend, maybe she and her mother could too.

"You makin' my Leesy happy?" Uncle Vic asked.

"Leesy?"

"My middle name, Elise? He'd always trip up mine and Marcus's names because they were so similar—thinking faster than he could talk—so he started calling me Leesy to keep us straight."

"Don't know why I'd ever call her Marcus, though," Uncle Vic said, shaking his head. "You were clearly the prettier one!"

"With my haircut—"

"Ain't nothin' wrong with your haircut," Uncle Vic said with a frown. "Your mama still givin' you grief about it?"

Margot rolled her eyes but smiled when Cole's hand slipped into hers. "Mama and I haven't had an actual conversation in years, Uncle Vic. You know that."

"Humph," Uncle Vic grunted. "Never even liked that ol' hoity-toity woman! Claimin' *my* Marcus wasn't good enough fo' you. But he was, wasn't he?"

"Very much," Margot agreed.

"Though I didn't think you'd last long," Uncle Vic admitted. "Thought you was slummin' to get back at Mommy and Daddy; but you loved my boy, didn't you?"

Margot took a deep breath and squeezed Cole's hand. "Very much."

"And now you here wonderin' if I'm okay with this latest development o' yours?"

She glanced at Cole. "I didn't want you to think—"

"Don't really matter what I think," Uncle Vic said with a shrug. "But since y'all here, I'mma give my dollar."

Margot caught Cole's confused look and grinned. "Uncle Vic claims his thoughts are worth a hell of a lot more than two measly cents!"

"Ya damn right! My brilliance knows no price, but the masses can only handle a dollar of it at a time," Uncle Vic said with a wink.

Cole laughed. "I like that. Might have to steal it."

"Hmm. You young. Sixty-three cents for your thoughts."

"Have my thoughts appreciated to seventy-five yet?"

"Eighty. You a bright girl, Leesy," Uncle Vic said, eyeing the ring on her hand. "You found love again when for a while there I thought you'd never go out searching for it. Marcus wouldn't have liked that, seeing you turn into the shell of the woman he loved. I was scared for you."

"Uncle Vic..."

"Naw, now, let me finish. I still got ninety-five cents' worth of wisdom to impart!"

Margot smiled. "I'm sorry."

"That's all right. But girl, when you called me just the other day, I knew somethin' good had happened because you sounded like the Leesy of old, but even better. I said that gal found some love in her life because you'd only sound that way with Marcus. Now did I expect...er...Cole, *no*, but he must be somethin' special if you fell in love with him."

Margot nodded, willing the tears to stay at bay. "He actually found me," she said with a choked whisper. "I definitely wasn't looking for romance when we met." Cole kissed her temple in support.

"I know, honey," Uncle Vic said, sobering a bit. "But who are we to talk about timin' and schedules? God saw fit for you to meet this boy at what was probably the darkest and lowest point in your life. I remember you after Marcus's death, baby, and I was real worried for ya. When I heard about Georgie and Oscar, gal, I had half a mind to go up to Boston to see about ya!"

"Why didn't you?"

Uncle Vic sighed. "Things had gotten so busy at the shop, and you know I ain't trust nobody but Marcus to run my shop in my stead. Then Gail said you had a friend looking after you…" He turned his attention to Cole. "Thank you."

Cole wrapped an arm around Margot's shoulders. "No need to thank me."

"Yeah, I do. You just the kind of man my Marcus would've wanted for Margot. Don't matter your age, color, or how much money you make to me. That girl right there is family; and if I hear you doin' some shady shit, I *will* close this shop and hunt you down, you hear me?"

Margot let out a watery laugh. "Don't think he doesn't mean it. He told Marcus the same thing!"

"You may as well be my daughter, girl," Uncle Vic said, shaking his head. "Don't care she married my nephew or that he dead and gone. Marcus was a son to me and you my daughter. So that means I'm about to be a granddaddy!"

"Yes," Cole said, brushing away some tears that had slipped down Margot's cheeks. He smiled softly. "In about a month or so."

"Well, I'll be," Uncle Vic said, then he coughed. "And speaking of granddaddy, I saw your father not the other day."

That surprised her. "You did? Why?"

"He needed his transmission checked. I'm shocked he still drives that late-model Volvo as sadiddy as they are!"

"He comes all the way out here?"

Uncle Vic shrugged. "Not all the time. Just when he go see Marcus."

Again guilt assailed her. "I couldn't—"

"You hear me fussin' at you about that? I told you time and time again I understood! Ain't no set time period fo' grievin'!"

"I know."

"But even though that Robert Butler is a sadiddy son, I know that's a man tryin' to atone for some mistakes."

Margot took a deep breath. "And there's the not-so-subtle push to see my folks."

"Richmond ain't but a two-hour drive away. And just by lookin' at Cole, I can tell he ain't the follows-speed-limits type!" Margot had to giggle at Uncle Vic's guess because it was spot on.

"They're just suggestions," Cole said glibly.

"Yeah, well, I *suggest* you don't get in an accident! We've reached our quota for the next ten years, haven't we!"

"And then some!" Margot insisted, standing with the help of Cole. Uncle Vic stood as well and the pair shared a long, intense hug. "I love you so much."

"We'll do better with visiting each other, yeah?"

"Yes, sir."

"And I want pictures of my grandbaby when she's born. And I get to buy her, her first car."

"Car!" Margot exclaimed. "She's not even here yet and you're trying to get her behind the wheel!"

"You damn right! Gotta keep this shop in the family after all. I ain't said it'd be a *working* car!"

Cole laughed and held out his hand. "It was very nice to meet you, Mr. Reed."

"None of that! I'm Uncle Vic, now. You marryin' Leesy; that means you family. But don't think I'm playin', either. The *second* you mess up, this shop's closin'. You don't want my shop to close unless it's a Sunday or Christmas, son!"

"Duly noted," Cole said seriously.

The three of them exchanged current contact information, and with a final hug and handshake, Cole and Margot were off to the cemetery.

Though she hadn't been there since the funeral, Margot knew the way instinctively. Cole held her hand as they went down rows of headstones, a quick left, a few more headstones, then a right and two more rows.

Marcus Darian Reed—The best husband, nephew, and friend anyone ever knew.

The sob she let out surprised even her, the sudden emotions overwhelming. She knelt slowly, hugged his headstone, and cried. She cried for all the missed times, apologized for not coming to visit sooner, and promised she'd do better in the future.

"I love you so much," she whispered, feeling the cool granite against her lips. "You have no idea how much I've missed you."

In her imagination, Margot saw those usually mischievous brown eyes staring at her without their usual twinkle and she moved back. It was then she realized Cole had knelt down next to her and she leaned against him for support.

"I'm sorry, baby," Margot whispered, wiping away her tears as she traced the engraved letters of the headstone. "I'm sorry I couldn't see you until today. I hadn't been able to, as if seeing you here, this headstone, would all bring it to a head. It wasn't as if I was in denial about your death. How could I be when the past four years have been without your arms holding me as we slept, or the familiar grease stains all over the house that I'd fuss at you about and now miss, because they were reminders of you?"

Margot leaned more into Cole and continued. "Then when I lost your baby, I really couldn't face you then. I never knew how I could actually *lose* the one gift you gave me, entrusted to me. What kind of wife and best friend could I be to lose something so precious and wonderful?"

Cole squeezed her shoulders, giving her the strength to continue.

"I guess you, Georgie, and Oscar are reunited now," Margot said, chuckling slightly. "How are they, honey? Are they good? I hope so. I miss them too. Tell them I'm sorry I couldn't spread their ashes on the Fourth, but I reckon they would like their daughter to at least...I don't know. Think that's weird? I hope it isn't."

She shifted so she sat fully on the ground, uncaring of the grass and dirt. "I'm pregnant. You already know that, though, don't you? I'm also engaged."

The wind began picking up and Margot took a minute to enjoy the breeze. It felt good to feel it caress her face and skin. She smiled, pressing a hand to her belly. "I hope that means you like him?"

Margot drifted into silence for a moment, just taking in everything. Cole had yet to speak, as if knowing she needed to get this out and would patiently wait for her to do so. He cocooned her with his body, his chin resting on her shoulder and his hands cradling her belly. Right then Margot felt like the world's most blessed woman, feeling Marcus and Cole's love surrounding her, protecting her. Any lasting concerns she had blew away with the wind and she smiled.

"Thank you, baby," Margot whispered to the headstone. "Thank you for teaching me how to love, that I *am* someone worth loving."

Another stretch of silence claimed them and Margot began feeling drowsy. The absolute peace in her soul was beguiling. She'd fall asleep right there if she weren't careful.

"Want me to place the flower down now?" Cole's soft voice asked in her ear.

"Please."

Cole moved from around her and placed the calla lily they'd brought down gently at the base of the headstone. He remained crouched there unmoving, as if preparing to say something but was having difficulty finding the words.

"Hey, man," Cole said, clearing his throat roughly. "I...don't *know* you, know you, but Mar has told me many stories about you. And since you were actually able to experience Margot's love, I know you were a good man."

He touched the dates on the headstone and frowned slightly. "I'll do my very best to pick up where you left off, man, and take care of her as she deserves. We both know what a special woman she is, and we've both committed to loving, honoring, and cherishing her for the rest of our days. Give me some guidance too. Advice. Like what not to do to get her mad; or if I *do* get her mad, how to make her *not* be mad anymore!"

Cole chuckled and Margot rolled her eyes, though she couldn't stop a tiny grin from forming.

"Anyway, I just...I love her, and I'll do my very best by her. I promise you that."

Cole nodded, squeezed the headstone one final time, and stood. He helped her to her feet and they hugged each other tightly.

The wind seemed to hug them too.

Margot had wanted to go directly to Richmond after they left the grave, seemingly inspired to see her parents, but Cole decided against it. They went back to the hotel and spent the remainder of the day in bed watching in-room movies while holding each other. Midway through the third movie Margot had fallen asleep, and he'd spent more time watching her than the television screen. He'd awakened her so she could eat something because the last time she'd eaten was before going to Uncle Vic's house. He didn't make her eat all of the pasta they'd order for room service, but he meant what he'd told Marcus at the cemetery—he'd take care of her as well as possible, even against her wishes.

He heard the buzz of a cell phone and he looked around the room until he realized it came from Margot's purse. He checked the ID and smiled slightly before answering the phone.

"Hi, Gail."

"Hey, Cole! Margot up?"

"No. Out like a light. Will we still see you this weekend?"

They'd planned to have dinner with Gail in Richmond after meeting with her parents. They were going to tell her about the engagement then.

"Of course. I'm actually on my way to my mama's house now. Y'all still in DC?"

"Yeah. We visited Uncle Vic and Marcus's grave."

Gail grew quiet for a few moments. "She all right?"

Cole nodded even though she couldn't see him. "I think she needed it. She's much more relaxed now. Invigorated. In fact, she wanted to go to Richmond immediately, but I told her to wait. She needed rest. She's in her eighth month. I don't want anything happening to her or the baby."

Gail chuckled. "Boy! If I ain't know any better, I'd swear you were her husband!"

Cole bit his tongue to keep from blurting out the news. "Anyway, how are you?"

"Boy, I'm so tired! Drivin' all day. All I wanna do is climb into bed after I eat my mama's cookin'. Nobody can throw down like my mama, though Margot comes close. She taught Mar how to cook because Miss Faye is about as worthless as a fish on land in the kitchen!"

He laughed at Gail's analogy. "Perhaps your mother will teach me some things?"

"Heck yeah! She loves it. Y'all know how long you staying at her folks'?"

He said he didn't, but he hoped it wasn't going to be a stressful visit. He'd tried to get Margot to hold off this meeting until after the baby was born, but she'd told him in a serious voice that "later" was never a guarantee.

"You'll be there with her. You'll be the rock she needs," Gail said confidently. "That was how Margot got the strength to leave the first time. If they try to pull some mess, all she needs to know is you'll be there with her and she'll leave again. She doesn't need all that negativity in her life, anyway."

"I'll always be there for her," Cole vowed.

Gail chuckled. "Lawd, first Marcus, and now you. Margot sure knows how to pick 'em!"

"I'm not complaining!"

"I know. I'mma need her to set me up with someone. Too bad Marcus ain't have any brothers or cousins. What about you? You got cousins?"

"They're either female or married," Cole said apologetically.

"Damn. One of those times I wish I swung both ways!" Gail sighed. "Anyway, let me get off this phone. I'm *still* driving—stupid detours. Give Mar my love, okay?"

Cole promised he would, then ended the call. After using the bathroom and changing into his sleepwear, he slid into bed next to Margot and slept.

They left early the next morning for Richmond, though Margot was a little lethargic in her movements. He kept sending her concerned glances, but she merely smiled and told him it was taking her a bit longer than usual to rev up.

Eventually, they got on the freeway, Cole driving and stealing more looks her way. She was sound asleep, her head tucked between the window and the headrest. His gaze dropped to her left hand where the sunlight played with the diamond facets of her ring. He turned his attention back to the road and smiled. His fiancée. *His.* Together, they would be able to face anything—starting with this meeting with her parents.

They hit a bit of traffic along the way, coming to a standstill. This roused her from sleep and she looked around, anxious.

"Probably an accident," Cole said, touching her cheek gently. "You sure you're okay?"

"I thought we were home," Margot said sheepishly, and then she smiled. "I'm fine. You?"

He paused a beat before he reached out his hand and squeezed her knee. "Just fine."

Her left hand cupped his cheek and he reveled in the cool platinum against his skin. "You nervous?"

"No."

She took a deep breath. "I'm trying not to be."

"I'm right here, sweetheart. No need to be nervous."

Her smile didn't reach her eyes this time, but he pecked her lips once more before turning his focus on his driving. The cars were starting to move again; and after thirty minutes of stop and go traffic, they found their original speed once more.

Margot remained awake for the rest of the trip, taking in the rapidly passing scenery in silence. Every so often she'd comment about a new landmark, reminisce over one lost, or smile at the one that had remained the same.

"We're getting close," she said as they passed the large green sign that said, "Richmond 20." His heart began to beat double at the prospect of seeing her father again and meeting her mother. Cole didn't know what to expect from this meeting, but he erred on the side of the worst. He knew this was something Margot needed to do, one last-ditch effort to repair something Cole had a niggling suspicion was irreparable. He hoped for Margot's sake he was wrong, especially about Faye Butler. At least Robert was trying, even if his visit hadn't ended very well. Cole couldn't blame Margot's reluctance to answer her father's phone calls, either, but she was ready to take that step now.

They exited the interstate and Margot became the navigator, telling him they were heading for the West End near the University of Richmond. Cole couldn't help the butterflies starting hurricanes in his stomach as he made turn after turn toward the Butler house. He turned onto a street full of nice, sharp homes with clean lawns, plentiful deciduous green and evergreen trees, and high-end cars. All the houses were significant in size, and Margot pointed to a red-brick Georgian three lots up on the left.

He pulled into the driveway and shut off the engine, looking at the champagne-colored old model Volvo and the newer model navy Buick parked beside it.

Margot took a deep breath. "That wasn't here when I last visited."

Cole looked at her and took her hand. "Are you sure you want to do this, baby?"

Margot nodded, still staring at the Buick. "I have to. I won't get any peace if I don't."

He squeezed her hand and then got out of the car. He went around to her side and helped her out as well. He closed the car door and watched her looking at her childhood home. There was a wistful longing in her eyes and her hands cradled her tummy.

He wrapped his arms around her. "I'm right here, honey."

"I know."

"I love you."

She rubbed her cheek against his in response before pulling away. He stepped beside her and linked their fingers together again. Margot's walk was one of a determined woman. Cole had never felt more proud of her.

When they reached the door, Margot took another breath. She let her hand hover over the doorbell for a few seconds before pressing it and dropping her hand quickly. A few seconds passed before the door swung open and an older black woman in a gray uniform appeared before them. She looked very surprised to see them, her eyes dropping to Margot's middle briefly, and she shook her head quickly to get her bearings.

"May I help you?"

"Yes, ma'am. Are the Butlers available?"

The woman frowned. "May I ask who is visiting?"

"Margot Butler Reed. Their daughter."

The woman's eyes widened and she looked to Cole as if to confirm it. Cole squeezed Margot's hand and nodded slightly.

"Ah—oh. I'll...tell them you're here. Come inside and wait a moment, please?"

Margot looked around the foyer and pressed her lips upon entering it. He felt her lean a little into him and he accepted her weight. He wished she didn't feel like such a stranger in her own home.

"Are you all right?"

"Nothing's changed and yet....This foyer doesn't have very good memories, Cole."

"Hopefully, that'll change today."

Margot started to say something when footfalls made her pause. Her breathing became shallow and her hand tightened around his. A few moments later a woman appeared. Cole blinked at how much she resembled her daughter—all except for the eyes. The woman's hair was loose and free around her shoulders, and the gray slacks and plain pink shirt hung well on her slender frame. The woman's eyes skipped over him briefly before settling on Margot.

"Faye? Faye who is—?"

Margot's hand tightened around his again as Mr. Butler stood beside his wife. His hands slid into his trousers and his face was expressionless.

No one spoke.

If Cole had felt awkward when Mr. Butler had visited, he felt downright bewildered now. These were two of the most intimidating people he'd ever met, but not in the same way Margot had been. He felt lacking, especially when Mrs. Butler's dark eyes looked at him again. With Margot, he'd felt on the brink of something monumental, yet excited to face it. Now he wished they could just turn around and leave.

Finally, Mrs. Butler spoke. "When are you due?"

"Middle of October."

Cole's lips quirked at that. His birthday was October 14th. He secretly hoped their daughter's birthday would be the same.

Mrs. Butler let out a breath and she shook her head. "Well, come on. Off your feet. If you're anything like I was, you get winded every three steps."

When Mrs. Butler turned to lead the way, no one moved. Margot blinked. "Mama?"

Mrs. Butler looked at Margot, then her entire body sagged. The older woman shrugged her shoulders and let out a mirthless chuckle. "For seven years I've been hoping you'd walk through that door, and when you finally do I don't know what to say to you."

Margot stood straighter. "You could've practiced something with me every time I called instead of hanging up on me."

Faye's smile was pinched and she nodded. "You still got that mouth."

"You gave it to me."

Mr. Butler coughed, but Cole noticed amusement in his eyes. "You really should sit, Margot. You, too, Cole. You must be tired from the drive."

Margot nodded slightly, and the four of them went into the living room. The furniture was plush and a deep crimson color that nicely offset the forest-green rug on which the cherry coffee table stood. Cole helped Margot sit in the easy chair, then he brought over a straight-back chair from a nearby desk so he could sit next to her. Margot's parents sat on the couch and regarded them intently.

He would not squirm...he would not squirm...

"Have you been taking your vitamins? Going to Lamaze?"

"Yes, ma'am. I've been given a clean bill of health and so has the baby."

Mrs. Butler nodded and licked her lips. Cole felt Margot tense and he squeezed her shoulder in support. Was this just the calm before the storm? Who would break first? He really didn't want a repeat of Margot's meltdown when her father had left, and he felt if it did happen again, it would be worse if caused by her mother.

Mrs. Butler's eyes fell upon him. Cole met them squarely. "And you've been taking care of my daughter during this time?"

"Yes, ma'am."

Mrs. Butler glanced at her husband briefly. "What do you plan to do after the baby is born?"

Cole reached into Margot's lap and picked up her left hand. He brought it to his lips as he grinned at her. "Marry her. Or I can marry her before the baby's born. I'm not too particular over that."

He saw Margot's eyes sparkle as she shook her head, and he chuckled softly. He was glad he brought a little light into her eyes. He didn't want her spirit dwindled because of this, even if her parents had been civil to her thus far. He thought the grandfather clock's ticks behind him were little more than counting down the impending boom he was sure would happen.

There was a space of silence before, "At least this one gave you a ring."

"Faye—"

"Don't even *fix* your mouth to say something about Marcus. Don't even say his name!" Margot said, giving her mother a hard look.

Mrs. Butler sighed. "First you marry a borderline thug, now you're about to marry a white man? Who next after him? A woman? Are you going to turn gay like your brother—?"

"*Turn gay?*"

"Faye!"

"I had plans for you!" Faye said, standing and looking at her daughter sharply. "I'd worked so hard! Put you in the best schools, taught you all the manners to be bestowed upon a lady. Even got you in that damn cotillion and you throw all that in my face? Margot Elise Butler!"

"*Reed* and soon to be Patterson!" Margot added. "And guess what, Mama, you're about to be a grandma whether you like it or not. I'm having your gay son's child! You can deny me, ignore me, disown me all you want, but there will be a child in about a month's time that has the same DNA you do. You deal with *that!*"

Cole saw the tears starting to pool into Margot's eyes and he pressed his face into her cheek, murmuring comforting words and rubbing his hand along her tummy. She shouldn't get so upset, and he almost regretted not putting his foot down and denying her this visit. They could've waited until after the baby was born at least, but Margot had been insistent. So far, this was going as badly as he'd expected, and he didn't know if it could ever be turned around.

"Why do you do this, Mama?" Margot asked. She'd calmed down somewhat; but when she closed her eyes, tears trailed down her cheeks. Cole brushed them away with a gentle thumb. "Why...why can't you just be *happy* for me for *once*? After all that's happened, after the way you've treated me, I'm *still here* trying to be a daughter to you! Why am I? I don't know other than the fact I love you." Margot shook her head and sniffled. "I probably shouldn't, especially when neither of you could talk to *me*, but you could talk to Georgie? *Georgie*? I don't see how what he did and what I did weren't the same. Is it because he's the beloved son? The aspiring doctor? The one who had always done what you told him to do, even if it went against his deepest wishes—?"

"Margot—"

"No, Daddy," Margot said softly. "I tried to be the daughter you wanted. I tried for almost twenty years, and it didn't matter how unhappy I really was. I was making *you* happy, and I thought that would be enough to sustain me. And then Marcus came and allowed me the freedom to be who I was supposed to be. He *scared* me because *he* was the one who first showed me what unconditional love is. *You two* were supposed to do that, but you didn't. Took me a long time to come to grips with that, especially after you all but erased me from your lives."

Cole noticed Mr. and Mrs. Butler wince, but he felt no sympathy for them. They were long past the time for hard, honest truths.

"I decided to come because soon I'm going to be someone's mother," Margot said, looking down at their joined hands. "I'm going to be someone's mother and Cole is going to be someone's father. Neither of us had planned on being such at the beginning of the year. Neither of us planned to know the other ever in our lives, and yet...things happened. I lost the remainder of my family except for Gail. Cole lost a brother. Yet through all of that, we found each other."

Cole nodded his agreement. She wouldn't lose another family member again if he could help it.

"These past six months have been full of so many changes. Sometimes I felt adrift, so completely unable to handle everything. In those weak moments I reached out to you, only to have you hang up on me, ignore me. If it hadn't been for Cole and Gail, and even Cole's mother Jill, I don't know what would've happened to me."

"Margot, honey—"

"Daddy, I need to say this," Margot said softly. "I need this opportunity to say what I need to say, especially to Mama."

Mr. Butler dropped his eyes and nodded sadly. Cole felt a little bad for him, but he needed to hear what Margot had to say just as much as his wife did.

"This is it," Margot said, looking at her mother. "If you let me walk out the door this time, I'm not coming back. I'm not calling. And you may as well consider me, this baby, and any other children I have nonexistent to you because I'm not going to put *my* children through what you're putting me through right now.

"Daddy, I know you're trying, and I thank you for it. I may need a little more time to be so open with you, but I am willing to start now. I meant what I said to Mama, though' so if you want to be in my life, you need to come to *me*."

Margot let out a harsh breath and shrugged, her expression firm. "What's it going to be?"

Chapter Seventeen

Margot prayed this wasn't déjà vu. She prayed she wouldn't walk out of this house in tears with her love consoling her because her parents had done away with her. Again. She meant it, however. If they didn't want her in their life, especially her mother, she'd stop trying to be there. Seven years' worth of pleading and begging was enough for one lifetime, even if they were her parents. She'd inherited some of their pride after all.

Margot felt Cole's eyes on her but she couldn't look at him. She'd cry at the love she'd see in his gaze, and she needed to maintain at least a modicum of calm as her future and her family hung in the balance. Her mother's behavior thus far had been disheartening. She claimed she'd waited for her daughter's return, and yet she was still chastising and denigrating said daughter. It didn't make any sense to Margot, but she vowed this would be the last time she'd endure it too.

A cell phone rang, disturbing the tense silence. Margot watched Cole check the ID on his phone and frown.

"Take it," she murmured. "It's okay."

Cole sighed. "I'll be really quick. It's Mom. I hope everything's okay." Margot nodded, smiling a little when he kissed her forehead before leaving the living room.

This was the first time she'd been alone with both of her parents in so long. Robert's expression was so contrite, but as usual, Margot couldn't read her mother. Faye had never been the warmest of mothers, behaving more like a strict headmistress instead. There had always been lessons to learn, etiquette to remember, classes and after-school activities for her to attend—the things every woman of culture should learn in order to leave a favorable mark on society. Margot had always felt suffocated by it, yet she'd wanted so much to make her mother proud of her. She'd heard of the Hollis humble beginnings since she was in kindergarten, and Margot hadn't wanted to be the cause of the regression Faye had threatened her with should she not succeed.

"There's nowhere for you to go but up! My mother and I will not have our work in vain!"

Work! That was all Margot had ever done. Though she'd never had a job during high school, oboe practice and debate team and mock trial and yearbook staff and every other "college-friendly" activity had sucked up every free moment not dedicated to education. It wasn't enough Margot went to college, and preferably Faye and Robert's alma mater, at that, but scholarships and grants would distinguish her even more. There was no time to paint, to date, to just *be*. There was that goal of success as defined by her parents, and she would attain it, by God.

Had Faye Butler ever been proud of her daughter?

"I had felt disrespected in my own home."

Her mother's voiced drew her out of her thoughts, and Margot looked at Faye incredulously. "Disrespected?"

"You brought that boy here, deliberately embarrassing me and your father in front of Earl and his family. You *knew* what we were trying to do, and then you brought...*him*! If you hadn't wanted to marry Earl, you could've said something—!"

"I did! You didn't listen to me! You kept going right on with the plans and to hell with what I thought!"

Faye frowned at her daughter's comment. "And then painting! *Painting*! How many successful black painters you know other than those from the Harlem Renaissance! You didn't work so hard and land such a plum job at that consulting firm to throw it away drawing!"

Margot kept her mouth shut, allowing her mother her opportunity to say her piece. If this was to be the last time they spoke, they need to say everything, put it all out in the open. She could handle it. With Cole by her side, Margot could handle anything.

"I thought he was poisoning you, that boy, and you were just too busy trying to prove us wrong to see it!" Faye whispered harshly. "So there was the ultimatum, and you didn't back down. I wasn't going to stand around and watch him destroy your life."

Her father had confessed this already, and Margot scowled. "Didn't want to see your investment go down the drain—"

"No!" Faye said emphatically. "I tried to give you *everything* I didn't have growing up. Maybe I was a little overzealous, but I wanted you to have *every* advantage so you didn't have to work beneath your talent like my mother and I did! You were going to do the Hollis name proud. Why else do you think I gave you my mother's name? I saw greatness in you, Margot Elise, but I couldn't watch you throw that all away, dishonor all the hard work my mother and I did so you wouldn't have to."

Margot shook her head. "Marcus supported me. His family's auto shop always had a steady stream of business, and they weren't lacking for anything. So maybe they didn't have a house in the West End and maybe Marcus didn't go to college, but that didn't mean he wanted to keep me down. That didn't mean he wasn't going to be there for me. He *loved* me, Mama. Doesn't every mother want a man who loves her daughter with all his heart?"

Faye's eyes softened. "It took me a long time to admit he did."

The admission blindsided Margot. "What?"

"Shortly after you married, Marcus wrote me a letter. As angry as I was about your leaving and elopement, I couldn't bring myself to throw it away." Faye chuckled and glanced at her husband. "I couldn't throw away anything you mailed to us. I know your father thinks I did. I hid them. I couldn't talk to you...but I could read from you. I still needed to know you were okay."

Margot frowned. Her parents were very odd people. "Seven years of ignoring my phone calls and proclaiming you didn't have a daughter and you expect me to believe this?"

"No. I don't. Just because I kept the letters doesn't mean I read them immediately. I didn't start reading them until after I learned of your miscarriage."

Margot winced. "And even that wasn't enough for you to contact me."

"By that point, almost five years had passed, Margot! I didn't think you wanted to hear from me, especially not then. What could I say to you? You lost a husband and a child and I hadn't been there for you. I was ashamed of myself. I still am."

Margot looked at her father. He was watching her carefully as if wondering if she were buying the story her mother was telling her. It did seem to corroborate the one he'd told her earlier, but none of this made any sense to her. "It's not as if I hadn't given you multiple opportunities to talk to me."

Faye left the couch and sat in the chair Cole had occupied. Her mother's small, warm hands framed her face and Margot felt tears spring into her eyes. She hadn't known how she'd starved for a maternal touch until Faye had done so. Even though she had a wonderful relationship with Jill, Jill wasn't her mother.

"Your heart wasn't the only one broken when you walked out, Margot," Faye said quietly. "I know we brought it upon ourselves, but we still...never thought...you'd choose him over us. That's what it felt like, baby, so for you to call us as if that hadn't happened...I was very angry with you. That image of you walking out with Marcus has been on loop in my mind every single day. That hurt has been with me every single day. I couldn't bring myself to talk to you, and a part of me wanted you to feel that hurt. It's wrong for a mother to say and admit, but I've been human longer than I've been a mother."

Both women were crying openly now and Faye brushed away her daughter's tears with her thumbs. "I am sorry for being too prideful and consumed by my vision for you that I was blind to yours," Faye whispered. "I'm sorry for being stubborn and entrenched in my hurt that I rejected every attempt you gave me. I know you probably don't believe me and I don't blame you. I made many mistakes with you and George. I'm finally ready to start rectifying them.

"After Georgie's dead," Margot said hollowly. "You kicked him out too."

"We didn't kick him out," Faye said with a frown. "I was angry with him, yes, but we didn't kick him out. He left."

Margot opened her mouth to contradict her, but she paused. Georgie had never actually said their parents had disowned him; he'd just said he couldn't take it with them anymore. Margot had automatically assumed the worst.

One hand left Margot's cheek to touch her swell. Faye smiled softly. "Middle of October."

Margot nodded.

"Have you chosen a name?"

Margot nodded again. "I haven't told Cole, though."

Faye glanced at Robert. "This time, I'm not so blind. That boy loves you, Margot."

"I know."

"Two men I wouldn't have chosen for you; but that's not my job, is it?"

"No."

Faye took a deep breath, her thumb caressing Margot's tummy. "I've really done an awful job."

It was Margot's turn to sigh. "Mama—"

"My mother had said I was working you too hard, pushing you further and further away from me. Turns out I pushed you right out the door, and I took all that anger I had for myself out on you, on Robert, Georgie—everyone *but* me. I'm sorry for that too."

Cole returned, obviously surprised by the change in the seating arrangement, and he stood awkwardly by the couch.

"Is everything okay?" Margot asked.

Cole nodded. "Mom was talking about something for the campaign—"

"Campaign?"

"My dad is running for attorney general in Massachusetts."

Robert smiled. "Good luck to him."

"Thanks."

"And what do you do for a living Cole?" Faye asked.

"I'm a consultant for financial firms."

"Really! You must have a lot of connections!"

Cole blushed slightly. "I have some."

"Is that how you met Margot?"

Margot shook her head. "We met in the hospital. After the accident."

"Oh."

Margot was glad her parents didn't ask her to explain further. That was a conversation for another time.

Another stretch of silence filled the room, but Faye's hand still caressed Margot's belly. Margot looked down at her mother's soft hand and then covered it with her own. They still had a long way to go, but both were now ready to make that journey. Some of Faye's truths hurt, as Margot was sure some of hers did, but the healing process was rarely without that initial, and sometimes long-suffering, pain.

"You'll do a much better job than I have done," Faye said quietly. "If for nothing else, I've shown you what *not* to do."

"You're not done being my mother yet," Margot said. "And I don't think you ever stop learning how to be one, or how to be a daughter."

"Or a father," Robert said.

Margot looked at Cole and smiled. "You hear that, baby?"

Cole returned her smile. "Can't wait."

For the meantime, the conversation turned away from heavy matters to the baby's upcoming birth. Said baby started using Margot's bladder for a trampoline, and Margot left to go to the bathroom. Faye insisted she help her to it, and Margot didn't argue. The walk down the hall to the downstairs bathroom was silent; but for the first time in a long time, the underlying tension between them was almost nonexistent. On the way back from the bathroom, Faye made a detour and led her into the dining room, confusing Margot briefly before she spied the art on the opposite wall.

It was a painting of the Boston skyline as seen from the Longfellow Bridge. It was one of the first paintings Margot had done after arriving in the city. Margot had been waiting for the train at the Charles/MGH stop on the Red Line going to Downtown Crossing, and it had been such a beautiful and clear day that the artist in her had decided to take a picture of it. It hadn't been until weeks later that she'd decided to put the image on canvas. She'd given the painting to Georgie afterward.

"He sent it to us in the mail," Faye said. "You know how your brother was—show rather than tell."

Margot chuckled breathlessly. She hadn't asked about the painting after she sent it to him, trusting him to take care of it, and too busy working with Oscar on the books to investigate further. To know her parents had had it all this time surprised her.

"Marcus was right. You are talented. We have some of your children's books too. Mr. Felton's daughter had a baby, and I bought the first one you and Oscar did as a baby shower gift. I supported you in the ways I could, Margot. I did."

Margot sniffled.

"Margot?"

She turned to her mother, who had an unsure expression on her face. This was Faye's attempt to start fresh. She didn't want a repeat of seven years ago, either, it seemed.

Wordlessly, Margot went to her mother's arms and hugged her hard for the first time in far too many years. She didn't know how long they stood that way, but soon another, stronger pair of arms enveloped them, and the remainder of the Butler clan cried for their trespasses and with the hopes of starting anew.

~SJF~

Cole sat at the dinner table nursing a glass of sweet tea as he watched Margot laugh and joke with Gail and Sasha Stewart while they prepared dinner. It was to be a miniature version of a Labor Day barbecue with spareribs, potato salad, dinner rolls, and pecan pie. When Gail had asked if they wanted a big dinner with all the guests and festivities Margot had said no, apparently much to Sasha's relief. Her husband was away at a conference, anyway, and the usual Stewart barbecues were more for his friends and colleagues than for hers.

Nevertheless, it was enlightening listening to the women gossip and tease each other. Granted, both Stewart women had screamed almost to ear-splitting decibels when Margot had shown them her engagement ring, but the three women had settled down considerably after Margot had recited a long, every-minute-detail account of Cole's proposal and her acceptance. The easy conversation and banter here was so different from the heavy, formal discussions at the Butler house.

That meeting had gone expectedly and unexpectedly. What had started out as a firestorm of emotions had settled into something very moving. Both sides had held on to their hurt and anger, had shared both, and it wasn't until they had that painful and honest discussion could either move on. Both he and Margot had prepared for that phase to be with the two of them alone, but it seemed Mr. and Mrs. Butler wanted otherwise. There had been years of miscommunication and worst-case scenarios for everyone, and while Cole would be forever on Margot's side on the matter, he couldn't help but empathize with her parents a little. He saw his father in Mrs. Butler, and Mr. Butler was a little like his mother in that he'd allowed certain things to happen. Margot's situation had been the extreme of his own, a glimpse of what could have happened had Jacob not died and everyone had decided enough was enough. Cole didn't know if Margot and her parents would ever be very close, but he did think there would never be another break as there had been. Phone calls, letters, and e-mails would be answered now. Maybe there would be mutual holidays shared.

Maybe her parents would attend the wedding.

"I still can't believe it, though," Gail was saying, breaking into his thoughts. "I can't believe your parents, paragons of civility and 'I'm Right-ism,' actually said they were *wrong*—"

"Gail—"

"I'm serious, Ma! You're way more forgiving than I am, Margot."

"It gets tiring carrying all that weight around," Margot said quietly. "I was exhausted. Cramped. I have a baby coming. I won't have the energy to nurse that pain anymore."

Sasha shook her head. "I'm not saying what your parents did was right, Margot, but I'm glad you all are turning over a new leaf. They were proud of you though...both of you. It's hard for them to admit when they're wrong. Pride. Faye always thinking she's got to prove something to someone—mainly herself."

Gail arched an eyebrow and joined Cole at the table. "I see you made it out virtually unscathed."

"Mrs. Butler got a nice little hit in at the beginning," Cole chuckled, recalling her passing jab to Margot about turning gay after she was done with him.

"Margot is a saint. I woulda been told them to screw themselves."

"They do have a long way to go," Cole admitted, "but Margot is definitely happier now. She has her parents back. I can't hold that wish against her, no matter how undeserving I think her parents are. That's not my call."

"Not anybody's call but Margot's and God's," Sasha said, looking at her daughter pointedly. "Now you come and take over for Margot so she can sit. Can't believe she got a month left as big as she is."

Cole laughed softly at Sasha's comment as he watched the younger women switch places. He slid the chair next to him, smiling cheekily when Margot rolled her eyes at him as she sat.

"You are so silly."

"You love me anyway."

They held hands atop the table, Cole tracing the lines of her palm while Margot stared at a faraway point. He traced the platinum band of her ring before lifting her hand and kissing its palm.

"I can't believe it."

"Believe what?"

"This is happening. This is my life. My dad and I are starting to talk more now. You all but got your parents back. *We're* about to be parents...and married. Unbelievable."

Margot smiled at him and kissed his cheek before resting her head on his shoulder. He held her close, rubbing her belly as they took in the smells, sounds, and space of the Stewart kitchen. He wondered what their home would be like. Although Margot's apartment was nice, it wouldn't be big enough. She deserved a house with a yard so their kids would have a space to play, and maybe even a room for her painting.

Would she want to move back to Virginia? Though Boston was his home, he wasn't married to it, and he liked the slower pace and the warmer weather and people of the state. He liked Uncle Vic very much, and Sasha and Gail were wonderful for Margot's spirit. Of course he'd miss his parents, but Cole had to start thinking about his own family now.

"You're quiet, baby. You okay?"

"Yes," Cole said, squeezing her hand. "Thinking."

"About?"

"Us and our family. Would you want to move back here?"

Margot lifted her head from his shoulders, a frown marring her features. "What about Boston? Your family?"

Cole shrugged. "It doesn't have to be immediate, but...I like it down here. It can be closer to DC if you like. Businesses will always need financial advice, and you can paint and illustrate from wherever. Besides, there's a shuttle from DC to Boston and New York, so if I need to meet clients I still can—"

"Cole."

"We have to start thinking about these things, don't we? A place for us to live. It doesn't have to be here or Boston. Pick a place. Think about it."

For the rest of the night, Sasha and Gail regaled Cole with stories of Margot and their childhood, and Sasha told them of the comings and goings since Gail and Margot left. There was much laughing and teasing, some moments of solemn reflection, but this was mostly a time to share and enjoy being in each other's company. At the end of the visit, Cole was just as sad as Margot was. When Sasha pulled him aside, he was almost as nervous about her opinion as he'd been was about Uncle Vic's.

"Mrs. Stewart," he said, looking the shorter woman squarely in her light-brown eyes.

"Sasha," she corrected gently with a smile. He returned it. "I'm invited to the wedding, right?"

"Of course!"

"Good. I was mad I didn't get to go to the first one! I really liked Marcus, too, bless his heart."

"The more I hear about him the more I like him too."

Sasha smiled again and looked at the two women who were forehead to forehead speaking in low tones. "Talk about sisters from different misters! Those two were joined at the hip when they were younger. You can usually tell when relationships will last from the start, and I saw that when Margot first came and sat at that kitchen table as they worked on that school project. Couldn't even tell you what it was, but I saw it then."

Sasha turned her eyes to Cole. "I thought she couldn't do better than Marcus, and then here you come. Y'all got it too. Race and age aside, y'all got it too."

"Thank you."

Sasha laughed. "You're welcome. I don't sugar coat my words, and I only want the best for my girls. I got one squared away, and now I'm working on Gail."

"I wouldn't worry about her. She's an incredible woman."

"I know. Wish the men in Jersey would wake up to it!"

After a slight pause, Sasha wrapped him in a hug, pleasantly surprising him. He chuckled a bit and returned it. "Don't be a stranger, Cole. You or Mar ever need anything at all, don't hesitate to call me. I know when Margot left she thought she was leaving all of Virginia, but she didn't. You aren't, either, okay?"

"Yes, ma'am," Cole said, squeezing her once more before separating so Margot could get in her own hug.

"And don't y'all mess around and get married without me," Gail said as got her own hug from Cole. "Margot has a tendency to have random, unannounced weddings!"

"We'll make sure *our* wedding fits *your* schedule," Margot teased.

"You better! I got maid of honor on lock!" Gail said, giving her friend one last hug for the road.

It was a painless drive back to Alexandria, and the next morning they were on their flight back to Boston. It was if the trip to Virginia had invigorated Cole, and he began making the necessary arrangements for the rest of his life.

The first thing he did was put his condo up for sale. He wasn't really living in it anymore, and it wasn't a family friendly dwelling. Though there were more vacancies in his building, many of them big enough to support a family of three, he knew Margot was a house dweller at heart. He also began talking to his father about drawing up documents so he could adopt Margot's baby. She'd already decided to put Oscar as the father of the child on the birth certificate because he was, and Cole understood that. However, the sooner Margot's child was legally a Patterson, the better.

Next, he began looking at house listings in Massachusetts, Maryland, and Virginia during free periods at work, though he hadn't told Margot yet. She and his mother were so busy making the apartment baby ready that he hadn't yet had the opportunity. He'd begun putting out feelers to his clients about their business relationships should he move, and the majority of them didn't object. Finally, there were the appointments with Dr. Dennison and the child-birthing classes that took up multiple nights during the week. Dr.

Dennison assured them the baby was healthy and on schedule, and Cole even had a tiny bet with her about the birth date.

"I can't wait for my box seats at the Red Sox–Yankees game, Patterson," Nan would tease, certain the baby would come earlier instead of later.

"You just produce my Patriots' fifty-yard-line seats against the Jets, Dennison!" he'd shoot back.

Margot, per usual, had taken everything in stride.

Maternity definitely agreed with her; and as the days passed, the more awed and breathless Cole became. Witnessing Margot's transformation had been a humbling, almost sacred experience, but these last few weeks had him thanking God and whatever other deity necessary for allowing this woman in his life. He doted on her completely, borderline smothering as she told him, but she never refused his efforts. He'd even remained home from a major fundraising dinner his father had been hosting because Margot had been experiencing awful cramps and he wouldn't leave her side.

"Epson salt baths should help with that," Frank had said when he'd called that evening. "And a cold compress. Your mother had really bad cramps when she was pregnant with you, but that seemed to work."

Whereas before Cole would've thought that was a snide comment, now he accepted it as Frank stating a fact. "Thanks, Dad."

"Anytime, son. Tell Margot Jill and I hope she feels better."

Margot and Frank had grown closer upon their return to Boston. He'd approached her to tell her how thankful he was for the portrait she'd painted, and had even commissioned her to paint another for the law office. It turned out Frank was an art buff, something Cole hadn't known, and the two had spoken for a long time about the newcomers into the art world, the old favorites, and the ones who perplexed them because of their fame or lack of it. Frank had told Margot he'd try to get her showings in some of Boston's more prestigious galleries—well, after the baby was born—and Margot had been truly thankful for his support.

"Our parents are something else," Margot had murmured after that visit, and Cole couldn't help agreeing.

Now, almost a week before Margot's due date, they were in bed with Cole lying laterally across it as he spread body butter on her tummy, sometimes dropping kisses and nuzzles as he progressed. Margot was smiling at him and drawing her fingers through his hair. He'd never felt so content.

"In a week everything will be different," she said quietly.

"I can't wait."

"Of course. You have the easy part!"

Cole smirked. "You think so?"

"You don't have to push this baby out and endure all that pain!"

"But *you* do. And trust me, honey, I'd do it for you instead if I could. I can't stand seeing you in pain."

Her hand cupped his cheek. "Wow. I really do love you."

"You should. I'm a catch."

"And what am I?" Margot said, arching an eyebrow.

Without missing a beat, Cole pressed one tiny kiss to her tummy before crawling up the bed and brushing her lips with his. "Priceless."

She smiled adorably and framed his face, kissing him more firmly. They exchanged leisurely pecks until she gasped.

"Kissed you breathless, did I?" Cole said, chuckling at his own joke.

"Baby..."

"Hmm?" Cole said, having too much of a good time kissing her and wishing to get back to it.

"Baby!"

Her urgent tone made him pull back and open his eyes. "What?"

"*The baby*! My water just broke!"

Chapter Eighteen

A hand squeezed his shoulder and he smelled coffee. He took it without looking at the bearer, muttering a thank you before blowing the black liquid and taking a sip. Bitter. Gritty. Just as it had been the last time he'd sat in a hospital waiting area.

"Relax, Cole. Everything will be all right."

"You can't promise me that."

"Cole—"

"Dad. Please? I just...I need..."

He needed Margot and the baby to make it through this. He needed them to be healthy and safe and as beautiful as he imagined them to be.

When Margot had said her water broke, panic had gripped him like a barnacle whereas Margot had been relatively calm. She'd called Dr. Dennison and his parents to tell them she was in labor, and then she'd called Gail, Uncle Vic, and her parents on the way to the hospital. Everything had been going well—the vitals were steady and strong, the epidural was working, and Margot was teasing Cole about treading a path into the floor with his incessant pacing.

Then the beeping had started.

Margot had begun going into distress around the fourth hour of her labor, her brows and temples beading with sweat and a perpetual grimace on her beautiful face. Cole had done his best to relax her and get her focused on him, but the distress was too great. Nan had ordered him out of the room while she and her team attempted to stabilize her;

but after fifteen minutes of trying, they'd opted to take her into surgery.

"If something happens—"

"Don't think like that, Cole," Jill said, squeezing her son's knee. "You have to think positively—"

"That didn't work with Jacob," he muttered darkly. No amount of positive thoughts could bring Jacob from the brink of death. Those two hours waiting for word about Jacob's status had been among the worst two hours of his life, and to find himself waiting in the very same hospital for news of another loved one was almost more than he could take. Yes, the baby was early, but only by a week. Every checkup had said the baby and Margot were in excellent condition, so why did there have to be a problem *now*?

His cell phone rang and he passed it to his father. He was in no state to speak to someone, let alone Margot's parents. Once he'd called to tell them about Margot's surgery, Mrs. Butler called almost every five minutes, only increasing the stress and anxiety he felt. Yet, he couldn't blame her. She'd just regained her daughter and wasn't too keen on losing her again.

Jill kissed his temple and he sighed, dropping his head into his hands as he prayed to God and cursed himself for not doing...something that would've prevented this. They'd talked about him being in the room for the birth, about holding Margot's hand, encouraging her, and letting her curse him for his manhood and anything else she wanted. He was supposed to *be there* with her.

"I'm going to get more coffee. You need anything?"

He needed Margot. "No. Thanks."

Jill left only for Frank to take her seat.

"I told Faye we'd call as soon as we got news. She can't do anything but pray while in Virginia, anyway."

Cole nodded but didn't respond. At that moment, he was glad his father was there. Frank knew about the waiting and the helplessness at a time like this; and though Cole was aware that neither his nor Jacob's deliveries had sent their mother into surgery, Frank could still empathize about what his son was experiencing.

Frank's hand squeezed his shoulder. "Margot's a fighter, Cole. She's not going to give up on herself or your daughter."

"But Dad, I don't know how much longer I can sit here and do nothing."

"Then you pray too."

Burying his face in his hands once more, Cole did just that. It became a mantra, the same prayer over and over again, thinking if he said it enough times, God would eventually hear him and have mercy.

Footfalls had him stopping in mid-sentence, and he looked up to see Nan approaching them. He stood quickly, his parents flanking his sides. He couldn't discern anything from Nan's face, but she gave them a soft smile when she reached them.

That smile could mean anything.

"Nan…"

She took a deep breath. "When we got into surgery, we ran into some complications because the umbilical cord was wrapped very tightly around the baby's neck. Also, there was unforeseen bleeding— so much so we had to work to stop it before we could continue with the cesarean…"

As Nan rattled off the medical play-by-play, Cole started to feel dread settle in the pit of him. None of this was sounding good, and his parents' tightened hold on him seemed to confirm that suspicion.

"Nevertheless," Nan's voice permeated his thoughts, "we were able to deliver the baby—"

"And?"

That was Frank, whose question mirrored Cole's own.

"Eight pounds, three ounces of pure and healthy beauty," Nan said with a smile. "She's in NICU for observation, but she shouldn't be in there for longer than a day."

His parents breathed sighs of relief, but Cole couldn't, not until he knew the status of his other baby. "And Margot?"

Nan's smile softened. "Medicated and resting in the hospital room. She should be out of it for a few hours, but she'll be fine."

"And she knows the baby's status?"

"Yes. She knows everything is fine."

Cole left his parents and hugged the doctor who had become a friend to him. "Thank you."

"You're welcome. I may even let you off the hook for those Red Sox tickets."

Cole, for the first time since this entire ordeal began, laughed and kissed Nan's cheek.

His parents opted to go home when Nan offered to take them to see Margot, saying Margot had had enough excitement for one day. Frank also promised to call the Butlers to tell them the news. Cole all but ran to Margot's room, ignoring the obstetrician's chuckle at his anxiousness. He was a father and his fiancée was safe and healthy. Why wouldn't he be excited? He did calm down a little when Nan opened the door to the room, and there was Margot: a little pale, clearly exhausted, and never more beautiful to him than at that moment.

"I'll give you some privacy," Nan said. "And congratulations."

Cole didn't even hear the door close when Nan left, his focus completely on Margot. She looked very peaceful, so different from the distress in which he'd had to leave her during the labor. He pulled up a chair to her bedside and took her hand gently in his, kissing its back and palm before resting his forehead upon it. He felt the pulse point in her wrist and was comforted by it. Life flowed through her still.

His eyes skipped to her middle, and he was momentarily startled by the absence of her belly. He'd been so used to the sight of her swollen with child that it was a little disconcerting not to see it now. Cole reached out a hand and touched her middle, missing the lack of movement underneath his hand briefly before smiling slightly. The cause of the movement was a healthy baby girl down in NICU for observation. He'd be able to hold her soon.

As the adrenaline finally ran its course, Cole's eyes became heavy as the events of the past few hours hit him. He kissed Margot's hand one last time before resting his head beside their clasped hands, allowing himself a little catnap. He dreamed of holding his daughter in his arms, falling more completely in love than he'd been, and making mother and daughter legally his once and for all.

"Cole."

That, and the feel of gentle fingers pulling through his hair, roused him from sleep. He turned his head to see a relaxed Margot grinning at him.

He smiled and yawned. "Hey, Mama."

"Back at ya, Daddy."

He went to the head of the bed and framed her face. Margot's eyes were so open and full of love as she stared at him. Unable to resist, he kissed her softly. The feel of her breath against his lips was so very welcome considering how close he'd been to losing her.

"I love you, Margot."

"I love you, too, Daddy."

He smiled, his blue eyes starting to fill with tears, a cathartic reaction to the emotions he was feeling. "Are you going to keep calling me that now?"

"Sometimes. Aw! Don't cry, honey!"

He kissed her again and allowed her thumbs to brush away his tears. They were happy tears, relieved tears. He wasn't a man who usually cried, but this was a very extenuating circumstance, and he really didn't give a flying fig.

"I was scared," he admitted.

"I'm sorry."

"Your parents called every five minutes to see how you were doing."

"Really?"

"Yeah."

Margot let that sink in. "That was nice of them." Her tone was level and frank, like she was still getting used to the fact her parents were back in her life.

"Faye was downright annoying," Cole chuckled.

"She's a very demanding woman," Margot said with her own small smile.

"Not unlike her daughter."

"And now there's another to the line. Think you can handle three demanding women in your life?"

Cole grinned and kissed her harder than before. "With pleasure."

A knock on the door had Cole pulling away, though not before sneaking in one last kiss. "Come in," Margot called, allowing him to take her hand.

The door opened and a nurse entered, rolling a wheelchair. "Let's go see your little one."

Cole and the nurse helped Margot into the chair, and then they were on their way to NICU. After several long moments, Nan approached, holding a bundle wrapped in a white cotton blanket. Cole's heart began racing, his eyes fixed on Nan's precious cargo.

"I think this darling is up for some visitors," Nan declared, winking at him.

"I hope she is," Margot cooed, sitting straighter in the chair. Cole couldn't breathe as Nan placed the baby in Margot's arms. When Margot pulled away the blanket, Cole became dangerously close to crying again.

The baby's eyes were big, liquid brown, and framed with inky black lashes. Her skin was a few shades darker than her eyes, about Margot's tone, and a riot of curly black hair adorned her head. She blinked at him slowly like she was trying to commit his face to her brand-new mind.

Cole was a complete goner.

"Oh..."

Cole saw tears streaming down Margot's cheeks and he wiped them away. Nan squeezed her shoulder.

"Like Oscar spat her out," Margot said brokenly.

"She's gorgeous, Margot," Nan added.

"She has that Butler nose, though," Margot noted with a little chuckle, and touched the nose with her finger. The baby scrunched up her face and let out a yawn. The adults laughed softly.

"They would've loved her," Margot said, looking first to Nan then to Cole. "They would've loved her so much."

Cole kissed Margot's temple. This indeed was a bittersweet moment filled with a plethora of conflicting emotions. Yet one was present above all else, and that was love. This baby would be loved so much. Both he and Margot would see to that.

"Have you chosen a name yet?" Nan asked after a few moments.

Cole nodded, looking to Margot with a smile. When she'd told him the name, he'd thought it poignant and perfect. Now that the little one was here, he knew it was even more.

"Marcia Grace," Margot said, kissing her daughter's forehead. "After Marcus and Oscar's grandmother Graciela."

Nan nodded. "That's a lovely name for a lovely girl."

"Very lovely girl," Cole murmured, giving his finger for the baby to hold.

"Well, I'll give you a moment alone, then I'll send a nurse to help you breastfeed. The baby should be hungry soon."

"Okay."

The door shut softly, but neither Margot nor Cole removed their eyes from the baby she held. Marcia enthralled him, her grip strong around his finger. He found this fitting because he was completely wrapped around all ten of hers.

"Do you want to hold her?" Margot asked.

He nodded. Margot transferred the baby carefully, telling Cole to support the head. Cole let out a small breath once Marcia was settled in his arms, and he looked at Margot full of wonder.

"I never knew...I feel so much..."

"Yeah," Margot murmured, pressing the backs of her fingers against his cheek.

He turned his head and kissed them, then lifted the baby's hand and kissed it as well. If someone had told him at the beginning of the year he'd have a wife and child by the end of it, he would've thought them insane. Now imagining his life without them proved impossible.

"I am going to love you and your mother so hard and so much," Cole vowed to his now sleeping baby. He looked to Margot. Her eyes were closed, but a soft grin was on her face. His grin matched hers, perfectly content to watch over the two slumbering girls he most adored.

-SJF-

Five years later...

"Marcia Grace Butler-Patterson, you have *five minutes*!"

Margot closed her eyes and counted backward from seven slowly, clenching and unclenching her hands. The coolers still needed to be packed. The sunscreen and bug repellent needed to be applied. Snacks still needed to be prepared. She'd woken everyone up from napping with more than enough time to get ready, so why was she the only one in the kitchen being productive? They'd had hours!

Her daughter had promised to help her make sandwiches, yet she'd gone into her room to finish packing her knapsack over ten minutes ago. Sighing, Margot pulled out the bread and began making peanut butter and jelly sandwiches. They had precious few minutes to spare.

"Marcia—!" The giggle at her legs cut off her call. Margot looked down and gasped. "*Why* is your face full of chocolate!"

Another laugh and an excited clap. Margot rolled her eyes and groaned, picking up the child and tearing off a paper towel. She wet it and wiped the dark-brown substance from the deceptively cherubic face.

"You think you're cute, don't you?" Margot mumbled. Another giggle. Margot nuzzled the child with her nose. "You do, don't you!"

"Cute, Mommy!"

Margot couldn't help but agree with her twenty-month-old son's assessment. Paul Jacob Patterson, named after her and Cole's brothers, was his father's coloring, yet looked very much like her. He was her sweet little boy, precocious as all get out, and would only have to flash those pretty brown eyes at her to garner her forgiveness.

"How did you get that chocolate, PJ?" Margot asked, getting one last stray streak of chocolate from his golden-tan cheek.

"Daddy."

"Daddy!"

"He's lying!"

Margot turned her attention to the voice. Cole entered the kitchen while holding Marcia in his arms, trying to look innocent and failing miserably. Margot narrowed her eyes. "I don't believe you."

"I didn't!"

"He did, Mommy! PJ was crying and Daddy gave him chocolate to get him to stop!"

"Traitor!" Cole exclaimed and began tickling his daughter in earnest. Marcia's happy giggles were joined by PJ's, and the parents gave each other amused smiles. Cole approached Margot and kissed her forehead. "Sorry."

"It's all right," Margot said, trailing a finger down her daughter's cheek. At four going on five, she was looking more like Oscar every day. Her mass of curly black hair reached the middle of her back, but Margot kept it braided so she could play safely. She was wearing a blue shirt and pink overalls and blowing raspberries on Cole's cheek, very happy despite the day.

It was the Fourth of July and they were in the White Mountains again. This time, however, they would spread Georgie and Oscar's ashes with a much larger group present. Along with Margot, Cole, and their children, her parents were here as well as Cole's. Gail, her parents, Nan, Nathan, and Kelly were there, also. Uncle Vic couldn't make it, unfortunately, having come down with a very bad cough, but he'd called earlier that day saying he was thinking about them.

Margot and Cole had reserved four cottages to accommodate everyone, though they would alternately eat in one cottage where they shared large breakfasts and dinners.

The first time the combined families had gotten together was the Thanksgiving after Marcia's birth at the Butler household. It was then that Margot had broken the news about the role Cole's brother had played in Georgie and Oscar's deaths. The Patterson family had asked for forgiveness—especially Frank, who had broken down and sobbed—but to everyone's surprise Faye had taken Frank in her arms and allowed him to cry. They'd both lost sons, yet their remaining children had found each other, and they now shared a beautiful granddaughter. Margot had asked if they were in the Twilight Zone, so surprised by her mother's lack of an outburst and drama, but Faye and Robert had dealt with their son's death in their own way; cursing the surviving Pattersons wouldn't bring back Georgie, Oscar, or Jacob.

"God doesn't give us more than we can bear," Robert had said as he held his granddaughter in his arms. "And there's always a blessing in the storm."

During the next five years, the families had grown close, especially when Margot and Cole moved to Silver Spring, Maryland. With them being located near Margot's family and Gail, as well as a short shuttle ride from Boston, there were plenty of opportunities for all sides of the family to bond—especially since Frank had decided not to run for a second term as attorney general. Because of that bonding, Margot felt contentment and peace this Independence Day instead of the overwhelming sadness she'd felt five years ago. *This* was the right time for Georgie and Oscar's final sendoff, when everyone who loved them could be together for it.

"Sunset's soon," Cole murmured, pulling Margot from her thoughts.

"Yes, and you all were too busy feeding each other chocolate to help!"

"I'm sorry, Mama," Marcia said, her eyes full of sorrow.

"How can I not forgive you when you look at me like that, heart?" Margot said, kissing her daughter's forehead, then her son's light-brown curls. She set her little boy on the floor and Cole set down Marcia on a stool so she could put together the two sides of the sandwiches Margot had already prepared.

"I'll go change PJ's clothes—"

"No more chocolate! That's what pacifiers are for!"

Cole's blue eyes darkened a bit. "A little chocolate never hurt anyone."

Margot ignored the shiver that went through her at that. It was hard to believe she still held her husband's attention and devotion considering body parts were starting to sag, wrinkles were starting to appear around her eyes and forehead, and she'd seen more than a few strands of gray in her still-cropped hair. At thirty, Cole looked even better than at twenty-five, and she didn't miss the glances younger women would send his way. Yet his focus was always on her and their children, and she fell more in love with him every day.

"Yeah, well," Margot said, cursing the huskiness in her voice she knew he heard. "None right now—for either of you!"

Cole smirked and captured her lips with his. "Later tonight, we'll let them stay at grandmas and grandpas'."

"Mommy and Daddy are kissin' *again*?" Marcia asked, using the spoon to plop blobs of jelly onto slices of wheat bread.

"And again," Cole said unapologetically, kissing Margot once more before winking and walking with his son to the rooms.

The two Butler-Patterson women worked in tandem quickly, Marcia chatting away about a dream involving a large blue dragon, castles, and puffy clouds.

"And you weren't scared?" Margot asked.

"No. Papa Oscar and Papa Georgie were riding the dragon with me!"

Margot bent and rested her forehead atop her daughter's head, touched by her story. Margot and Cole had never made Georgie and Oscar a secret, nor about her true parentage. Margot had been adamant Marcia knew the truth as early as possible, and Marcia had taken the news with the grace and acceptance of a child who knew nothing but love. With Margot's parents and Gail sharing stories about Georgie, and Uncle Vic and Nathan sharing stories about Oscar, Marcia had a very firm idea of who they were and what they meant to her life. She called them "Papa" to honor them, her guardian angels. Margot learned much from her daughter about empathy and resiliency.

They finished the rest of the sandwiches quickly, and Cole and PJ returned to the kitchen. Cole packed up the cooler while brother and sister watched a children's program on the television. There was a knock and Nathan, Kelly, and Nan entered, Nathan immediately going to Cole and helping.

"You ready for this?" Kelly asked, hugging Margot in greeting.

"Yes, ma'am. I made some peanut butter and jelly sandwiches just in case we got hungry during the hike," Margot said, hugging Nan once Kelly let go of her.

"It's a beautiful day out," Nan said, squeezing Margot softly.

"It is. Nothing but the best for them."

Soon everyone was gathered at the trail where they would make the short hike to the spot Georgie and Oscar had designated all those years ago. Nathan and Cole pulled the wagon with the cooler inside while Marcia sat on Grandpa Frank's shoulders and PJ was snuggled tight in the baby carrier around Grandpa Robert's front. Gail carried Oscar's urn while Faye carried Georgie's, and everyone's pace was unhurried. When they reached the open clearing that overlooked the mountain peaks, all took a few moments to bask in the view and the atmosphere of the place.

The early-evening air was surprisingly cool, and the sky was starting to turn from bright blue to reddish-gold and purple. The sun was low, hanging just behind the mountaintops, and beautiful. The setting was perfect.

It was a simple, poignant ceremony. Anyone who wanted to speak could. Nathan had gone first, leaning on his wife for support as he shared first one very comical story, then about his feelings when he'd been informed of Oscar's death. Nathan's confession led the way to countless others, and by the time all had said what they wanted or needed to be said, the sun was setting over the mountains.

"It's time, heart," Margot said as she squeezed her daughter's shoulders. Mother and daughter went to the guardrail. Gail handed Margot Oscar's purple urn and she lifted the top. She bent to her knees next to her daughter, and after a quiet count of three, they tipped over the urn and watched the ashes float on the wind toward the valley below.

"See you later Papa Oscar! I love you!" Marcia cried. Margot couldn't have stopped her tears if she tried. Given the sounds of sobs and sniffles behind them, neither could the others.

Faye approached with Georgie's urn, tears streaming down her face. She kissed it one last time before handing it to Margot. She squeezed her mother's hand and nodded before taking off the urn's top and holding it out for Marcia to grasp. Three more soft counts and Georgie's ashes followed Oscars.

"See you later Papa Georgie! I love you!"

Margot wrapped her arms around her daughter's waist from behind and hugged her. Marcia took her mother's embrace and weeping in stride, even patting Margot's hands and proclaiming everything would be better in the morning.

Margot chuckled. "Is that right, heart?"

"Yep! Papa Georgie and Papa Oscar said so in my dream!"

Margot turned Marcia around and hugged her again, standing with her daughter in her arms. Marcia wrapped her tiny legs as much around Margot's waist as she could. Out of the corner of her eye,

Margot saw her father and Nathan re-top the urns and hold them, their eyes solemn as they looked at the dusky valley.

"Definitely the perfect time for this," Robert said, smiling at his daughter and granddaughter. "That was beautiful." Nathan nodded his agreement.

"Very," Margot affirmed, kissing her daughter's nose.

"I wanna go with grandpa."

"You do?"

"Yeah."

Robert, now sans the carrier as Jill now had PJ, welcomed his granddaughter gladly. "We got hamburgers waiting at the cottage with your name on them," he enticed.

"*Oooh!*"

The group started its way back to the cottages, but Margot wasn't in so much of a hurry. A pair of strong arms settled around her waist and soft lips caressed the skin underneath her ear.

"That was amazing," Cole murmured.

Margot nodded, tightening his arms around her. She felt so safe in his embrace, so cherished. "They're all looking down on us...Marcus, Jacob, Georgie, and Oscar. I feel them, even now."

Cole sighed and squeezed her. "Me too."

They remained standing there for a few more minutes, enjoying the warm night and each other. On the walk back to the cabins, Cole laced his fingers through hers and hummed a horribly off-key tune she couldn't recognize.

"Baby, please."

"You don't like my humming?"

"No."

"Mar!"

"Cole!"

He yanked her to his side and kissed her temple, Margot giggling at his antics. "If I didn't love you so much..."

"What? You'd be able to hum better?"

"There's no hope for my hum."

"That's unfortunate."

"You still love me, though."

"Utterly."

He tipped up her chin and kissed her, then continued his humming with a cocky wink. Margot rolled her eyes but soon joined him, giddy and happy that God and the universe had sent someone to help lead her out of her loneliness and despair to a place filled with nothing but joy and love.

ABOUT THE AUTHOR

Originally from Blythewood, South Carolina, Savannah J. Frierson has been writing since she was twelve years old, releasing her debut novel *Being Plumville* in March 2007 with iUniverse, Inc. She has released more publications since then, and they are available at all online book retailers or by request at brick and mortar bookstores. For more information about other titles, please visit Savannah's Web site at **http://www.sjfbooks.com** or contact Savannah by e-mail at me@sjfbooks.com.

Chapter One

Righteous indignation swirled inside of Norma Jackson five seconds before reluctant curiosity took over. She narrowed brown eyes at the e-mail and read it again, slowly, to make sure the three lines said exactly what she'd initially processed.

Happy birthday!
Have a night on us.
Contact Max Worthington for more details.

Love,
Murph & Gids

Norma saw the e-mail had come from her cousin Gideon, with her sister Murphy carbon-copied on it, which meant this really was a Gideon Jackson production that Murphy had been coerced into cosigning. How much coercion and with what, Norma couldn't be certain, but it said a lot that neither had bothered to call her directly to warn her about such an extravagant, completely *ridiculous* "gift."

Bad enough Murphy was stuck in Europe on tour with her jazz quartet and Gideon had booked a photo shoot in the Bahamas—both last-minute once-in-a-lifetime opportunities that an off-year birthday could never supersede—but now they were throwing her into the clutches of a stranger? Happy birthday, indeed! Norma understood life could come at a body fast, but hers was going so slowly the tortoise had already lapped her twice and the hare was gearing up for the next race.

Sighing, Norma clicked on the link, rubbing her left hand over the closely cropped curls atop her head. The feel of her natural tight coils soothed her as the site for Dream Dude LLC popped up on her monitor.

An escort service.

She blinked at the provocative poses of mostly shirtless men with their come-hither stares and too perfect everythings. They were *not* the dudes she dreamed of whenever she went to sleep.

There was no point in e-mailing Gideon back. She was most likely in the air by now and Norma still wasn't quite sure where Murphy was, other than given the hour, Murphy was probably performing or asleep. Shoulders hunched over, Norma began perusing the "Dream Dudes" with a soft scowl on her face. Some of them—*most* of them—were too pretty. Intellectually, she understood why clients would go for them, but the conventional flawlessness they presented left her feeling *meh*.

Norma snorted at her gall. She hadn't been on a date in nigh six years, having grown bored and disillusioned with the slim pickings the South Carolina Lowcountry offered. Gideon had always accused her of having too-high standards, but Norma could only like what she liked. She was a personable person, friendly enough, and understood her generous ass could compensate for the generosity everywhere else on her person. She worked as an intake nurse at the one urgent care center in Moncks Corner to pay the bills but squirreled enough away to pay for studio time in Summerville to throw clay.

She made ceramics, really nice ones if the small stable of clients she'd gained had anything to say about it. In fact, that was where she'd been for the majority of the evening, hoping to finish up a project and check on a few others before coming home. Clay was still under her fingernails and upon her palms, but she didn't mind. It was such a soothing, productive way to wind down from the workday.

Her cousin and her sister had said she could quit her job and pursue her art full time, but turning down a decent, steady paycheck over a passion seemed the peak of irresponsible. She wasn't the beauty Gideon was or the talented musician Murphy was. Norma had only been doing ceramics for two years; that wasn't nearly a long enough track record to make that switch feasible. Nevertheless, there probably was a lot to be said that most of her disposable income, the little she had, went to studio time and supplies. At least if she made this an official business, those expenses could become deductions at tax time.

Norma then groaned and shook her head before snickering. A Web site full of attractive men and she was thinking about her career, such as it was. Maybe she *did* need a night out.

Refocusing herself, Norma began scanning the men's names instead of their bodies, figuring it was best to go directly to the Dream Dude mentioned in the e-mail, except no one was named Max on the site. She did click on others, especially the images of the few men of color featured, and Norma blanched at their rates. The cheapest was two hundred dollars an hour, with zeros being added the longer the time requested.

Now she *really* felt some kind of way and wished she could call Gideon or Murphy for an explanation. She knew things had been picking up for both women, but enough they could splurge on a Dream Dude for a night at *these* rates? One night alone would cost more than Norma's monthly rent, and she wasn't prepared for anyone to drop that much money on a date that might not even go well.

She shook her head, covering her face with her hands. She shouldn't think that way. Hell, maybe thinking that way had doomed her previous dates at the start. It would be nice to do something exotic on her birthday for once, instead of the customary movie and milkshake she'd been treating herself to these past few years. Even last year for her big three-oh she'd been fairly pedestrian, although treating herself to an all-day throwing session at the studio and a nice take-home dinner from Carrabba's had been a highlight. She'd even taken off work to celebrate, giving herself a nice, three-day weekend since it'd fallen on a Friday. Her sister and cousin had been slated to come help her celebrate with a night on the town, but Gideon had gotten sick days before just as Murphy had booked a career-breaking gig with a major jazz star that Norma had insisted she not give up for the sake of her birthday.

A regular martyr, she was.

Norma shoved her hand between her thick thighs and bit her lip in contemplation. What would be the harm in this, truly? She was grown, officially on the other side of thirty come the weekend, and what could it hurt to at least learn a bit about what Dream Dude LLC actually was?

If only she could find this Max character!

She clicked back to the e-mail and read through it again, this time making it down to the bottom of the page. She finally noticed the attachment, and .pdf. She opened it to see Max Worthington's business card. He was the Founder/CEO of Dream Dude LLC.

Of course he was. Gideon might not have graduated from a university, but she had a PhD in Doing the Most.

The .pdf was two pages showing the front and back of the card. The front was all typed text in a clean serif font with the company's logo and Mr. Worthington's contact information—all business related. On the back, however, was Gideon's blocky script that composed a cell phone number and the directive of "CALL HIM TONIGHT!"

Norma checked the time on her smartphone. It was a little after eight. Not too late, but it was a Thursday night and maybe he had things to do? Or maybe he was expecting her call because why else would Gideon tell her that?

Licking her full lips, Norma unlocked the screen of her phone and pulled up the number pad. She typed in the area code, paused to take a deep breath, then added the other seven digits.

"Max Worthington."

Norma gasped. She really and truly didn't mean to do so, but the bass in his voice was so resonant her entire body vibrated from it. She hadn't expected that at all, and it'd caught her off guard.

"Norma?"

Oh, *absolutely not!* He couldn't say her name out of the gate like that! Even with the tone was full of doubt like it was, the two syllables of her very staid name sounded damn good from his mouth.

She cleared her throat. "Yes, hi. My cousin Gideon told me to call?" That didn't sound raspy or aroused at all. *Good job, Norms!*

He chuckled and she bit her tongue to stifle a whimper, squeezing her thighs tight together. She didn't know what the hell was going on, but if it could stop post-haste, that would be *great*. She did have a thing for voices—the deeper, the better—but something about Max's voice hooked her and wouldn't let go.

"I'm sure she did," Max said on the ending hills of his laugh. "She's an...*assertive* person in that regard."

"You're too kind. Everyone else just says bossy," Norma mumbled.

"You said it, not me," Max confirmed, another laugh floating on the line. "She told me to put your number in my cell so I'd pick up the phone because this is your birthday and it's *important* you have a good one."

"Every birthday I make is a good one," Norma said.

"That's a very good point. I'll remember that for myself," Max said, and only then did she notice the hint of a Southern accent of some sort. It didn't sound quite like what she was used to hearing where she was, but the way he stretched out some words and ended others with the consonants optional implied his home region.

"Sorry, I tend to do that," she said with a wince.

"What?"

"Get philosophical a smooth minute into a conversation," Norma explained, cringing. "I'm working on not being so serious all the time."

"There's nothing wrong with philosophy or thinking deeply," he said. "I find it refreshing."

Norma bit her lip, now curious. "Would your Dream Dudes think the same?"

"Ah," he said, humor back in his voice. "My Dream Dudes will be whoever they need to be in order to make your time pleasant."

"So, they're actors?"

He laughed again. "Some of them. Mostly, though, they're attentive. They won't be rude; and if the Date isn't going well, they'll leave early and prorate the fee. Can't get paid the full amount if they don't stay, you know."

"Well, that's fair," Norma conceded.

"We try to be," Max said. "Dream Dude LLC is all about making sure our clients get exactly the experience they want, but we know sometimes what's on paper doesn't always translate to live action. I don't believe in penalizing people just because a connection isn't made."

"What if the person is being rude or obnoxious?"

"The Dude or the client?"

"Either?"

"If the Dude is, he's fired and the client gets a full refund. If it's the client, then they're put on a probationary ban and they don't get that Date's fee refunded. First and foremost is respect, Norma. It must be mutually given to be received."

With those words, a great bulk of her anxiety eased out of her system. She exhaled slowly and nodded, even though Max couldn't see her. "So you get clients of all shapes, sizes, walks of life?"

"Yes," Max said. "I know the rates can be high for some of the Dudes, and that's because they tend to be the most popular, but we have a referral service and sometimes we even do promotional Dates."

"Why haven't I heard of this before?"

"I don't think Charleston is a market city for us, unfortunately."

"Well, I can assure you there are women here who would definitely appreciate the service!"

"Like yourself?"

"I suppose so, or else my cousin wouldn't have orchestrated this entire thing and I wouldn't have called you."

He laughed once more, and Norma was unaware she was as funny as he'd thought her to be. "There's a vast misconception about the services an escort provides. I'll spare you from that spiel right now in favor of asking you, who is your Dream Dude?"

"I don't have one," she said automatically.

"Really? No ideal date with an ideal partner?"

"Is this to help you match me with someone? Are they coming up to Charleston? I saw those rates for a travel overnight date! I wouldn't do that to my sister or cousin, even if they are paying for this experience!"

"Let's...slow down for a sec," he suggested. "Actually, do you mind getting on camera?"

The anxiety must not have gone far because it was creeping back inside. "Why?"

"It'll help me get a read on you, and then you can get a read on me too. This isn't a one-way interaction, after all."

"Do you do this with all of your nervous potential clients?"

"I do offer it as an option," he said, "although it's not me who's usually doing these interviews."

"Well, don't I feel special?"

"Well, that *is* the goal of a Dream Date."

It was her turn to laugh and she started to relax again. It turned out his voice could be as soothing as it was arousing. Really, what could be the harm?

"That seems to be the question of the night," she muttered to herself.

"I'm sorry?"

"I said, that should be all right," Norma amended aloud. She looked down at the top she wore, white tank splotched with gray and brown clay. She should change her shirt. She then eyed the foot of the bed where there were clothes draped on the comforter. She'd been in the process of packing, thinking she'd be meeting Gideon at the train station in Miami tomorrow evening before she'd read the e-mail. She would *not* dress up, but she would put on a clean shirt.

Except, the screen flashed and the video chat request popped up. Norma considered it for a moment, then shrugged and accepted it. He might as well get authentic!Norma right off the bat.

For more on *Escort to Tenderness*, please visit
http://www.patreon.com/sjfbooks